# SCOUTED

## REVENGE, SCANDAL, AND THE RISE OF A SUPERMODEL

## JAMES HOUSTON

*This is a work of fiction.*
*Names, characters, organizations, places, events, and incidents are either products of the author's imagination or are used fictitiously.*
*Text copyright © 2024 James Houston*
*All rights reserved.*

*No part of this book may be reproduced, or stored in a retrieval system, or transmitted in any form or by any means, electronic, mechanical, photocopying, recording, or otherwise, without express written permission of the publisher.*

*Published by James Houston*
*Cover design by Camilla Monk*

*ISBN: 979-832-706-6571*

**I wish to dedicate this book to all the amazing agents and bookers that I have worked with over the years both in the modelling and photography world.**

I have been lucky enough in my career to have worked with incredibly talented and professional individuals all over the world who have helped me to book great work and build a career both as a model and then as a photographer.

Like in any industry you come across people who are not doing the right thing and taking advantage of their power and the situation. In my eight years modelling all over the world I personally never experienced any kind of abuse, and as a photographer I got to work with numerous model agents, stylists and talent and never had any issues. The fashion industry is an exciting place and an amazing platform that offers so many people a place to shine and achieve success.

Even though this book portrays some bad apples in the business I can confidently state that the majority of the industry is professional and respects and looks after their talent. I'm grateful for all that everyone has done to support my career and I value the friendships we have created.

# CONTENTS

CHAPTER 1 ............................... 9
CHAPTER 2 ............................... 16
CHAPTER 3 ...............................25
CHAPTER 4 ...............................32
CHAPTER 5 ............................... 41
CHAPTER 6 ............................... 50
CHAPTER 7 ...............................60
CHAPTER 8 ...............................68
CHAPTER 9 ...............................73
CHAPTER 10 ............................... 77
CHAPTER 11 ............................... 84
CHAPTER 12 ............................... 88
CHAPTER 13 ...............................97
CHAPTER 14 ...............................107
CHAPTER 15 ...............................116
CHAPTER 16 ............................... 122
CHAPTER 17 ............................... 130
CHAPTER 18 ............................... 139
CHAPTER 19 ............................... 146
CHAPTER 20 ............................... 153
CHAPTER 21 ............................... 162
CHAPTER 22 ...............................170

CHAPTER 23 ...............................177
CHAPTER 24 ...............................182
CHAPTER 25 ...............................188
CHAPTER 26 ............................... 195
CHAPTER 27 ...............................202
CHAPTER 28 ............................... 207
CHAPTER 29 ............................... 215
CHAPTER 30 ...............................225
CHAPTER 31 ...............................232
CHAPTER 32 ............................... 238
CHAPTER 33 ...............................245
CHAPTER 34 ............................... 251
CHAPTER 35 ...............................255
CHAPTER 36 ............................... 261
CHAPTER 37 ...............................266
CHAPTER 38 ............................... 275
CHAPTER 39 ............................... 281
CHAPTER 40 ...............................286
CHAPTER 41 ...............................294
CHAPTER 42 ............................... 304
BOOK CLUB CONVERSATION.... 309

# CHAPTER 1

*1994 Rio Brazil*

March was always hot in Rio, but today seemed more humid than usual as the midday sun streamed through the window, the sheer patterned curtains casting shadows on the floor. The old metal fan on the side table offered little relief from the heat; its low rattle could be heard just above the sounds of children playing out on the street. Ronny sat upright on his small bed in an old tank top and shorts, shuffling his prized Nikon FE2 camera nervously around in his hands. *I can't believe this is happening. It's like a dream.* He glanced up at the black and white photographic prints taped to the cracked wall in his small cream-colored bedroom. To distract himself he tried to remember taking each photograph: the beautiful blonde tourist he had met on the beach last summer and photographed at sunset, his friend's grandfather with a lifetime of deep wrinkles, and the middle-aged woman who lived in his building whose striking light green eyes couldn't hide the pain of her recent divorce.

Rio offered such a wide variety of characters for Ronny to photograph. He set out to capture the vulnerability and beauty in his subjects, even if they didn't appear that way to most people. He often lay there looking at his photographs, daydreaming about traveling the world photographing people and getting paid to do what he loved, but today was different. Today he would be watching his favorite photographer Santo Diaz taking photos. Ronny dreamt of one day assisting a fashion photographer working at that level.

That dream, however, seemed so far away from his reality as a nineteen-year-old kid living with his parents in their small two-bedroom apartment in Praça do Vidigal on the coast just below the slums of the Rocinha favelas. The plain white concrete apartment building had six floors crowded with families that overlooked the busy street full of small stores and street vendors. The area was safe enough in the daytime, but at night the silence would often be broken by police sirens and distant gunshots that could be heard ringing out from the nearby favelas. When he was very young his mother would tell him it was the sound of fireworks, until he was old enough to know it was gunfire exchanged between the local gangs and authorities.

"Which one is your favorite?" asked his mother, Adriana, who appeared in the doorway, nodding toward the wall of portraits in her worn blue dress, holding a soda bottle in her hand. He thought she looked older than her forty five years, her curly brown hair pulled back in a loose bun. Her kind blue eyes had lost their spark and her face looked tired.

"I think the one of the old woman who works at the fruit stall on the promenade." Ronny pointed with pride to the close-up black and white portrait of the woman's wrinkled smiling face.

"I would have thought it would be the young blonde girl or maybe the one of me on the roof? Such beautiful photographs."

He smiled at his mother, noticing the sadness in her face, feeling torn in so many ways, knowing he was only living at home now to protect her from his father. He remembered happier times when he witnessed his mother and father in love, hearing the house filled with laughter. Ronny and his older brother, Luiz, had grown up together enjoying summers on the beach and family holidays traveling up the coast to Bahia to stay with his cousins. Back then his father was a happy man and someone he loved to be with. That all changed about five years ago, when Ronny's mother discovered his father was having an affair with a woman from his work. That's when Diego's drinking became a problem and the fighting began. His mother was never the same; she became insecure and angry, which pushed Diego farther away. So many nights, after he was sent to his bedroom that he shared with Luiz, Ronny lay silent in his bed listening to his parents fighting, praying that his father didn't hit his mother. Eventually the front door would slam, signaling that Diego had left to go out, often not returning until the early hours of the following morning.

It wasn't long before Luiz turned eighteen and began to stand up to his father, who in a drunken rage would knock his brother down with a quick backhand. The first time it happened, Ronny gasped in shock to see his brother get hit; warm tears filled his eyes as the hatred for his father grew. He cursed under his breath, wishing he were physically able to stand up to him. The violence continued to escalate over the following months, and at one point his mother tried to break up a fight between Diego and Luiz and was knocked to the floor. Ronny rushed to see if she was okay. He was only fifteen. It was too much. A few months later his father hit Luiz for the last time. After taking so many beatings, with tears in his eyes and blood on his lip, his brother connected a punch that left his father winded on the floor.

Luiz had had enough and left that night to move in with some friends. Unfortunately, a few months later he got caught stealing a car with those same friends and spent six months in prison. When he got out of prison, he managed to get a job working at a local restaurant. Luiz and Ronny had kept in touch, and he had always offered to come stay with him if things at home became too difficult. "There's always a couch here for you," his brother would say when they saw each other. Ronny didn't understand why his mother stayed. For some reason she felt loyal to Diego—*blind love*. His father was a handsome man that could turn on the charm when it suited him, especially around women. He made promises that things would get better, that things would change, but they didn't. Ronny had lost respect for his father a long time ago and in many ways resented the fact that people would tell him he had inherited Diego's charm and good looks. His father was sleeping around behind his mother's back, and the last thing Ronny wanted was to end up like him.

"What time is it?" Ronny asked his mother. "Milo is swinging by to pick me up at two," He felt excited and nervous about the shoot.

"It's almost one-thirty. So what exactly are you guys doing anyway?"

"I was playing volleyball with the guys yesterday down at the beach and this man came up to us who works as a producer for a photographer and asked if we wanted to play volleyball in the background of a photo shoot. He offered us fifty dollars cash each to make sure we turned up." Ronny had seen many photo shoots being done on the beach; he always enjoyed sitting at a distance and watching the way the photographer worked, listening to the way the models were directed. He smiled to himself. "I could definitely use the cash," he added. What he didn't tell his mother was that the photographer, Santo Diaz, was his favorite fashion photographer. His magazine covers and fashion spreads always stood out in *Italian STYLE* magazine. He thought if he told his mother about his dream of assisting someone like Santo, she might ask him about leaving and Ronny knew that she had enough to worry about without causing any extra stress.

"Good for you. I know you will do something amazing one day." She added as Ronny watched her looking at his photos on the wall, her smile slowly fading. "I used to feel that way when I was your age. I used to love to paint," she added with a broken tone of regret.

"I remember you did that painting of the ocean at night with that big orange moon. It was beautiful," said Ronny.

"You remember that? You must have been about ten. It was a long time ago."

"There is still time to do anything you want." He didn't want to directly confront the situation that she was in. His mother had always taken an interest in his photography. Her face lit up when she listened to him talk passionately about his work, and yet he could tell that it pained her in a way to acknowledge that she had dreamt of more than what she ended up with. Ronny had always been able to confide in her and respected her opinion. He missed their long conversations and seeing her laugh freely. After his father's affair, she had changed from a positive young woman who loved to dance with him in the kitchen to a broken person who had lost confidence in herself and now seemed trapped by her circumstance.

"I don't know." She looked back at him and changed the subject. "Will you be home for dinner?"

"I'm not sure how late it will go, so don't count on me being home."

"There will be leftovers anyway. I'm cooking your favorite chicken tonight. Hey, how's it been going with Danilo?" Danilo was an old friend of his mother who ran a small commercial and portrait photography business nearby shooting weddings and low budget commercial jobs. Ronny had been working with him for a year now, and even though most of the work wasn't that inspiring, Danilo taught him a lot of technical things and gave him his old Nikon camera and lens to use. He was able to develop his film there and do some printing for free.

"I appreciate you hooking me up with him. It's good experience, but I'm trying to think of ways to get some extra cash, without ending up in prison." Ronny regretted the words as soon as they left his mouth. His father had forbidden her to see his brother, and hearing he had spent time in prison was devastating for her.

"I know Danilo only works on smaller jobs, but he says you have a great eye; you should stick with him and learn as much as you can. I don't want to see you getting sidetracked like your brother."

"Danilo's been great. I've already learned a lot, but I need to get some more work. I want to travel." For a while now he had wanted to escape his life here—get out of Brazil, experience the world, and try to get a break to start his own photography career.

"Just keep out of trouble and work hard."

"I'd better get ready." He stood up to get changed before Milo arrived, placing his camera down on one of the large piles of international fashion magazines next to his bed that he had collected from the newsagent near Copacabana Beach who saved the outdated issues for him. Occasionally Ronny took a magazine spread to Danilo and ask him what lighting he thought the photographer had used. He wasn't sure if Danilo knew exactly what he was talking about, but he appreciated that he always had time to answer any questions he had.

"Olá, Ronny. You ready?" Milo called up from the street.

"Coming," he called out the window. He walked through the living area of the apartment that joined the small open kitchen. His mother embraced him and held him longer than usual. Something felt different, like she was afraid of losing him. He unlocked his bike that sat outside the front door and made his way down the old cement stairs out onto the street where Milo sat straddling a red push bike. His huge white smile beamed across his friendly tanned face, his thick dark hair tied back in a small ponytail.

"Hey, is that a new bike?"

"Yeah, I got some extra cash. Sweet ride."

Milo was more of a hustler than Ronny and he knew better than to ask how he got the extra cash. He slapped Milo's hand as the they jumped on their bikes, dodged an oncoming taxi, and headed off down the busy street. Milo and his other friends had no idea what a big deal this was for him—a dream come true. *Who knows what might come from meeting Santo Diaz.*

# CHAPTER 2

Milo liked to ride fast. Ronny tried his best to keep up despite the occasional pedestrian and swerving scooter that would obstruct his path. Normally he preferred to ride a little slower so he could survey the people going about their lives; he studied their faces, taking imaginary photos in his head, seeing the beauty beyond their often-challenging reality. Rio was such a melting pot of the poor, the rich, and everything in between.

"Ronny," called out a man standing on a corner at a fruit stall.

"Olá, Benicio," he replied. He had made this ride down to the beach almost every day and knew most of the local vendors by name. As he turned the corner past a line of colorful old buildings, he caught a glimpse of the ocean through a web of powerlines that crossed randomly above the street. His heart started racing with excitement. As scooters and motorbikes passed them, he wished he had the money to afford one. The ride downhill on the bike was easy; coming back up took a lot more effort, especially after a long beach volleyball game.

*I wonder how Santo Diaz got started. Maybe I can ask him.* He could barely contain his excitement as they finally arrived at the end of Ipanema Beach and rode their bikes up onto the promenade.

The long stretch of white sand separated them and the ocean as they rode around the tourists and locals that were coming and going from the beach. He looked at the tall high-rise buildings lining the road to the left, imagining the amazing view the people who stayed in those apartments and hotels woke up to every day.

"Olá, beautiful," Milo called out to a group of local teenage girls walking toward the beach in bikinis. The girls turned to see who called out and quickly averted their eyes from Milo to look at Ronny and smiled. "Always the ladies man," added Milo as he turned back to Ronny. The last thing on Ronny's mind right now was picking up girls.

"I hope Bruno and Javier are on time; I don't want to mess these guys around."

"They'll be there. Don't worry, they need the money." Milo didn't seem to worry about much. Ronny had always admired the way he seemed to cruise through life. Even when he got his girlfriend Ana pregnant two years ago, he didn't seem fazed. He was impressed that Milo had stayed with her to raise their kid. As hard as that must have been, he managed to somehow make it work.

In the distance Ronny could see a production tent set up on the beach near the volleyball courts with a few armed security guards around it. He quickly scanned the scene and finally saw Lucas, the producer who he had met the day before, on a walkie-talkie standing in front of one of the location vans.

"Maybe I should have asked for more money," he added when he saw the size of the production.

"Oi," called out Bruno as he and Javier appeared. Bruno wore denim cut-off shorts on his tall, lean frame; the sun glinted off his blonde hair, as well as Javier's shaved head and gold-rimmed glasses. Ronny felt a wave of relief that they had actually shown up.

"Thanks for coming." He slapped each of their hands.

"If someone's going to pay me to play volleyball next to a hot model I'll be there," said Javier. Milo looked at Ronny, rolled his eyes, and laughed. They chained their bikes up to the railing and walked up to the producer who seemed to be freaking out about something. Lucas was a handsome, dark-haired man in his thirties wearing a wide brim straw hat and black tank top.

"Just get her down get down here before Santo loses his shit. We have a lot of shots to do." Lucas put down the walkie-talkie and wiped the sweat off his brow. "That Tiana Taylor will be the death of me," he muttered as he turned and forced a smile. "Thanks for showing up. Sorry about that. Tiana isn't happy with her hair; you know how these supermodels are." He started walking down the promenade.

*I wish I knew how these supermodels are,* thought Ronny, his excitement growing. He knew Tiana Taylor from the magazines—she was the first black supermodel and one of his favorites. They followed Lucas past the security guards to a large silver location trailer. He held the door open as they entered. "This is Flavio. He will be in charge of dressing you," Lucas called out as they walked in.

"I don't want any of you stealing any of this stuff. Got it!" snapped Flavio as his eyes surveyed the four friends.

Ronny couldn't help but stare at his hard, sharp face, shaped eyebrows, and slicked back black ponytail. He was dressed in a blue silk robe that looked like a kimono over white tennis shorts and a tank top. Ronny looked around the trailer, savoring the moment. This was the first time he had been in a wardrobe trailer on a professional shoot. *I wonder who else has changed in here.*

"Let's get you boys dressed so we can get you on set. Santo is down at the location now and we need something to distract him from Tiana being so late." Flavio locked eyes with Ronny and held his gaze; he smiled back, then averted his eyes. They were ushered to the back of the large trailer, past the banquet seating and bathroom at the front to where racks of clothes lined the walls. Flavio passed a pair of black speedos to each of the guys. His eyes remained focused on Ronny who was searching for somewhere to change. He quickly realized Flavio didn't intend to close the privacy curtain, and rather than make a scene he moved to the side wall, turned away, took off his shorts, and slipped on the speedo. He noticed his friends looking lost, then eventually they followed his lead, turning toward the wall and quickly changing. Bruno burst out laughing, breaking the silence.

"Let me check those," said Flavio as he moved closer and slid his hands over Ronny's butt to smooth out wrinkles. As uncomfortable as Flavio's touch made him feel, he didn't want to say anything that may cause a problem and get him thrown off the set before he could meet Santo. "Let me see the front." Ronny turned around. "Seems to fit well enough. I might need to adjust," added Flavio. He pulled the speedos down slightly on Ronny's hips and without warning went to adjust Ronny's package.

"Hey, easy man," said Milo. Ronny pulled away and indicated to Milo to not make a scene as he tried to deflate the situation.

"What the fuck?" Javier added.

Flavio mumbled something under his breath, and everyone looked up.

"Let's go!" called out Lucas from outside the trailer.

"I got this!" Ronny put his hands down to tie the speedo cord, knocking Flavio's hand out of the way and moving past him to head outside. The others quickly followed. "Asshole," he muttered, trying to not let Flavio ruin his mood. He was on a high finally getting to meet the man behind all the amazing photographs he had admired for years. He would look over his collection of fashion magazines each night, studying the photographs, observing how the models were positioned and how each photograph was created. Santo's work had always stood out; his photographs always seemed to capture the energy of the moment.

"What happened back there?" asked Bruno.

"Nothing, man...all good," replied Ronny. They followed Lucas down the beach to the volleyball courts where Santo was talking to his three attractive male assistants. He recognized him from the social pages of *Italian STYLE* magazine. In his mid-forties, Santo was tanned and lean, with dark features. He wore a white linen shirt with a bandana scarf around his neck, and white jeans. Seeing him in person was surreal and a little intimidating. *Don't say I'm a photographer too—that sounds desperate.*

"Lucas, where the fuck is Tiana?" Santo called out in a Spanish accent.

"Sorry, there was an issue with her hair."

"Fuck, she's a pain in my ass. I should have brought Claudia." Santo shook his head.

"Here are the volleyball guys you requested," Lucas motioned to Ronny and his friends standing behind him. Ronny tried not to appear starstruck.

"Well, things are looking up." Santo smiled as he walked up to meet the guys; his eyes surveyed the group and then focused in on Ronny. "What's your name?" His eyes briefly glanced down to his body then back to his face.

Ronny felt the blood rush to his head and his face turning red as their eyes met. He composed himself. "I'm Ronny and this is Milo, Bruno, and Javier." Santo quickly acknowledged the guys with a polite nod but came back to continue looking at Ronny. "I'm a big fan of your work, Mr. Diaz." *That's enough. Don't say any more.*

"Oh, well thank you, and please call me Santo. Mr. Diaz makes me feel so fucking old," Santo replied with a charming smile. Ronny caught one of his assistants rolling his eyes and then turned back to see Milo and his friends looking somewhat amused by the situation.

"The light's great, let's start shooting. Why don't you start playing against each other." Santo's tone became direct as Ronny watched his assistants move quickly into action, prepare his cameras, and move the reflectors into position. He watched closely and took note of the four Pentax 6x7 camera bodies sitting on the equipment cart under the umbrella and the lens he was using. Even though he was there to be photographed, Ronny didn't want to miss this opportunity to watch Santo and his team work and pick up a few tips.

"Javier and Bruno against me and Ronny," said Milo.

Santo stood on the sideline for a moment watching, one of his assistants shaded him with an umbrella. He slowly began taking photos to capture the action of the game.

"Hey, get your head in the game, bro," Milo called out as Ronny missed another shot.

"Sorry, man." It was difficult to remain focused when all he wanted to do was watch Santo work. Santo moved to the end of the court behind Ronny and Milo, coming in close to photograph them as they continued playing. Ronny was trying his best not to hit Santo with the volleyball.

"Ronny, hold the ball and walk back towards me," Santo started directing as he kept shooting. "Okay, now stand facing me. Keep the ball on your hip. Can everyone stand around near the net in the middle of the court like you're hanging out waiting to start playing?" They followed his direction. "Ronny, look past me to the trailer, let's see you laugh."

Ronny stood there feeling self-conscious. This was the first time he had been photographed in this way by a professional. There were so many questions he would have liked to ask Santo, but for now he tried to stay focused and do a good job.

"Bigger, come on, open your mouth." Santo laughed as his camera clicked away. "Perfect," he added as he came in closer to push the hair back that was falling on Ronny's face. He briefly made eye contact and offered a warm smile before moving back to continue directing and shooting. Santo's expression seemed genuine.

"Ronny, give me a serious expression. Keep the strength in your eyes and tense your stomach for me." He felt Santo's hand touch his stomach and linger long enough to make him feel slightly uncomfortable. He glanced back quickly to see that Milo was watching him. How could they know how much this meant to him. *Breathe. Focus.*

"You look great with your facial hair. Don't shave it off," Santo added softly as he ran his fingers down the side of Ronny's jawline to his chin.

"Thanks," Ronny replied. Santo then stood back and took a few more photographs of Ronny.

"Belíssimo," he exclaimed before putting his camera down. As flattered as he was, Ronny felt self-conscious. He looked back to his friends—the extra attention he was receiving from Santo hadn't gone unnoticed. He smiled uncomfortably as they stared and nodded back.

"Let's see you all standing on this side of the net as a group just hanging out, like a rock band. Come closer together. Milo, put your arm around Ronny's shoulder, that's it, Ronny hold the ball and move it in your hands, slouch your stance a little more. Relax, don't smile, give me serious expressions. Perfect!"

Ronny studied the way Santo orchestrated the dance in front of the camera and directed everyone. He worked quickly, effortlessly going from shooting one roll of film to the next as his assistants continued to pass him a new camera body as soon as his film ran out. It was so exciting to watch him work. He glanced to his side to see Milo and Javier offering up their best strong expressions. Everyone appeared to be under Santo's spell.

"Santo, darling!" called out Tiana Taylor as she appeared walking down the beach toward the guys in a tiny gold bikini followed by Flavio and her hair and makeup team. She was finally ready. Until now Ronny had only seen her in magazines. She was a strikingly beautiful girl with feline features, tall and muscular but sexy and feminine at the same time. Her long hair trailed straight down her back, and her eyes were dark and intense.

"Sorry I'm late," she said. "I just wanted the hair to be perfect for you, darling."

Santo passed his camera to his first assistant. "Okay, let's not waste any more time. Tiana, come meet everyone."

He did a quick introduction as Tiana offered them a polite smile. Santo started directing again, telling them to start playing on the court in the background while Tiana walked toward him and posed for the camera. He snapped off a few polaroids, showed them to Flavio, and then continued shooting. It was getting harder for Ronny to keep his eyes focused on the game as Tiana walked back and forth modeling in front of the camera. He couldn't believe his luck—here he was watching a famous photographer work with a supermodel. After the first setup Tiana got changed on set into another bikini behind a sheet that the stylist assistant held up around her body. She came back onto the court and Santo directed her to stand close to Ronny.

"Do you like Brazil?" Ronny asked her, breaking the silence.

"I've been here a few times; it's a bit like Miami but I like it here better. Miami is a bit sleezy," Tiana answered without making eye contact as she touched her hair and adjusted her bikini. He could tell she wasn't interested in talking, for Tiana this was just another day on set, but for Ronny it was the most exciting day he had in years. "I want to go to America one day and take photographs."

"Great," Tiana responded flatly without making eye contact.

*Fuck, why did I tell her that? As if she cares. Just stop talking.* Ronny wasn't in her league. He imagined with her looks and supermodel status that she had been given everything she could possibly want without having to work that hard to get it. Milo shot him an amused look affirming that he was being given the cold shoulder. Santo directed them to stand around behind Tiana as she began to flirt and dance to the boom box music that had been brought down to help her get in the mood. Ronny studied her face and her body, trying not to stare. Tiana put her arms around him as she laughed and flirted. Ronny couldn't tell if she was faking it or really enjoying touching his body. He found himself getting distracted as she worked her body against his and Santo quickly took more photographs, shouting out directions.

She was incredible to watch. He was a fast learner and, following her lead, he started to model for the camera with more confidence. The energy and the music made it feel more like a fun time with friends than a photoshoot. Santo did another four setups, with Tiana changing each time into a new outfit. Just when Ronny thought the afternoon couldn't get any better, Santo passed his camera to his assistant and called out, "You all look amazing, great energy, thank you! Ronny, let's get you and Tiana changed and do some shots together up on the promenade."

## CHAPTER 3

A huge smile appeared on his face as he turned to look at Tiana. She didn't look impressed that she would be sharing the spotlight with an unknown kid from the beach. Everyone started walking back up toward the trailers. He couldn't believe his luck. *Was this really happening?* He looked around him at his friends and the crew walking up the beach. He walked up next to Santo's second assistant who was carrying his camera.

"Is that an eighty-five millimeter lens?" he asked as the assistant looked around and Ronny nodded toward the camera.

"Yeah, he loves this lens and I'm glad it's not too heavy." The assistant smiled.

"Easiest money I've ever made," said Javier as he slapped Ronny on the back and high-fived Milo.

"I think someone's working it a little harder than we are," added Bruno as he messed up Ronny's hair and laughed. Ronny shook his head and playfully pushed him away. His friends knew he did photography as a hobby, but he had never really shared with them his dream of becoming a working photographer traveling the world. He didn't think they would take him seriously.

"Lucas, ask Flavio to change Tiana into that silver sequined

Mancini cocktail dress, and can you ask his assistant to get a pair of black Mancini jeans and shirt for Ronny," called out Santo as he lit a cigarette. The sun was slowly setting as Ronny went into the wardrobe trailer with Flavio's assistant and quickly changed into the jeans and a see-through black top. Fortunately, Flavio was busy with Tiana so he didn't have to deal with him adjusting the jeans. He walked back on set and stood next to Santo who was waiting for Tiana to appear.

"So how did you get started in photography?" Ronny asked nervously.

"When I was a kid, I used to look at magazines in my dad's barber shop and I always loved the fashion photos. They transported me away from my simple life to another world. I imagined traveling to amazing locations and taking photographs like that. When I finished school I moved to Paris and worked as a waiter at night and assisted a local photographer during the day and started test-shooting models until I got my first break to shoot a magazine editorial, and it went from there. It's what I always wanted." Santo paused and looked at Ronny with a smug expression. "I usually get what I want."

Ronny nodded at Santo and averted his eyes. "I would love to get to travel to all over the world, too." He avoided telling him that he wanted to pursue photography for fear he wouldn't take him seriously. *I'll wait for the right time. Who knows when he might be needing a new assistant.* Suddenly Santo moved closer and reached out and touched his face.

"How did you get this scar?" His fingers traced the curved scar that ran across his cheek. Ronny was caught off guard and pulled back slightly. He saw Milo was looking at him and wondered if he could hear their conversation.

"I got it playing sports," he answered before quickly changing the subject. "Where is your favorite place to shoot?"

"That's easy. Brazil. The people here are so free and sexy." Santo took a final glance down at Ronny's chest before moving toward Lucas. "Now where the hell is Tiana? We are going to lose the light!" Lucas raced off in the direction of Tiana's wardrobe trailer.

Even though Ronny felt an overwhelming excitement being on set with Santo and getting to speak to his idol, his advances made him feel uncomfortable. He looked back to Milo, who was now talking to their other friends standing off to the side. He touched the scar on his cheek. He thought back to that night a few years ago when it had been cut by a blade during a street fight between Milo's older brother Pedro and a gang member. Ronny happened to be on the scene and tried to step in to break up the fight and defend Pedro. He punched the gang member who pulled out a blade and cut his face. Pedro grabbed him from behind but ended up getting stabbed in the struggle. The gang member was consequently shot by someone as he tried to run from the scene. Life on the streets of Rio was unpredictable and often dangerous.

Later that night Pedro died from blood loss. "He had it coming," Ronny remembered his father saying. Pedro was a member of a local gang, and a few times Milo and Ronny had run errands for him to make extra money until that fateful night. After that they had avoided any association with his brother's friends for fear they would end up with the same fate. As tough as that night had been, it had brought Milo and Ronny closer together.

"Serge, can you check Ronny's hair? Grazie," Santo spoke to the hair stylist who stood next to him waiting for Tiana. He was a calm unassuming man in his forties with a bald head and a kind face, wearing a black T-shirt and shorts.

"Nice to meet you, Serge." Ronny smiled politely, recognizing his name from magazine credits.

"You too, Ronny. I wish I had your head of hair," said Serge in a French accent. He began to run his fingers through Ronny's hair. "It's a little easier to deal with than Tiana's." Serge winked at Ronny and smiled.

He instantly liked Serge; he felt he was friendlier than most of the other people working on the set, and he didn't feel as uncomfortable as when Santo had touched him. He was quickly learning there was a big difference between touched and being touched up. There was no denying how talented Santo was and how much Ronny admired his work. Maybe because Ronny and his friends were just background extras, he thought they could be taken advantage of? His mind raced as he tried to justify Santo's advances. He did say Brazilians were free and sexy. *Not all Brazilians,* Ronny thought as Milo and the others moved to the side of the set to watch the rest of the shoot and wait for Ronny. Finally, Tiana appeared from the trailer looking incredible in a short silver sequined dress and high heels.

"Ronny, why don't you sit on the wall, and Tiana let's see you in close to him standing between his legs," Santo directed as his assistant handed him a camera with a flash attached to it. Ronny quickly tried to see what settings his assistant had put on the camera and what kind of flash he was using until Tiana approached him and offered a brief smile. Ronny couldn't deny his excitement as she turned back toward Santo. She looked amazing.

"Is my hair okay at the back, Serge?" Tiana asked in a short tone.

"It's perfect, darling—"

"Let's shoot this before it gets dark," Santo interrupted in a frustrated tone. His patience waiting on Tiana's hair was apparently running out. "Tiana, move in close to him. Ronny, look at Tiana. Start with your hands on the railing and then put them on Tiana's waist and flirt with her."

Ronny felt the blood rush to his head as the boom box music played and Javier, Milo, and Bruno stood next to Lucas watching Tiana position herself between Ronny's legs. Santo started taking photos and the flash went off and lit up the couple. As hard as it was, Ronny tried to focus and not get distracted by Tiana or his friends. After Santo had pulled a few polaroids, he quickly continued shooting. Tiana openly flirted with him for the camera and her body gyrated up against him. *If the modeling thing doesn't work out, she could always be a stripper.* Ronny glanced across to see Milo raise his eyebrows and give him a nod.

"Let's change Tiana and lose Ronny's shirt," Santo directed. Tiana quickly changed.

"Okay, Ronny, stand up and let's have you close to each other, like you're dancing together, about to kiss. Tiana, work your body against his. Let me see the sex." Santo quickly took another camera that was handed to him. Ronny stood up and Tiana started moving to the music, turning around while keeping her body close to his. She put her arms around his neck and brought her face up close and her lips close to his mouth.

"Ronny, keep your mouth open and look down at her lips," instructed Santo. Everyone on set was quiet. Tiana came in close so he could feel her breathing, almost like she was going to kiss him, and then pulled back and turned her body around pushing herself back into him. He put his arm around her waist, and she brought her hand up into his hair and pulled his face down close to her again. Even though Ronny knew that Tiana was performing for the camera it was hard not to be turned on by her self-confidence and ability to take command of the situation.

"Bring your eyes to me, Ronny. Strong expression," called out Santo as he continued shooting, moving in to get some close-ups of the pair. As Santo's camera clicked away, Tiana moved around him, changing her positions and expressions, almost like a dancer.

Suddenly Santo called out, "Bellissimo. We have it!" The shoot was over. Everyone on the set started clapping as Santo's assistants took his cameras away. Ronny joined in clapping.

"Tiana, it was amazing to watch you work," said Ronny. She quickly shot him a fleeting smile and started walking off to her trailer, stopping briefly to give Santo a hug and kiss. Santo walked up to Ronny who was still standing shirtless near the railing and put his hand on his shoulder and kissed him on both cheeks.

"You were great today," Santo said as he touched Ronny's arm and felt his bicep, momentarily glancing down at his bare chest. "I'm having a wrap party tonight at my hotel if you'd like to come by around ten o'clock. Lucas will give you the details. Bring your friends if you like." Santo offered a smile, then walked away.

"I always said you should have put those big lips and bedroom eyes of yours to good use," said Javier as he pushed Ronny in jest. Ronny nodded but didn't say anything. He was high on adrenalin, his heart racing, trying to comprehend what had just happened. He felt conflicted about what to do about the wrap party and Santo's advances. Lucas escorted the guys back to the wardrobe trailer to change into their own clothes and handed out model release forms for the guys to fill out. At the back of the trailer, Flavio shamelessly position himself so he could watch Ronny take off his pants. He turned away feeling his gaze upon him. *Kiss my ass.* Ronny thought as they collected their belongings and Lucas handed him an envelope that contained their cash for the job.

"Santo invited you along tonight to the wrap party in his hotel suite," Lucas said. "He is staying at the Copacabana Palace. Come by at ten if you and the guys want and just mention to the concierge that you're there for Santo Diaz in the penthouse. I'll leave your names on the guestlist." Lucas collected the signed release forms and left the trailer. Ronny's mind raced as he considered who might be at the party.

"I bet that's going to be an awesome party—we should go!" said Milo.

"I'm sure there will be some hot girls there. Maybe Tiana will finally let you kiss her, Ronny, and if she won't I'm sure Santo will." Bruno laughed and hit Ronny on the shoulder. "Javier and I can't make it, but you guys have fun."

The friends got back on their bikes and headed off down the promenade laughing about the fact that they just got paid for playing volleyball on the beach all afternoon with a hot model. The shoot today had given Ronny a glimpse into a new world, a better life, doing something that made him feel alive. As he thought about the party, he was torn between the opportunity to get closer to Santo but hesitant about the sexual vibes.

# CHAPTER 4

At 10:15 p.m. he and Milo arrived at the Copacabana Palace, a luxury hotel right on Copacabana Beach. He was freshly showered wearing a black vintage button-down shirt and jeans, his thick dark hair slicked back away from his face. Milo wore a blue collared shirt, cream pants, and a little too much cologne. The uniformed concierge saw them walk through the front door and walked up quickly to stop them. Ronny knew he was on the lookout for opportunistic street kids that often came to the hotel to sell drugs or sex.

"Can I help you gentlemen?" asked the concierge in a stern voice.

"Ronny and Milo here for Santo Diaz in the penthouse," answered Ronny, his heart racing.

"Stay here," said the concierge. Ronny was shuffling nervously on his feet as Milo put his hand on his shoulder.

"Calm down, bro. We'll get in," Milo said. Ronny nodded and forced a smile.

"Follow me," the concierge snapped as he walked in front of them, heading toward the elevator; his heels clicked on the polished marble floor. The opulent foyer was a grand room filled with flowers, large botanical paintings on the walls, and a huge chandelier overhead. It was hard not to be impressed by the luxurious décor. Even though he was wearing his best clothes, Ronny still felt out of place; this was an unfamiliar world. Milo winked as they headed into the wood-paneled elevator. The ride up to the penthouse didn't take long, and when the doors opened they could hear the party going on down the hall. The concierge knocked on the large white double doors.

"Hey, guys. Welcome!" Lucas the producer said as he opened the door. He appeared well on his way to getting drunk and a lot less stressed than he had been on the beach. "Come in, come on in. What do you guys want to drink?" he asked.

"Just two beers. Thanks," answered Milo as a handsome nearby waiter in a black tank top handed them two cold opened beers.

"Enjoy, guys." Lucas slapped Ronny on the back and stumbled away. Ronny nodded and then quickly scanned the room to see if Santo was anywhere in sight. The glamorous, sexy fashion crowd looked like they had been partying for a while. Ronny felt self-conscious as a few people turned around to briefly check them out. *What am I doing here?* A wave of insecurity washed over him. He took a few gulps of his beer and wiped his mouth. The penthouse suite was a large stylish room with rich décor and French doors that opened to the outside terrace and small private pool.

"So this is what a penthouse looks like," Milo said just loud enough for Ronny to hear. He was reminded just how poor he was as they headed outside where the DJ was located. A few people were already dancing in front of the incredible view of Copacabana Beach. He closed his eyes momentarily and breathed in the cool ocean air. *I could get used to this,* Ronny thought to himself as he nudged Milo who was standing with his mouth slightly open, obviously impressed with what he saw.

"This guy takes photographs and makes this much bank? I need to buy a camera." Milo looked back at Ronny and smiled.

"He's the biggest photographer in the world," Ronny added proudly.

"You should show him your photographs."

"I'm sure he has better things to do than look at my photos," he replied, deflecting attention away from his own work. He couldn't imagine showing someone like Santo his work. It just wasn't good enough. *Not yet anyway.* Suddenly Santo appeared behind them, putting his hand around Ronny's waist.

"So glad you could make this little party we are having up here." He moved in closer to Ronny and kissed him on both cheeks then did the same to Milo. Then he positioned himself next to Ronny and let his hand slide down to rest on the top of his ass.

"Hi, yes hello," replied Ronny as he tried to pull away from Santo's touch. He took a long swig of his beer, not wanting to say anything that might offend Santo. Ronny returned a forced smile trying not to appear uncomfortable. *Maybe this was a bad idea.*

"Thanks for the invite, Mr. Diaz," added Milo.

"Pleeeease call me Santo," he replied as he sniffed and stared back at Ronny with an intense look on his face. He suspected that Santo had been doing a lot of cocaine, His hand casually explored Ronny's back and then slowly made its way back down again to the top of his ass. *Fuck!* He came in close and whispered in his ear, "The photos today were so sexy." Santo felt his arm again.

"Thanks. I can't wait to see them." He felt a knot in his stomach, unsure whether he should move away or stay. It was obvious that a conversation about photography was the last thing on Santo's mind.

"You know I could do a lot for you in this business," Santo sniffed again and pressed his crotch into Ronny's hip. Ronny slowly pulled his body away realizing that Santo was definitely looking for a lot more than he was willing to give. A part of him wanted to leave as he turned and noticed Milo standing quietly beside him taking another sip of his beer. It was an awkward situation. At that moment Tiana appeared wearing a slinky body-hugging black dress that showed off her flawless figure. She looked incredible.

"Santo, darling, I need a tour of your beautiful suite." Tiana offered the guys a fleeting smile before moving in to embrace Santo. She was accompanied by a stylish tanned woman in her forties with blonde hair and a sharp angular face. The blonde woman moved in closer to Ronny and spoke in an Italian accent.

"Ciao, Ronny. I'm Sylvia."

"Nice to meet you. This is my friend Milo." Sylvia nodded at Milo then moved in close to Ronny.

"Tiana showed me some of the polaroids of you from the shoot today and Santo said you will be featured in the story." He noticed Santo and Tiana entering a side room together and closing the door. *More cocaine. I guess this was a waste of time.* Sylvia touched his arm.

"I'm a model scout from Europe. I discovered Tiana. Have you ever considered becoming a model?" Ronny was caught off guard—it had been such a surreal day.

"Um, you know I hadn't really considered modeling." The shoot had been fun but the best part of it was getting to watch Santo work and picking up some photography tips that he would get to experiment with.

"You should think about coming to Milan for men's fashion week. I think you would do really well, especially with the editorial of you and Tiana coming out in *Italian STYLE* magazine." Ronny couldn't believe that his photographs would be featured in his favorite magazine. "Can I give you my card?" Sylvia asked. Ronny nodded, smiled, and took the card and slipped it into the pocket of his jeans. Even though he wasn't really interested in modeling, he didn't want to appear rude.

"Do many young photographers go to Milan?"

"Darling, it's Milan, the fashion capital of the world. The town is full of models and photographers. It's where everyone goes to be discovered. Some models who go there actually end up becoming photographers. You have my card, so think about it." Sylvia gave Ronny two kisses and walked away. *Is modeling my ticket out of here?* He thought for a moment then remembered how uncomfortable he had felt earlier in the day on the shoot with all the touching that was going on. *Im sure all shoots aren't like that.* He considered this might be his only way out of here. *Whatever helps me get closer to being a successful photographer.*

"See any girls here you like?" asked Milo.

"I was really hoping to speak to Santo about photography, but he's pretty messed up." It was hard to hide his frustration. Two good-looking muscular young men with tattoos wearing tank tops approached them at the bar.

"Hey, Milo, how's it going man? Nice digs, eh?" said one of the guys.

"Olá, Enzio." Milo introduced Ronny to him and the other guy he was with. They were Brazilian but he didn't recognize them. Milo seemed to know them pretty well but appeared a little uncomfortable as he stood talking to them. Eventually they moved on leaving the two friends in silence.

"You know, man, it's been tough since the baby arrived trying to make ends meet," Milo spoke without making eye contact. "A friend knew I was struggling and suggested I come down and check out the club where he worked. He makes good cash and has a few private clients that pay him really well when they come to town."

Milo paused then touched Ronny on his arm. "I didn't have many options, you know." Ronny kept his eyes down on his beer.

"What's the name of the club?" he asked in a quiet tone. He didn't need to hear the answer.

"Club 117," Milo replied as Ronny finished his drink, caught off guard learning that Milo was working at a well-known gay brothel in Rio. He wasn't sure what to say. He finally looked at Milo, trying not to sound condescending.

"Do you need some cash, man? You okay?" It was hard not to pass judgment.

"I'm okay. Actually, the people that come there are pretty cool, and some are really generous. It's more money than I could make anywhere else."

"I guess Santo is a regular there?"

"I haven't seen him, but Enzio told me that Lucas came to the club to find some guys and had invited them."

Ronny knew that in Brazil, to survive you had to have something to sell. Those who didn't have a degree or a job often resorted to selling themselves. He himself had slept with an older female tourist a year ago when she had propositioned him for sex on the promenade. She offered him $100 and Ronny had gone back to her hotel, had sex with her, and took the money. As soon as he left her hotel, a wave of guilt washed over him and he regretted what he had done. He remembered looking down at the cash in his hand. *Dirty money.*

Milo must have been desperate. He remembered how cheap he felt after sleeping with that woman for money. He couldn't imagine having sex with men for a living. It was hard to accept this was now Milo's life. What about his dreams? Did he ever have any dreams? He couldn't remember Milo ever sharing anything about what he wanted to do with his life besides playing beach volleyball. He needed some air.

"I need to use the toilet," Ronny said as he put down his empty beer and walked across the room, down the hall, and into the marble bathroom. As he turned to close the door Santo appeared out of nowhere and forced his way into the toilet with Ronny, closing the door behind him.

"You want some coke?" asked Santo as he reached into his pocket and retrieved his stash.

Ronny was taken aback but tried to play it cool. "I'm good, thanks. I just need to use the toilet." This was exactly the kind of situation he wanted to avoid. Santo blocked the door and snorted a large bump of cocaine off his hand as Ronny stood there hoping he would leave. *Fuck, what do I do now?* "I don't want any coke, I'm good, thanks." *Why did you have to turn out to be such an asshole.*

"I thought you had to use the toilet?" Santo sniffed. Ronny thought about the scenarios playing out in his head and what his next move should be. He decided he had had enough and tried to leave. Santo grabbed his arm to stop him and started moving his hand down toward Ronny's jeans. He leaned in and whispered in his ear. "You want to make some extra cash?"

His dream of speaking with Santo Diaz about photography quickly turned into a nightmare. He could feel his face getting red as he grabbed Santo's wrist and forced his hand away trying to get past him. *Get me out of here!* Santo freed his hand and quickly put it on Ronny's crotch and proceeded to start massaging him. He moved in closer. Ronny felt violated as the smell of cologne and cigarettes filled his nose. He opened his eyes that were starting to water.

Suddenly overcome with rage he snapped, "Fuck you." He grabbed Santo by the shoulders and slammed him into the wall knocking the wind out of him. The impact seemed to sober Santo up; he looked shocked and grabbed for his chest. Ronny resisted the urge to punch him in the face and pushed his way past him and out of the bathroom shaking with anger. He slammed the door behind him and walked back to where Milo was standing. Dealing with his father was bad enough, but now the man he idolized had tried to abuse him and pay him for sex. He was crushed.

"You okay, man?" Milo said as he touched his shoulder.

"I'm going to leave."

"What? I'll come with you."

"I'm okay. You should stay here with your friends and hang out." Ronny nodded toward Enzio and the other escort. "You guys could probably make some extra money. I'll catch you later," Ronny added before walking out of the room, not giving him a chance to respond. He regretted saying it as soon as the words left his mouth. He knew he had hurt Milo. His anger and frustration at the whole situation caused him to lash out. He felt somehow betrayed. Maybe Lucas had seen Milo at the club when he was organizing the escorts for Santo and when he saw him on the beach with Ronny he would have told Santo and the stylist. *Maybe that's why they were trying to take advantage of me? They think I'm an escort. Guilty by association.*

As the elevator doors closed, he punched the wood paneled walls. Ronny walked out of the hotel, retrieved his bike, and rode along the promenade. *Did everyone here just want a piece of flesh? Is that how this works?* He stopped his bike and put one foot on the railing as he looked out at the ocean, still shaking. He breathed in the ocean air deeply, trying to clear his head. His face grew hot as tears filled his eyes and blurred his vision; he blinked and wiped his face with his hand and took another deep breath. It was late.

He took a final look at the dark ocean, then pushed himself off the wall to ride his bike home. He knew what he wanted more than anything else, but surely after what happened tonight Santo would not use any of the photographs of him in the magazine, so his chance of using modeling to get to Milan wasn't going to be an option.

# CHAPTER 5

Ronny barely slept. He tossed and turned most of the night, kept up by his thoughts on what could have happened and the reality of what did. *I shouldn't have gone to the wrap party. What was I thinking? I should have known there would be drugs there and Santo would be messed up. He must have thought we were escorts.* He got up and went into the kitchen, trying to distract himself with food. His father was already sitting at the small dining table eating his breakfast. Diego looked up.

"Bom dia," Ronny tried to sound upbeat. Ever since Luiz had left, he tried to become invisible in the house and not do anything to aggravate his father. The last thing he wanted was to upset him in any way and cause his mother more trouble. He suspected that he was still having an affair, but he kept his thoughts to himself.

"Where did you go last night? I heard you come in late," asked his father who sat shirtless on his seat. His once fit physique had softened and his handsome face looked bloated.

"I was at a party at The Copacabana Palace with Milo," Ronny answered. His mother entered the room and went to the stove to serve him breakfast.

"Fancy. I think it's time you got a full-time job and started to pay rent here."

The truth was Ronny couldn't wait to leave, and paying rent would mean it would take longer for him to save up money to be able to travel, and his hopes of pursuing his dreams would be crushed. *Asshole. How can Mom stay here?*

"He's working assisting Danilo," his mother said.

"That's only part time. I'm talking about a real job, not a hobby," Diego replied.

"I'm trying to get a second job so I can still work with Danilo and make some more money," Ronny said.

"Are you really looking?" Diego muttered. Ronny took a bite of his scrambled eggs that his mother had just put down and nodded at his father who he presumed was probably dealing with another hangover.

"I am." He knew Diego was looking for an argument; he had seen the same playbook with Luiz. Ronny was determined not to engage.

"How's Milo's baby?" asked his mother, doing her best to change the subject.

"Um, I think he's doing okay. Milo seems to be making it work." *I wonder if his girlfriend is okay with him working at the club.* Ronny was still processing Milo's predicament. He remembered when they were running errands for the gang his brother was in. They had become so close. The idea of Milo sleeping with men for money was hard to accept and he tried to not focus on what exactly he was having to do for the cash.

"Has he got a job to support his family?" Diego asked as he looked up.

Ronny imagined how his father would react if he knew what Milo was doing. "He is doing a few different things." Diego grunted and Ronny ate quickly. It was obvious he wanted to get out of the house as fast as he could. The tension was escalating between him and his father, and he knew it was only a matter of time before he would say something that pissed his father off and he would fall to the same fate as Luiz.

"Thanks for breakfast, Mom. See you tonight." He raced out the front door with his camera hidden in his backpack and grabbed his bike. As much as he felt sorry for his mother, he had come to accept that she was in denial that Diego was having an affair. He could see she was trapped and every time he tried to have a conversation about it, she quickly justified why she stayed with her husband. He loved his mother but didn't know how much longer he could deal with staying there.

Ronny rode down to the promenade to the exercise area on Copacabana Beach as he had done on most days, either to work out, hang with Milo and his friends, play volleyball, or take photographs. Even after what happened with Santo last night, Ronny wanted to take some photographs and try out a few ideas he had got watching Santo shoot on the beach yesterday. He was nervous about seeing Milo again. For a moment Ronny considered his own future and wondered what his options were. How desperate would he have to be to consider having sex with men for money? *Maybe if I had let Santo have his way with me last night I'd be in a different place today?* His mind raced as he questioned his actions. When he arrived at the volleyball courts, he saw Bruno and Javier, but Milo wasn't there.

"Hey, how was the party?" Bruno smiled as he approached them.

"Did Tiana finally come around?" Javier said and laughed.

"No, I only saw Tiana for a second. The party was cool, but by the time we got there everyone was pretty messed up. I actually didn't stay long."

"Hang on, hang on. Sounds like you're leaving something out."

"Not much else to tell," Ronny answered, wishing the topic of conversation would change. The whole experience with Santo had been traumatic enough without finding out about Milo.

"Whatever, Romeo," Javier added.

"I brought my camera down—can I take some photographs of you guys?" He quickly changed the subject.

"Sure, man, but my rate went up to a hundred dollars." Bruno pouted his lips, giving his best modeling expression, then burst out laughing. Ronny started directing Bruno, Javier, and the other players to start playing volleyball as he ran around in between them photographing the action and stopping them occasionally to take portraits of each of them. There were a few girls they knew standing beside the court watching. He directed Javier and Bruno to put the girls on their shoulders and move into the ocean to try and push each other off. He changed film rolls and continued taking photographs, calling out directions. This is when he felt most alive—creating and capturing moments. Once everyone was wet he brought them back on the beach and took some close-up portraits. He loved to capture the realness of a scar, sweat on skin, freckles, and emotion. Whether happy or sad, the eyes couldn't lie, and when you really connected with someone they let you in. He looked through his camera lens and directed his subjects, watching how the light changed on their face and remembering how Santo had directed and composed his shots. After an hour of shooting, he had used all the film he had brought with him, though he could have happily continued taking photographs. He was lucky to have been working for Danilo—he allowed him to develop film for free. Without his generosity he wouldn't have been able to afford to do it.

"That was incredible. Thanks, guys!" As he walked back up the beach, he saw Milo offering a wave. Ronny felt uncomfortable seeing him.

"Hey, man," Milo said as he approached. "You get some good shots?" Ronny fist-pumped his hand. He could tell Milo held no resentment toward him even though he would have been hurt by what he had said. He acted like nothing had happened.

"I'm sorry for what I said last night. I was just so angry about Santo being so messed up. I really thought it might have been a chance for me to talk with him about photography. I'm really sorry for what I said," Ronny added.

"It's cool, man. I'm sorry I didn't tell you earlier about everything. I was worried Ana wouldn't let me see the baby if I didn't start to make some money. I didn't have a lot of options."

Ronny thought about what Milo was saying. It was true, there were only so many jobs available and because people knew Milo's brother was in a gang and that they had worked with him it was tough to catch a break. Nobody wanted trouble. That reality and the few opportunities available upped the ante on Ronny wanting to leave. "Does she know about it?" he asked.

"I didn't tell her for a few weeks, and when I finally did we had an argument. She didn't approve, but ultimately we needed the money so she let me keep working but she didn't want to have sex with me. I think she was worried she would catch something. I told her I was being careful, but we haven't really spoken about that again." Milo scratched the side of his face; he looked tired. "It's not easy. I didn't know what else to do."

Ronny saw that Milo was having a hard time. "I know how it feels to need cash. I've got to sort something out so I can move out of my home and get away from my dad." Ronny added. It felt like they were both trapped by their circumstance without a lot of options.

"You guys want to work out?" Bruno asked as he walked past them on his way to the outdoor exercise area farther up the beach close to the promenade. Ronny patted Milo on the shoulder, and they joined Bruno and began to work out together with Javier as if nothing had changed. He was glad that he and Milo had spoken despite not being comfortable with his predicament.

The next week Ronny managed to get a part-time job at a restaurant to keep his father happy. At least he could still get to work for Danilo and use his photo lab to develop his film and make photographic prints. Since he saw Santo work, he had become even more inspired to continue taking photographs himself and spent a lot of the money he made at work on film and photographic paper. Several months passed as Ronny focused on working hard and doing as much photography as possible. It was the best way to distract himself from the toxic environment at home. He could tell his father had been drinking more than usual. His mother accused him of gambling and their fighting had intensified. Ronny was finding it hard to stay out of their arguments until one evening before dinner his father burst into his room, already drunk, demanding that he pay more rent. He had been giving Diego almost half the money he was making, which didn't leave a lot once he had paid for photographic supplies.

"I'm doing all I can. Calm down," Ronny said as he stood up and put his two hands out in front of him.

"Maybe you should sell your camera and stop spending money on these stupid photographs," Diego said sternly as he reached out and in one movement ripped down two of the photographic prints that were taped to the wall above his small desk. Ronny moved forward to try and stop him. Even though Diego wasn't as fit as he used to be, he was still strong enough to hold him back. Diego reached down to grab the camera that was sitting on his desk.

"Give me back my camera. Please!" There was desperation in his voice as his father pushed him away. Ronny stumbled back and almost fell over.

"You're wasting your time with this photography thing. You're a loser just like your brother."

Ronny exploded as he returned the push with as much force as he could muster. Diego lost his balance and fell backwards into the corner and landed on the ground with a loud thud still holding the camera. For a moment Ronny thought he may have knocked him unconscious. A wave of panic hit him as he momentarily regretted pushing him. He was about to ask him if he was okay.

"You ungrateful little shit," yelled his father as he sat up and threw the camera across the room. The sound of it smashing into the wall was only drowned out by the sound of Ronny crying out.

"Nooooo!" His heart dropped as he ran to retrieve the camera that was now on the floor. Unfortunately, the lens was still on the camera body and he could tell straight away looking at the cracks in the glass that that it had been badly damaged.

"Fuck you!" Ronny slid down the wall and sat on the floor holding the camera, tears welling up as he looked back toward Diego. The man that he had once loved and looked up to had just broken his heart. He sat there on the floor holding the cracked camera lens. His mother entered the room with a shocked expression on her face. She raced forward to help Diego to his feet.

"You're done!" Diego yelled at Ronny as he staggered to stand up. "Get out of my house!"

"No, Diego," his mother called out, sounding desperate. She glanced back at Ronny; tears filled her eyes as her mouth hardened trying to compose herself. "He is doing all he can." Ronny's anger slightly subsided as a wave of pity for his mother washed over him. All of a sudden something inside him clicked and he felt almost numb.

"It's fine, Mom. I'm done." His father had crossed a line that he could no longer ignore. *I'll fucking show you who's a loser.* It was time for him to move out. As much as he feared for his mother's safety, he now realized he had to put himself first—his safety, his dreams, and his life. Diego stormed out of the bedroom and left the apartment as Adriana started to cry.

"I'm sorry," Ronny added. She picked up the photographs off the floor and moved close to Ronny as he got to his feet. "I love you but I can't stay here anymore. I just can't." He hugged his mother who squeezed him tightly. She held him as she sobbed quietly. "Why don't you leave with me?" he whispered in her ear. She didn't let him go.

"Your father doesn't mean what he said. I know this has been really hard on you but things will get better."

He knew there was nothing he could say that would convince his mother to leave. She had to make that decision for herself, she had to hit rock bottom. He took a deep breath, rubbed his mother's back, then pulled away from her, wiped his eyes, and began to pack up his room. He was shaking from the fight with his father. He carefully peeled each photograph off the wall, put them in a print box, and collected his film negatives and clothes. His head was swirling as he considered his next move. No home, no money, and a broken camera. He picked up the pieces of his camera and put it in his backpack. Thankfully his brother had offered for him to sleep on his couch; that would at least give him somewhere to stay until he had a better plan. He looked up at the now bare walls and felt alone.

Half an hour later Ronny walked out of his bedroom with a suitcase harnessed over his shoulder with two belts, not wanting to look back. He found his mother in the kitchen cleaning up, trying to distract herself. She was still quietly crying; her face was red and she looked exhausted.

"I'm going to stay with Luiz. I'll be okay. I'm sorry," Ronny said.

"I don't want you to leave," she said. "I know this has been tough on you, but it will get better."

"You've been saying that for a long time and it's only getting worse," he replied, sounding defeated. "He's not going to change. The man we loved is gone." Adriana stopped crying for a moment. Even though his comment was harsh, she needed to hear it and accept the reality of the situation. He looked down at his bag and moved forward to hug her. "I love you, Mom. Take care of yourself." He didn't make eye contact with her as he pulled back and walked out.

# CHAPTER 6

Warm tears slowly streamed down his cheeks as he rode the twenty minutes to Luiz's apartment feeling broken and lost, trying not to resent his mother for staying. As much as he wanted to scream, he wiped away the tears and took a deep breath to clear his mind. For years now he had been dealing with emotional stress by blocking it out, not wanting to show his father he was weak. But tonight he felt exhausted, tired of living in a toxic environment, witnessing his parents' relationship deteriorate. He was done. When he arrived at his brother's apartment, Luiz's girlfriend of two years, Maria, opened the door.

"Come in," she said and smiled. She waited until he put the suitcase down before giving him a hug. The one-bedroom apartment was small, but Maria had filled it with colorful eclectic furniture, art, and plants; it felt warm and inviting.

"Hey, bro. I missed you." Luiz appeared and embraced Ronny as Maria went to make up a bed for him on the sofa. "Stay as long as you like," Luiz added as he headed back to the kitchen. "You hungry?"

Ronny tried to offer a smile and nodded as he closed his eyes for a moment, relieved he had somewhere to go.

"Grab a shower if you like, then we can eat." Luiz had their mother's kind eyes and appeared to understand what it had taken for Ronny to leave. Nothing needed to be said. Ronny put his suitcase next to the couch and took a shower. As the warm water ran down his back, he thought of his mother. He suspected his father was out for the night and he imagined his mother would be sitting at home crying in the kitchen.

He felt his anger rise again as he thought about Diego throwing his camera against the wall. The one possession he truly valued besides his prints and negatives. He had disrespected his dream for the last time, and it was only a matter of time before he hurt his father or his father hurt him. Staying in that place was killing his dream and holding him back from living it. As hard as it was to leave his mother there, he knew it was time. He got out of the shower, got dressed, and joined Maria and Luiz at the small dining table. Maria served up a delicious chicken rice dish that Ronny ate, momentarily distracted from feeling unsettled and shellshocked. It was so good to see his brother, even under these circumstances. He felt safe for the first time in a long time, like he had someone to look out for him again.

"It was only a matter of time before you left. I'm surprised you lasted this long." Luiz touched him on his shoulder.

"He came home drunk again, ripped down some of my photographs, and smashed my camera against the wall. I was only staying there for Mom, but I couldn't take it anymore. I'll give her a call tomorrow after he's gone to work to let her know I'm okay. I told her I was coming here."

"Is your camera okay?" asked Maria as she passed Ronny a beer.

"The lens was cracked—I know it's broken, I'll get it checked out. I just had enough." He took a sip of beer to distract himself from crying again.

"Well, you're here with family now." Luiz raised his beer, and Ronny noticed how much he had grown up since he left home. After his stint in prison, he was forced to step up and get his life together. He and his brother had been close growing up; they had enjoyed so many adventures together, so many great memories. Unfortunately, when things changed with Diego, Luiz stayed away as much as possible until he finally left. Ronny remembered how crushed he was and how much he missed having his big brother around.

When when Luiz went to prison, he remembered how badly Diego spoke about him, trying to paint a picture of a good kid gone bad. He forbade Ronny from seeing his brother, but he skipped school on a few occasions to visit him in prison. When Luiz got out he managed to see him each week in secret, though he would let his mother know how he was doing. It had been a tough time for everyone.

At dinner Ronny talked about the photo shoot with Santo on the beach, he didn't mention the incident at the wrap party. He preferred to focus on the experience of watching Santo work and how inspired he had been. After the meal Luiz and Maria cleaned up the dishes then retired to their room while Ronny lay down on the couch, which was surprisingly comfortable. He considered the hard choices he now faced about his uncertain future. He rolled to one side, trying to shake off the worry about what to do, trying to get comfortable. He tossed a few more times then finally lay on his back as the ceiling fan spun overhead. He took a deep breath and closed his eyes, emotionally and physically exhausted. *I'm sorry, Mama.*

Ronny was woken up early by Maria's cat who jumped up on his legs.

"He's waiting for some breakfast." Maria smiled warmly as she walked out of the bedroom and went to the kitchen to get a small plate of cat food and set it down in the corner, her thick black hair tied back loosely in a ponytail. The energy in the small apartment was so much calmer than his parents' home. It was nice to wake up in a household with no tension.

Luiz appeared and smiled at his brother. "Sleep okay?"

"Hey, bro. Yeah, thanks. This couch is so comfortable, I may never leave," Ronny joked as Luiz tapped him on the leg and walked toward the kitchen.

"Coffee?"

"Perfect, thanks." Ronny got up and went to use the bathroom.

"Have you been seeing anyone?" asked Luiz as Ronny came out of the bathroom.

"No one serious. I briefly dated a girl a year ago but we broke up. She was way too jealous. Every time I would photograph another girl, she would go crazy." Ronny knew that he couldn't be with anyone who had an issue with his photography. He had slept with a few girls since then but nothing serious.

"I'm lucky Maria is pretty chill." Luiz didn't pry further. Seeing him and Maria together gave Ronny a glimmer of hope that a relationship could work. He had lost so much faith being around his parents over the last few years, seeing how his father had betrayed his mother's trust. "You'll meet the right person when its time."

Ronny nodded and smiled. "I've been trying to focus more on my photography and not to get distracted." It was easier to offer an excuse than to get into the details of why he didn't think a relationship was something he was interested in. At this stage the only person he felt he could really trust was himself. "Dad said I was a loser and should give it up my photography."

"That sounds like something he'd say. I remember how I grew

to hate him and the way he treated Mom. When I was in prison, I was able to make peace with my anger and ended up feeling sorry for him. You should always stay true to your dream. Fuck what anyone else thinks."

"Thanks, man." Ronny needed to hear that, especially now. Later that morning, when he knew his father had gone to work, he rang his mother to reassure her that he was okay and staying with Luiz. She sounded broken, exhausted, and close to tears.

"Your father's been under a lot of pressure lately as they cut back his hours at work."

He shook his head slowly. "You can leave, too, you know," he said, unable to hide the anger and frustration in his voice.

"I'm really sorry he threw your camera."

"I had to leave; I just couldn't take it anymore. I love you," Ronny said and ended the call. As hard as it was to leave her there, he knew he would not be going back. Nothing would change his mind. Hearing his father call him a loser had ignited a fire inside him and a determination to prove himself. Somehow, he would work this out, get the money together to fix his camera, and find a place to live. He pulled out a copy of *Italian STYLE* magazine from his bag to try and distract himself. He tried to focus on the photographs but felt overwhelmed by his situation. He closed the magazine and lay on the couch watching the ceiling fan overhead.

Later that week Ronny got news that the restaurant he worked at was closing down and his part-time work doing photo assisting was cut back because Danilo wasn't getting as many jobs. He walked his bike along the beach promenade, looking down at the pavement, trying not to be consumed with despair. He felt too embarrassed to ask his brother for money but maybe he'd know of somewhere he could get some work.

"Hey, stranger," said Milo as he walked up the steps off the beach. He looked tired.

"Hey, man," Ronny replied in a somber tone. He had avoided seeing his friends since he left home. He felt too depressed to be social.

"Are you okay? I went past your place a few days ago and your dad said he didn't know where you were."

"Probably because the asshole kicked me out."

"What? Sorry, man. Where are you staying?"

"I'm on my brother's couch. It's been a bit rough," Ronny answered as Milo stood quietly listening.

"Is your mom okay?"

"She's the same. She won't leave him. He smashed my camera," Ronny added then moved to the side of the promenade and sat down on the ground. He put his head in his hands and started quietly crying. He felt as if his world was closing in around him; he was freefalling and couldn't stop. Milo sat down next to him and put his hand on his back. They sat there for a while as strangers walked by.

"Sorry, man." Ronny slowly stood up and wiped his face. "I'm trying to get some work so I can get my camera fixed and get my own place. It's just been tough, you know."

"Hey, you know if you want, I can introduce you to the guys at the club. You could just come down and check it out. See how you feel." Milo added.

Ronny slowly lifted his head. He felt numb and alone, unable to see another way out. "I guess I could come down tomorrow night. Just to see the place." That was as much of a commitment as Ronny could muster.

"I'll be there from five," Milo said.

"I'll see you tomorrow night," Ronny replied as he touched Milo on the shoulder. He wanted to be alone and process everything. He didn't feel much like talking. He collected his bike, and started riding up the promenade back to his brother's house.

He imagined working at the club with Milo, letting the men there touch him, use him, pay him for sex. Every one of them had the face of Santo Diaz. The sun was almost setting, and he decided to stop next to the promenade wall to distract himself by watching the sunset. He sat on his bike shirtless feeling the cool breeze on his skin, one leg up on the wall to balance himself.

"Amazing, right?" A woman's voice with an American accent broke the silence. He turned around to see an attractive dark-haired woman in her fifties smiling at him. Foreign tourists in Rio were easy to spot.

"Bela." Ronny nodded back to the ocean as the woman walked up next to him and looked out at the horizon. She was attractive and fit for her age, and even though she wasn't wearing any jewelry Ronny could tell by her styled shoulder-length hair and nails that she had money.

"So I gather you're from here?" she asked.

"Yep, made in Brazil." He could sense the woman was flirting with him. He offered a forced smile; he had grown up seeing his father use his charm on women and as much as he despised his father, he knew he had the same gift. It came so natural to him.

"I'm Amanda." She reached out her hand.

"I'm Ronny." He shook her hand and when he locked eyes with her, he got a sense that she had been drinking. Her hand felt smooth and soft to touch. He released it and turned back around to watch the sun disappear over the horizon. When he turned back to Amanda, she was still looking at him. "You missed the sunset," he said.

"I didn't miss a thing." She reached out and felt Ronny's arm; he saw the hunger in her eyes. He was caught off guard and slightly turned on by her confidence. With all he had going on, having his ego stroked was a nice distraction. "So now that the sun's gone, what are you doing?" she asked.

"I was just heading home for dinner."

"Maybe I could make it worth your while to be a little late?"

Ronny didn't speak. He kept his eyes on her and gave a slight smile; his mind raced as he considered exactly what she meant.

"How would you like to come back to my hotel room? I could pay you a hundred fifty dollars for your time," Amanda added softly.

Ronny felt overwhelmed as he considered his options. *Maybe sleeping with a woman for money again will ease me into being able to do it with men?* The only thing he knew for certain was that $150 would allow him to get his camera fixed. Maybe it wouldn't be as bad as he had imagined. He remembered the last tourist he had slept with for money, and how dirty he had felt. At the time he hadn't planned on doing it again but now he really needed the money. He felt like a hypocrite after judging Milo for doing what he was now considering.

"Sounds interesting." He heard the words leave his mouth as Amanda's smile widened. She motioned for him to follow. He put his shirt on and followed closely behind her walking his bike, not speaking as he crossed the street and walked two blocks to her hotel. He didn't hear any of what she said—he was distracted, trying to process how he ended up in this situation. As he was chaining up his bike outside the hotel, he fumbled with the lock. He took a deep breath, acknowledging that his week had somehow gone from bad to worse. His mind raced as he considered another way to get back on his feet. Selling himself seemed to be the only option presenting itself to him.

"Everything okay?" asked Amanda.

"Yes, sorry," he replied. The sooner he got this over with the sooner he could get his camera fixed. The bike lock clicked shut as he stood up offering a polite smile. As the elevator door closed in the hotel, he caught a glimpse of his image reflected from a mirror on the paneled wall as Amanda ran her hand up his arm to feel his bicep. *I can do this. I need to do this.* An uncomfortable ache in his stomach made him wonder if it was nerves or the fact that he hadn't eaten since breakfast. As he entered Amanda's suite on the sixth floor, he was momentarily distracted by the spectacular view of the ocean and walked toward the balcony. The last time he has seen this view was at Santo's penthouse.

"Ronny, this is Darren," announced Amanda as she closed the door behind them. He turned to see a grey-haired, heavy-set man coming out of the bedroom wearing just a bathrobe.

"Well, hello, Ronny. Nice to meet you." Darren raised his eyebrows and offered a satisfied smile. Ronny looked back at Amanda with a startled expression. *What the fuck!*

"He's my husband, darling. Don't worry, he just likes to watch," she added as Ronny looked back at Darren casually walking toward the kitchen. He felt sick to his stomach.

"Um, I don't think I'm cool with this. Sorry."

"I'll pay you two hundred fifty," Amanda said as she stepped forward, reached out, and started massaging his chest. "You're so damn sexy," she whispered.

Santo's face came to mind as he remembered being groped by him in the toilet at the wrap party, and being offered money for sex. Here he was again. His mind raced as he considered the money he so desperately needed. Amanda came in close and started trying to kiss him, her hand moving lower to grope his crotch. He closed his eyes.

"You want a drink or some cocaine, Ronny?" asked Darren from the kitchen as Amanda continued to grope his crotch trying to get him hard. It wasn't working. He felt a deep sadness rising inside him. *What am I doing?* He swallowed and started to kiss Amanda back until his sadness was overcome with the feeling of resentment and anger. Anger toward his father for destroying their family. Anger toward his mother for not protecting him and leaving Diego. But mostly anger toward himself for ending up in this place.

"I want to feel you inside me," said Amanda as she continued trying to get him hard.

*I need this money. I need it.* Ronny opened his eyes and kissed Amanda back until the sound of Darren snorting a line of cocaine snapped him back to reality. He pulled back from her mouth.

"Sorry, I can't do this. I have to go." Ronny turned around and walked out of the suite and headed back down to his bike. *Fuck them.* He was willing to have sex with Amanda for the money, but the thought of her old husband masturbating while he watched just freaked him out.

He started second-guessing himself as he rode to a house he couldn't afford and a dinner he hadn't paid for at his brother's house. He swerved to miss an oncoming scooter. *What the hell am I doing? No job, no place to live, no camera...no money.* He felt numb.

# CHAPTER 7

When he entered Luiz's apartment, the smell of cheese bread reminded him how hungry he was.

"Just in time," said Maria as she came out of the kitchen. "Why don't you wash up and Luiz will set the table."

Ronny offered Maria a polite smile, relieved to be away from Amanda and her voyeur husband. He showered quickly, trying to wash away what had just happened—the dirty feeling of being used. He gargled some warm water in his mouth and spat it out. When he came out of the bathroom, he could hear Luiz and Maria singing along with the music laughing with each other. It reminded him of when he was young and his parents were in love. He remembered his mother's smiling face looking young and beautiful. The sound of her laugh was something he hadn't heard for a long time. He felt sad as he wondered what she was doing; he imagined her alone cleaning the kitchen. Ronny joined Luiz and Maria at the small dining table, and he could feel the cat moving around his legs purring loudly.

"Smells amazing. Thank you." He was grateful for the distraction as Luiz served him up some food.

"How was your day?" asked Luiz as Maria passed him a beer.

"Pretty chill—just out trying to get some more work." *Oh, and I was propositioned by an older woman who took me back to her hotel room and tried to pay me $250 for sex while her husband watched and jacked off.*

"You need some cash? You okay?"

"Thanks, I'm fine. You're already doing so much for me. I'll work it out." Ronny reached for a piece of bread, trying not to get emotional. He was embarrassed and overwhelmed by his predicament and could feel his brother's gaze still on him. Luiz touched him on the shoulder. Like his mother, Luiz could tell when Ronny had something on his mind. A few tears finally ran down his cheeks as he wiped them away.

"Just don't do anything stupid," said Luiz. "Look where that got me."

He nodded and took a slow breath. He wasn't going to tell Luiz about his plans to visit the club where Milo worked. Not yet. The phone rang, and Maria got up to answer it, then turned back to the table holding the receiver. "Ronny, it's your mother. She said it's important."

Ronny's heart dropped. He immediately thought that his father had done something to hurt his mother. He quickly got up and took the phone from Maria.

"Mom, are you okay?"

"I'm fine."

"Where's Dad?"

"Your father isn't here." Ronny felt a sense of relief that his mother wasn't in trouble.

"A woman named Sylvia called today asking for you. She is a model scout and had met you after the photo shoot you had done with that photographer."

Ronny was caught off guard. After what happened with Santo,

what could she want? "Yes, I remember her. What did she say?"

"She wanted to talk to you about a show or something. I have her number for you if you have a pen."

*A show? How did she even get my number?* He tried not to get too excited; it wasn't like things had been going well for him lately. He carefully took down Sylvia's number. He wasn't sure if he still had her business card or not and wanted to make sure he had it right.

"I need to go. Please give my love to Luiz and Maria. I love you," she said. The urgency in his mother's voice led him to believe his father was arriving home.

"I love you too." He hung up the phone.

"Is she okay?" asked Luiz when Ronny came back to the table.

"She seemed fine. She got a call from a woman who is a model scout who wants to speak to me about something."

"Do you know her?" asked Luiz.

"Yes, I met her at the wrap party after the shoot I did with that photographer I told you about. I'll give her a call in the morning if that's okay. I think she's based in Milan." Even though it had been months since they had met, Ronny remembered the brief conversation he had with her about Milan being the fashion capital of the world where all young models and photographers get started. He drew a deep breath, not wanting to get his hopes up. *What could this mean? A second chance? A way to get to Milan?*

"Talk to her as long as you need," added Maria.

After dinner Ronny stood in the kitchen with Luiz washing the dishes.

"Do you think about Mom?" Ronny asked Luiz.

"I think about her all the time. I was so angry at her for such a long time. Resenting her for letting Dad kick me out. Now I just feel pity for her. She is trapped and blind."

"I hope she will be okay there."

"You can't take it on. She made the decision to stay with him and you have your life to live now. You haven't been going out much lately. Are there any parties on with the guys?" asked Luiz, changing the subject.

"I guess there's things on, but I just haven't felt like going out much. I'm trying to get things back on track and going out is really the last thing on my mind."

"Things will turn around for you. Just don't lose hope and give it time." Luiz hugged him before heading to bed.

The following morning Ronny was up early and made himself a coffee before calling Sylvia in Milan. He hadn't slept well the night before as his imagination raced. He dialed the number his mother had given him, and Sylvia answered.

"I got your number from Lucas the producer and called your mother," she explained. "I wanted to let you know the editorial you shot with Tiana has just come out in *Italian STYLE* magazine and the photographs are amazing."

"Really?" Ronny said, relieved that Santo had still used the photographs despite the incident in the bathroom. "We don't get the new issue here for another month."

"I know I spoke to you briefly about modeling at the party. Well, the Italian designer Lorenzo Mancini just saw the magazine spread of you and Tiana and he wants to book you to walk in his summer fashion show. It's a huge deal." Ronny knew Lorenzo Mancini from seeing his ads in the fashion magazines. Sylvia continued, "I have already spoken to BAM models in Milan. They're the best agency for men here and they want to represent you in Europe. If you agree they will advance you the money for your travel and accommodation in Milan."

Ronny sat down in the chair next to the phone. Sylvia had no way to know how much this meant to him. "That's amazing news. I wasn't sure if my photographs made it into the magazine."

"There are eight photographs of you in the story and the cover with Tiana."

Ronny put his head into his hands and closed his eyes. *Is this really happening?*

"Ronny? Are you still there?"

He cleared his throat, trying to compose himself. "Yes, sorry, I'm still here. So when would I need to go to Milan?"

"Do you have a passport?"

"Yes." He had to get one when he visited his uncle.

"Great. If you agree to the contract terms you will need to get a tourist visa which takes five days to process, so you would be coming here in ten days so you could be in town before the shows."

"I'd love to come to Milan." Just yesterday he was at the lowest point he could remember—ready to start working as an escort at a gay brothel. Now maybe there was a chance he could get his dream back on track. Sylvia went over the general terms of the contract, and Ronny gave her the fax number at Luiz's work so she could send it through.

"I will start to get everything organized for you and get the details for the flight and accommodation. Does that sound good?" Sylvia asked.

"Sure. I can get the visa application started today." Ronny was shellshocked. He gave Sylvia his number and address and hung up the phone. *Milan men's fashion week. Seriously!* Ronny couldn't believe that he was already booked for the Mancini fashion show. He imagined meeting the designer and the contacts he would make that could possibly help him get a start in the business. Being photographed in Milan by successful photographers, watching how they worked, and getting to assist them. Walking the streets of Milan capturing the beauty of the city and taking portraits of the street vendors and photographing young models to build up his portfolio.

"How did the call go?" asked Luiz as he walked out of the bedroom.

"They want to pay for me to fly to Milan for a fashion show and will advance me for the air ticket and accommodation."

"What!? That's amazing!" Luiz moved forward and embraced Ronny. "You deserve it, man. Don't look back, just go for it."

"Thanks, bro. It would be a dream to go to Milan and have a chance to get a break with my photography." He looked down at the ground briefly, remembering that his camera was broken. His heart sank as he couldn't imagine going without a camera and he was unsure how much it would cost to fix or how long it would take.

"What is it?" Luiz asked.

"My camera. I'm just thinking how I can get that fixed before I leave."

Luiz paused as Ronny was again confronted with the fact that he had no money. There was still the chance he could work with Milo at the club. That would guarantee him some fast cash. *If that's what it takes, I don't have a choice.* Luiz touched him on the shoulder. "Why don't you let me pay to get it repaired?"

"You've already done so much," Ronny answered. He felt so much closer to his brother since he moved in than ever before. In some ways it felt like it was just the two of them now, supporting each other as family. Luiz had become the father he had lost.

"I know what this means to you—you can't go to Milan without your camera. Take the money and we will sort it out later. I couldn't be there to help you when I left home, so let me help you now. Please."

Ronny started to smile as he held back the tears, overwhelmed by the support from Luiz. He nodded and said, "I'll take it in today so I can get it back before I leave."

"I have a friend that does construction who just told me yesterday he needs some help on a new project if you want to pick up some extra money before you leave. It's hard work but it pays well."

"That would be amazing." Ronny knew he would need spending money in Milan, so the extra cash would help. And he'd certainly rather do hard labor than work with Milo at the club.

Maria came out and gave Ronny a huge hug when she heard the news. "I'll cook something special for you for dinner to celebrate."

"Sounds perfect." He was happy his brother had met such a sweet woman. Maybe a relationship could last...

"I'll make some eggs for breakfast," said Luiz. Ronny felt a renewed energy as he helped set the table. He hadn't felt like that in months.

"We will miss having you around here," Luiz said as he poured some more coffee.

"Rio will always be my home." Modeling was just a way he could do some traveling, build up his photography portfolio, and hopefully get the break he needed. At least something good came out of the whole Santo Diaz ordeal. But he didn't want to dampen his excitement thinking about Santo. For now he was just happy.

"You should call Mom," said Luiz. "I'm sure she will be wondering what happened."

After breakfast when Ronny suspected Diego had left the apartment, he called his mother. When she picked up the phone, she sounded unusually upbeat.

"It's good to hear your voice—did you call that woman?" she asked.

"I called her. I've been offered a modeling contract in Milan and I leave in ten days."

"Good for you."

He could hear a crack in her voice. A feeling of guilt slowly rose up inside him.

"I don't want to leave you here." *With him.*

"I'll be fine. You need to do this—it's something you've always dreamed about. Nothing will change here."

She was right, nothing would change.

"Mom—" he stopped himself, knowing his words would fall on deaf ears.

"I'll miss you," she said, sounding like she was about to start crying.

"I love you, Mom." He slowly shook his head as he put down the receiver.

# CHAPTER 8

After dropping off his camera to be repaired and getting a visa application, he went by Milo's house to let know he wouldn't be coming by the club that night. Milo looked exhausted when he answered the door, and Ronny could hear his baby crying in the background. They stood outside on the street in the shade.

"I got a call from that model scout I met at the wrap party after the photoshoot, and she offered me a modeling contract in Milan for men's fashion week," Ronny said. "I am already booked for a big fashion show so the model agency representing me there is advancing my air ticket and accommodation."

"What?! Good for you." Milo appeared genuinely happy for Ronny. "When do you leave?"

"I leave in ten days. I managed to pick up some construction work with a friend of Luiz's so I'll be busy until I leave."

"You nervous?"

"More excited than nervous. It's the first time I'm leaving Brazil by myself and I'm so ready. I'm hoping this modeling thing will help me get the start I need to do photography in Milan. Apparently a lot of young photographers go there."

"Imagine the girls, man. It's going to be crazy." Milo pushed his shoulder as Ronny smiled back. It had been a while since he had been focused on girls.

"How's things with you? All good?" Ronny asked.

"I'm hanging in there, keeping busy, you know." Milo looked past him, avoiding eye contact. Ronny didn't want to press for more details—it was obvious that things weren't going well. His usual carefree demeanor was gone, and he wondered if he was doing drugs at the club.

"I had a woman try to pay me for sex after I saw you at the beach. She offered me two hundred and fifty dollars. I would have done it but when we got back to hotel room her husband was there and wanted to watch." He felt sharing his story would somehow make Milo feel better about his own situation.

"That's a lot of cash," Milo replied, sounding numb, almost despondent.

"Is it always just about the money?" Ronny snapped. He could see a sadness in Milo's eyes as he stood silent and put his hands in his pocket and shuffled uncomfortably. Maybe he had a dream that he never got a chance to follow and now he was caught in a vicious cycle of survival. "I guess I won't need to come down to the club tonight, but thanks for offering to make an introduction," Ronny added. "Do you think you will stay working there for long? Isn't there something else you want to do?" Ronny tried to hide his frustration and judgement.

Milo shrugged his shoulders and shook his head. "It's the money, man. I've got a kid. I don't have much else going on." He sounded like he had given up. Ronny didn't want to press him further. It was still hard for him to accept the reality of the situation and what his friend was doing to survive. Many people came to Brazil for sex and there were just as many poor people willing to sell it. Ronny hoped opportunities would be different for him in Milan.

"I don't know exactly what's going to happen in Milan. But I know right now it's the best chance I have to get my photography career off the ground."

Milo looked at him. "Better than staying around here trying to hustle," Milo replied.

"Yeah. I guess," Ronny said before heading off down the street.

The next day Ronny started working doing construction with Luiz's friend. The work was hard and the days were long. His body was sore but he stayed focused on his upcoming trip and the money he was saving. The day before he left, he went to his parents' house to say goodbye to his mother. He arrived around 2 p.m., presuming his father would be at work, and rang the buzzer for their apartment. Ronny could hear his mother speaking and when she finally opened the door slightly with the chain lock still on, he heard his father's voice yelling something muffled in the background.

"This isn't a good time." Her face was flushed and her eyes were red from crying.

The last time Ronny saw his father was when they had the fight and he broke his camera. All the fears and anxiety about that night came flooding back. A wave of guilt washed over him.

"Are you okay? I wanted to come and say goodbye." Ronny reached out and touched her hand; his face began to get warm. He felt helpless. She closed her eyes.

"I'm sorry. Your father lost his job." A tear rolled down her face as he heard his father's voice getting louder. "I'm sorry." She pulled her hand away and closed the door as their arguing continued. A part of him wanted to kick down the door and beat up his father—make him feel some of the pain he had caused the family. But he knew that would only cause more problems for her in the long run. The guilt he felt for leaving was replaced by anger knowing she had abandoned him again. As much as he wanted to stay and look after her, he couldn't feel sorry for her anymore. He was heartbroken.

The morning Ronny was leaving Milo dropped by just as he finished packing his bag.

"I came across this and thought you might like to take it with you." Milo retrieved a small black and white photograph from his backpack and handed it to Ronny.

"I remember when this was taken—you told me we were going to play beach volleyball for Brazil together one day," Ronny said as he studied the image, smiling to himself as he looked at the faces of the two young boys standing together at the beach holding a volleyball. "I think it was your tenth birthday."

"I was so skinny," Milo laughed.

Ronny looked at the photograph, remembering how carefree life was then. He studied the bright-eyed hopeful expression on Milo's face. The smile slowly left his face. He didn't recognize that boy anymore. The two friends stood in silence looking at the photograph, caught up in the nostalgic moment.

"Don't come back until you're ready. There's nothing keeping you here," Milo added. He sounded so much older than his twenty years. It was a bittersweet moment; Ronny had managed to finally catch a break, a chance for a better life, and yet he was leaving Milo and his mother behind.

"Must have felt good to get your camera back," said Luiz as he walked into the kitchen.

"It's the longest I've gone without taking a photo since I got the camera."

Luiz touched him on the shoulder and handed him an envelope. "I know you saved up some cash, but this will help you buy some film when you get to Milan."

He glanced down to the envelope of money. "I can't take this."

Ronny was overwhelmed with his brother's generosity. His father had never believed in his photography, and with one simple gesture Luiz had shown him more support than his father ever had. It was hard to accept the love and generosity that he had been missing for so long.

Luiz embraced him. "We believe in you."

"It means so much to hear you say that. More than you know." Tears welled up in his eyes. When he really needed it, his brother had been there for him. He provided Ronny a safety net he would never forget. "I love you. I will pay you back," Ronny added feeling uncomfortable accepting the money though knew he needed it for his expenses.

"Hey, don't forget to have some fun." Luiz nodded and smiled, silently acknowledging there was no rush to pay him back.

## CHAPTER 9

Ronny slept all the way to Milan until a woman's voice with a heavy Italian accent came over the flight's loudspeaker welcoming everyone to Milan, first in Italian then in English. A wave of excitement mixed with fear of the unknown came over him. He had brought two issues of *Italian STYLE* magazine with him in his backpack next to his camera and box of photographic prints. He re-read the article in the magazine about Lorenzo Mancini, the designer that had booked him for his fashion show. It described his decadent lifestyle, love of powerful women, and his passion for design. The term "supermodel" had been coined by Mancini and a handful of female models, including Tiana Taylor, part of that elite group of girls that had taken on a new level of celebrity. They were fast becoming just as famous as the designers they modeled for.

After exchanging some money, Ronny headed toward the taxi stand but was stopped in his tracks when he saw an enlarged poster of the cover of the current *Italian STYLE* magazine. He approached and saw himself and his friends standing around Tiana Taylor on the cover as she danced in front of them in a bikini. She looked incredible. Ronny smiled to himself and purchased a copy. He looked at the cover then flicked through the magazine until he found the editorial spread, which was about twenty pages long. He was featured on eight pages with group shots, double shots with Tiana, and a single shot of his torso and face.

It was incredible to see the finished product after he had studied the way that Santo had set up and directed the photographs and captured the energy and magic of the moment so perfectly. The story was printed half black and white and half in color. He took note of how each photo was cropped and how the layout of the story flowed. He imagined seeing his first editorial spread in a magazine as a photographer and how incredible it must be knowing your work was being seen by so many people. He wished Milo and his friends could have been there with him. The short Italian man who worked at the magazine stand sat on his stool with a blank expression.

"Grazie." Ronny put the magazine in his backpack; he couldn't wipe the smile off his face. As he looked out the window of the taxi, he thought that Milan was more industrial than he had imagined. Eventually the taxi pulled up on a main street in front of a ten-story building with a large 'Residence Pola' sign on the outside that ran up the side of the grey-tiled building. Sylvia had told Ronny this was one of the hotels that agencies used to accommodate the models who were in town for show season. After pulling his bag out of the taxi, Ronny paid the driver and headed inside to the small reception area. The mustard yellow room smelled of stale smoke with a faint hint of bleach. There were two potted plants on the end of the chest-high, wood-paneled reception counter in the corner that looked like they needed some sunlight.

"Buona serata, signore." Ronny heard a husky woman's voice coming from behind the reception desk. An Italian woman with her grey hair pulled back in a bun sat behind a cloud of smoke wearing a dark navy blouse. "Mr. Ronny?" Ronny nodded with a smile.

"Welcome to Milan! I'm Mama Pola, and if you need anything you come to me, okay."

"Grazie," Ronny responded in his best Italian accent, wondering if everyone in Italy smoked. Listening to Mama Pola's voice he imagined she must have been smoking at least two packs a day. It was almost 7 p.m. and Ronny was ready for a shower and some food. Fortunately, he had managed to sleep on the plane despite the cramped seat and his close proximity to the toilet. After taking copies of Ronny's passport, Mama Pola came out from behind her desk to introduce her son Mateo who worked with her at the hotel. Mateo was a casually dressed, heavy-set, dark-haired man in his thirties who had a warm smile and laid-back demeanor.

"Ciao, Ronny," said Mateo as he took Ronny's bag and walked him to the small elevator door painted the same color as the walls. "So where have you come from?"

"I just arrived from Brazil."

"Ah, Brazil. Always beautiful people come from Brazil. Is this your first time in Milan? I don't think I recognize you from last year."

"Si, it's my first time here in Italy."

"Well, welcome to Milan. You will like your roommate, Mr. Chad. Very funny American."

Sylvia had told Ronny it was common for the new models to share rooms with other models to lower their expenses, which would be covered by the model agency and paid back from the model's earnings. That is unless they don't work, in which case the agency would be responsible for the bill. Ronny had enough money for about six weeks of expenses. He had to make this modeling thing work so he could afford to stay and build up his photography portfolio until he eventually started working as an assistant or shooting small jobs. *Failure isn't an option*, he thought as the elevator door opened with a bang. Ronny struggled to get his bag and himself inside the tiny wood paneled space.

Mateo pushed the button for the fourth floor and bade Ronny a good evening, handing him a room key. The elevator started with a jump and slowly crawled its way up. He maneuvered his suitcase out of the tight elevator and down the old cream hallway with worn burgundy carpet. He hadn't shared a room with anyone except his brother growing up, he hoped that Chad would be laid back. When he reached the wooden door with the brass numbers 402 on it, he felt obliged to knock.

# CHAPTER 10

To his surprise the door was opened by an attractive black girl wearing an old grey T-shirt. "Hello, you must be Ronny?" she had a sexy French accent.

*I gather this isn't Chad.* "Yes, um, hi, nice to meet you," he stammered.

"I'm Camille, a friend of Chad's. He's in the bathroom. Come in." Camille ran her fingers through her dark curly hair and tucked it behind her ear on one side and stood back as Ronny entered the room.

She had flawless skin and beautiful brown eyes, and her smile revealed a large gap in her teeth. There was a musky smell in the air and one of the two beds in the room was unmade with clothes on the floor. As Ronny looked back at Camille, he couldn't help but notice she wasn't wearing a bra and he could easily make out the shape of her breasts through the T-shirt. *Well, welcome to Milan*, he thought as he averted his eyes. The small cream-colored room was only about twenty feet wide; the two queen size beds were separated by a small wooden side table with a cream phone on it. The floor was some sort of fake cherry wood, and the large window that faced the street was covered with a light translucent fabric curtain hung over a pull-down blind. It wasn't exactly a five-star hotel, but it was clean, and after sleeping on Luiz's couch it would be nice to have a bed.

Chad appeared from the bathroom wearing only a towel. "Hi, Ronny. Nice to meet you, man." He spoke with an American accent as he walked up to greet him. "I'm sorry for the messy room—I thought you were coming in later. I'm Chad."

"Nice to meet you too." He shook his hand that was still wet from the shower. It became obvious that they had just finished having sex. *Lucky guy.* He glanced back at Chad who was fair skinned with an athletic build, broad nose, and cauliflower ears that Ronny imagined he got from playing sports. He had a handsome face with strong masculine features, piercing eyes and full lips.

"You already met the French beauty Camille, I see," Chad said, then gave a blinding smile with perfect white teeth as Camille hit him playfully on his shoulder. They were a beautiful couple about the same age as Ronny. "Even though it's called 'men's fashion week,' we are lucky enough to have a lot of beautiful girls in town to keep us company," Chad added as he touched her hand.

"Americans. You talk too much," Camille said as she smiled, shook her head and started collecting the rest of her clothes. Ronny enjoyed seeing them having fun with each other. He thought about the last few months and all the dramas he had been dealing with. He needed to remember to have some fun.

"So the agency told me you were coming in from Brazil. How was your flight?" asked Chad.

"It wasn't too bad. I managed to get a decent amount of sleep. I think I could fall sleep just about anywhere." He moved his suitcase next to the bed that was still made.

"Okay, so you're nice and awake then. Great! Are you hungry?" asked Chad.

"Actually, yeah, I haven't eaten for a while."

"Okay, grab a quick shower because I'm taking you out for a welcome dinner to my favorite restaurant...well, my favorite pizza joint." Before he could reply, Chad walked up next to his bed, turned away from Ronny, and dropped his towel to get dressed, exposing his backside.

"You're fucking crazy," laughed Camille as she walked past Chad, slapping his butt, and headed toward the door. "Nice to meet you, Ronny," said Camille as she closed the door behind her. Ronny lifted his bag up onto the patterned bedspread. He could see behind the little dining table against the wall was a small simple kitchen, and next to that was the tiny plain white bathroom with an old blue sink and silver taps.

"Did you start modeling in America?" Ronny asked as he opened his bag to retrieve his toiletry bag and a change of clothes.

Chad put on an Iowa State T-shirt and sat down on the end of his bed. "Yeah, I'm from Iowa where I was scouted to come here to Milan. I've never really modeled or been overseas before, so it's all new to me. I got here a month ago. How about you?"

"I was scouted after I did a shoot for *Italian STYLE* magazine in Rio with the photographer Santo Diaz."

"I heard he is a pretty big deal. Good for you," Chad replied.

Soon they were walking out of the Pola following Chad's lead. The streetlamps were coming on as the daylight disappeared. They passed a chic restaurant with tables spilling out onto the street. An old man sat on a stool playing a guitar as guests sat inside enjoying themselves. Ronny wished he had his camera to capture the scene. So many amazing characters. He took imaginary photographs in his mind, trying to savor each one. They walked farther down the street and came upon a group of women wearing overtly sexy clothes standing under a streetlight.

"Ciao, sexy," said one of the women in a deep confident voice. Ronny had photographed a few transexual prostitutes in Rio and always remembered their incredible stories of struggle and survival.

"Ciao," Ronny replied with a respectful nod, as they walked on for another block.

"We don't see that at home." Chad commented.

"They have had to deal with more than you can imagine. Better to keep them on our side than piss them off." He was quickly beginning to realize Chad had lived a pretty sheltered life in Iowa, but he seemed harmless enough. He reminded him of the carefree jock characters he had seen in American movies.

After another half a block they arrived at Bella Vita, a small Italian taverna on a corner with French doors that opened out onto an outdoor seating area. Most of the tables were full of Italian families dining out together. Some Italian music played in the background. The food that was being brought past by busy waiters looked and smelled amazing. This was obviously a local favorite that reminded him of many of the small open-air restaurants in Rio. They entered the old restaurant, Ronny noticed the mahogany paneled walls, small bistro tables in the center of the room, and old brown leather booths around the outer walls filled with people crammed in enjoying the food. The walls featured a mix of framed posters and a few vintage paintings along with some old sconces.

"Buona serata." A young, edgy, blonde-haired girl in her late teens, who reminded him of Madonna, walked up to greet them. They followed her to a small table in the corner. Chad openly flirted with her as she handed them two menus that were translated into English.

"Could we have two beers to start? Grazie." Chad smiled. *This guy's having a good time. I need to take a leaf out of his book.* They got settled at the table, and Chad suggested they order a large Margherita pizza and a side salad.

"Camilla brought me here and I've been back a few times. It's incredible." After their two Peroni arrived at the table, Chad turned to Ronny. "Cheers, Ronny. Welcome to Milan, bro." They toasted and Ronny took a long swig of his cold beer.

"So, are you seeing Camille?" Ronny asked as Chad put his beer down and raised his eyebrows and smirked.

"I'm not really seeing anyone. Milan is full of hot girls, and however the modeling thing turns out I wanted to make sure I have a good time. We don't have girls like that at home in Iowa. She's cool and only lives a few floors above us so we're just hanging out having some fun."

"Tell me about Iowa. Sounds like a happening place."

"Ah, that would be a no. It's pretty low-key, I live on a working farm with my parents and my little sister Claire. I had a wrestling injury a year ago and so I stopped competing and started working on the farm to help my parents. I wasn't sure what I was going to do after the injury and then this modeling thing came up so here I am."

Ronny watched Chad as he shared his story. When he spoke about his injury he could see his expression change and get more serious. "You were a wrestler like Hulk Hogan?"

Chad laughed. "No, like in the Olympics."

"That must have kept you fit. What did you do for fun?"

"Um, well, I wasn't really going out that much the last year. I was kind of recovering from the injury and just doing basic stuff like the movies and BMX. When I say it out loud it sounds like my life's boring." The pizza arrived, and the two stopped talking briefly to eat a few slices.

"Have you ever had pizza like this? It's insane!" Chad said

between mouthfuls. Ronny had to admit it was the best pizza he had ever tasted and nodded silently in agreement.

"How was it shooting with Santo Diaz?" asked Chad.

"He was actually pretty cool, I have to say." Ronny didn't feel he needed to tell Chad what happened on the shoot with the stylist groping him or Santo at the wrap party.

"How was Tiana?"

"She was amazing, but not exactly the friendliest person."

"Yeah, I heard she's tough. Sounds like a pretty cool afternoon, though, and I bet the photos are cool."

"Santo took some double shots of Tiana and me. I thought she was flirting with me but when the shoot was finished, she went cold and walked back to her trailer. So how did you get scouted in Iowa?"

"My dad went to school with this girl who moved to New York and became a big model scout, and when she was home for the holidays in Iowa she saw a photograph of me in the local newspaper after I had won a wrestling competition. She contacted my dad about modeling, but I was planning on going to college on a scholarship at the time so I wasn't interested." Ronny watched Chad's expression change. "I hoped one day to compete in the Olympics. Then I lost the scholarship. I recovered from the injury, and a few months later she contacted my dad and asked if she could take some test photos of me. I didn't really have anything going on, so she took some and I ended up here in Milan."

"Sounds like it was meant to be."

"Hey, when God gave you looks like this, baby, you can't let them go to waste." Chad pulled a modeling face, laughed, and took another slice of pizza.

"Have you managed to get any work since you got here?" Ronny was curious.

"I have done a few test shoots and a few catalogues—two for sportswear and one for underwear, which was cool except for this stylist creep that kept trying to grab my dick."

"I think I've met that stylist!" *I wonder if it's the same creep I worked with in Brazil. I hope I don't run into that guy.* "I got direct booked for the Lorenzo Mancini show from the shoot with Santo."

"Dude, that's amazing! I'm sure the magazine spread in *Italian STYLE* will help you kill it." Ronny hoped he was right. He disguised a yawn; the jet lag was hitting him hard after the beers and pizza. They made their way back to the Pola. It had been a long day and if it wasn't for Chad, he may have been missing home but instead he was excited to finally be here.

# CHAPTER 11

He woke early around 6 a.m. *I guess I wasn't dreaming, I'm really in Italy.* He closed his eyes again and lay there for a while, too excited to go back to sleep. He decided to go for a run, quietly got out of bed, and put on his running gear, then sat on the end of his bed to put on his shoes. Chad stirred and opened his eyes.

"Hey, man, where you off to?" Chad stretched his arms above his head.

"I've got some pizza and two beers to run off." He stood up and patted his stomach.

"Okay, when you come back, I'll take you to the gym close to here. They let models work out there for free. Then we need to be at the agency by eleven."

Downstairs at reception Mateo was about to end the night shift and greeted Ronny with a wave and a smile as he pulled out his Walkman. Soon his head was filled with his favorite songs from the mix tape and after a quick warm-up stretch, Ronny set off along the Via Pola toward the nearest park where he could run and not worry about being hit by passing traffic. A David Bowie track filled his head as he pushed himself to take each stride to match the beat. Running had been something Ronny enjoyed when he was younger, and now that he didn't have beach volleyball to keep him fit, he committed to running again. It helped him clear his head and gave him a chance to see the city sights and get his bearings. As he ran through the streets of Milan, many of the brown, grey, and black buildings reminded him of parts of Rio but a little cleaner and more organized. Many of the streets looked the same as he ran block after block, navigating his way past apartment and commercial buildings and the occasional park. He felt a sense of freedom; he smiled and felt lighter for the first time in months. The smell of fresh bread and coffee distracted his focus momentarily as he ran past cafés and bakeries with an interesting mix of old and young stylish Italians on the street going about their morning routines. Then he almost got hit by a driver at an intersection when he got distracted studying the faces of the people heading off to work. Ronny couldn't wait to find the local photo lab and get some film. Back at Residence Pola he took a moment to stretch out on the street. When he entered the building, Chad was in reception holding court, keeping Mama Pola and two other people amused.

"Hey, Ronny, how was your run?" called out Chad as he walked in.

"Those drivers are crazy out there. I almost got knocked over crossing a street." *Just as crazy as Brazilians.* As he approached the reception counter, he took a closer look at the guy and girl standing next to Chad and couldn't help but notice how attractive they were; they had to be models. Their features were chiseled and perfect. Chad made an introduction.

"Ronny, meet Josh from Austria and Ella from Australia, two more unattractive people living here with us here at the Pola."

"G'day, nice to meet you," Ella said as she smiled and elbowed Chad in jest.

Ronny tried to stop himself from staring at Ella. She was the quintessential beach girl with long dirty-blonde hair, freckles, and a warm smile. *I wonder if they are together.*

"Hi, nice to meet you," said Ronny. The two models left him feeling a little intimidated by their style and appearance.

"Welcome to Milan. Hey, congrats on the story with Tiana," said Josh, a handsome black guy, about six feet tall, wearing a gym outfit of layered shorts over tights and a cut-off shirt and headband; he looked like a gladiator.

"Thanks, man."

"Ready to hit the gym?" Chad asked before turning to Ella and Josh. "See you guys on the rooftop later." Ronny turned back to have a final look at Ella as they walked out of the foyer. The gym was a ten-minute walk from Residence Pola, so the guys set off at a good walking pace.

"When I see people that look like that, I totally get why they are models," said Ronny as they stopped momentarily at a traffic signal.

"It's crazy having so many models living in once place," Chad replied. "It's like a model fraternity."

"People here in Milan are good looking, too," Ronny added as he noticed the steady flow of business men and women who passed them on the street. Beautiful, chic, stylish Italians, flawless tanned skin, some with jet back hair and piercing blue eyes.

"Watch out, man, or you'll run into a pole," Chad joked as Ronny took in all the sights on the street. Finally, they reached the gym. "Time to get a sweat on!" Chad added. The gym was a decent-sized space set up with free weights, machines, treadmills, and mats. It was in an old run-down building with high ceilings and a large glass front facing the street that let in the natural light. As Ronny walked into the gym, he noticed a lot of good-looking young people working out, Chad waved to the manager and introduced him to Ronny. The two guys had different approaches to training. Ronny was used to working out at the outdoor beach exercise area using his body weight and doing some Capoeira, an Afro-Brazilian martial art that combined elements of dance and acrobatics. As they worked out together, Ronny felt more relaxed around Chad and enjoyed their connection.

"Ronny, this is Nick, another model from our agency that's here from London." Said Chad as he greeted another model.

"Hello, lads." Nick winked and shook Ronny's hand, his broad nose and scar through his eyebrow gave his handsome face a rugged edge. He had a pair of red training boxing gloves hanging around his neck.

"Ronny just arrived from Brazil," Chad added.

"Cool. I got here two weeks ago from London. It's my first time in Italy," Nick said.

"Were you a boxer there?" Ronny noticed the scars on his swollen knuckles.

"Yeah, I used to compete. I was going to go pro until I was knocked out. I'm still dealing with issues from a bad head injury. My doctor doesn't want me to fight again."

"I can relate to that. Let's catch up later on." Chad slapped him on the shoulder and started walking toward the exit. Ronny felt an ease with Nick and Chad. Initially he thought it might be hard to make friends, but he felt like he was fitting right in. They reminded him of Milo and how carefree their life and friendship used to be. After a shower and breakfast back at the Pola, Ronny went to the mirror to check his outfit and add some hair wax to tame his thick curls. He felt both nervous and excited about meeting his agency. They'd only seen him in photographs, and he hoped they wouldn't be disappointed when they saw him in person.

"Let's do this," called out Chad as he opened the front door and Ronny grabbed his backpack to head out.

# CHAPTER 12

After a few stops on the metro, the guys walked down a busy street to an old six-story building with an ornate stone front and a heavy security door. Once in the foyer they crossed the terrazzo floor and rode the tiny shaky elevator up to the fourth floor. The elevator came to an abrupt halt and the doors opened with a bang. Ronny shot a quick look to Chad with his eyebrows raised.

"I don't know if I'll ever get used to these elevators," said Chad as he led the way down a hallway of worn creaky floorboards to the two large paneled white doors with a 'BAM Models' sign on it. He pushed one of the doors open to reveal a small seating area and reception desk. There were a few other models sitting there who Chad gave a nod to. "Ciao," Chad called out to the receptionist who returned a smile. He had a natural way of lighting up a room.

Ronny quickly glanced around the room and then looked up the wall to see framed magazine covers of male models that must have been represented by the agency. He felt nervous knowing these were models he would be competing with. He remained quiet, still unfamiliar with the whole model agency world; he was content to let Chad take the lead.

"Ciao, Chad," called out a man who sat with a group of people around a table in the middle of the room. He waved them over and stood up. He was a black man in his mid-forties with a bald head, big smile, and light eyes. He was slightly overweight and wore an oversized button-down black shirt and jeans.

The room was all white with high ornate ceilings and tall windows along one side with lots of natural light and more poster prints of fashion magazine covers featuring male models. At the table six people were busy spinning around a large round filing system in the center as they retrieved folders and replaced them. Ronny watched as the man greeted Chad with a kiss on each cheek then turned to welcome him.

"Ciao, Ronny. I'm Paul, your agent here in Milan. Welcome! It's so great to finally meet you, and I see you're in good hands with Chad." Paul's accent sounded like a mix of American and European.

"Nice to meet you too, Paul." Paul moved in closer and gave him a kiss on each cheek. Ronny looked to see Chad giving him a wink then laughing. Paul seemed excited to see him in person as Ronny felt his hand running down his back to land just above his jeans. He felt slightly uncomfortable as he stood still and forced a smile, trying to appear unfazed. Paul's lingering touch reminded him of Santo. Whether it was affection or inappropriate, Ronny knew he needed to play along with it. He had too much at stake.

"How was your flight?" asked Paul. Ronny noticed his eyes casually moving down to survey his appearance.

"I pretty much slept most of the way, and I ran and trained this morning, so I feel good. Chad's been awesome showing me around; I feel right at home."

"The editorial with Tiana in *Italian STYLE* is incredible. I'm so glad Sylvia got a hold of you. Getting direct booked by Lorenzo Mancini for his fashion show is a really big deal. I have a test shoot lined up for you tomorrow with Francesco, one of Santo Diaz's old assistants, to add to your portfolio. I'm sure Santo is going to be glad to hear that you're in town too."

*I bet he will be.* Ronny wondered if he would be blacklisted from shooting with Santo after he didn't succumb to his advances and almost pushed him through a wall.

"Everyone, this is our new model, Ronny, who just arrived from Brazil." Paul turned to the booking table and raised his voice over the chatter of the other five agents who were busy engaged in conversations in English, Italian, and French. Paul went around the table giving the name of each agent; each one looked up briefly and smiled or waved. Ronny smiled and nodded as he tried to remember their names.

"Ciao. Beautiful photos with Tiana. Welcome," said a dark-haired Italian woman.

"Grazie. I'm excited to be here," Ronny replied.

"Well, hellooo, Ronny," called out an animated young booker named Brett, in an American accent. He had shoulder-length curly blonde hair, freckles, and wore a Madonna T-shirt. "Looks like double trouble to me."

"If you say so, Madonna," Chad responded sarcastically.

"Chad, you're breaking my heart," said Brett. Ronny remained quiet, amused by the banter. Paul turned to Ronny.

"So I know this is your first time with an agent so let me explain how this works. Every day we receive castings for upcoming jobs and we either send the models we think are right or a client may request to see you if they have seen your modelling composite card or portfolio and like your look. You then go for an appointment or what we call a 'go-see' to meet with the client so they can see what you look like in person, and they may ask you to try on some clothes and take some polaroids. Then if a client is interested in a model for a job, we negotiate the rates that are paid for the day's shoot and then put a hold or 'option' on their schedule for that time until the model is confirmed or released." Paul pointed to the alphabetically labeled folders in the center of the table. "These are the schedules for each model. We give the clients a first option on the model if there were no other jobs on the requested date or a second or third option if the model is busy or if we want to wait and see if something better comes along."

Ronny watched the bookers spin the filing system around, retrieving the labeled folders for each model.

"If a job confirms we will give you all the details for the shoot. Make sure you check in with us in the morning when we open and in the evening before we close at six. As you saw in your contract you are then paid when the client pays the agency, less agency commission and expenses or advances." Paul moved away from the booking table to a white wall with several rows of small shelves showcasing about fifty male model promotion cards.

"These are the composite cards for our models that we send these out to clients to get the models work or for you to leave behind at castings," Paul added as he stood in front of the display wall. Each card was about the size of a large greeting card. Most of them were black and white headshots and a few waist-up body shots. Ronny surveyed the wide variety of faces with chiseled features, lean defined bodies, smoldering looks, and full smiles. It was slightly daunting and intimidating to think that all these guys were in town competing for the same jobs. BAM was also one of many model agencies in town. Ronny felt a wave of insecurity wash over him mixed with the excitement that he might get to photograph some of these models.

Ronny noticed the composite cards were in alphabetical order and located Chad's, a shirtless black and white portrait of Chad looking like a young movie star. He looked so different with his serious expression.

"Here's the composite card we put together for you." Paul retrieved Ronny's card with one of the photographs from the *Italian STYLE* photo shoot on the front. The shirtless photograph in black and white of him with a serious look on his face seemed to fit right in with the other model cards on the wall. He felt more confident and a sense of relief.

"Looks strong, man," Chad chimed in as he looked over his shoulder. Ronny had to admit it looked good, and the shots on the back of the card with Tiana Taylor would surely help him get attention.

Paul continued, "Your card is great, Ronny. The industry has moved away from the skinny grunge look for guys, and clients are looking for a stronger, sexy, masculine look these days. With your body and face, your timing couldn't be better."

Ronny was aware of the grunge period for models after seeing the trend start to change in the fashion magazines he collected. He was never a fan of grunge himself.

"We think you will do well here. Do you have any questions?"

"Thanks, Paul. It all makes sense. Could tell me where the best photography lab is in town to develop film and order prints. I do photography myself on the side." Ronny felt a little self-conscious admitting that to Paul. It was the first time he had told that to a person from the fashion industry.

"Sure, I'll write down the address for Aldo Foto for you. I'd love to see some of your work sometime. You should shoot Chad; he could use some more photos."

"That would be cool. Thanks." Ronny tried to contain his excitement. This was his first day and already he had an opportunity to photograph someone and show his work.

"Before I forget, I need to take some updated polaroids of you and Chad to have on file. Clients like to see you in natural light with no studio lighting so they can see exactly what you look like." Paul picked up a polaroid camera and motioned to follow him to a white wall on the far side of the room next to the window. It wasn't long before Chad was removing his shirt, standing against the wall in his jeans.

"Let's take off your pants," Paul said. "I need to see your legs."

Ronny watched Chad take off his clothes and stand against the wall in his white briefs. He was glad Chad had gone first. As uncomfortable as he felt with the whole idea of standing there half naked while people looked at you, he accepted it as another necessary part of the modeling business. As he watched Chad he could tell that his defined body was the result of sports and manual labor and not just from working out. He turned around comfortably while Paul took a series of polaroids. He had a unique look with his broad nose, big lips, and strong jawline. *Definitely not a grunge model.* Ronny studied the way Chad moved in front of the camera and followed Paul's direction. He appeared confident with his poses and expressions. *Probably helped shooting those catalogue jobs.*

"Thanks, Chad. Let's get you in here, Ronny." Paul turned back around to watch him change. Ronny hesitated for a moment then slowly started to remove his clothes. As he stood up and walked toward the wall, he could sense many of the eyes in the room were on him. Were they looking at his proportions or something more? He stood in his boxer briefs against the wall feeling self-conscious. He could see Brett watching from the model table holding the phone against his ear. Paul stood for a moment in front of Ronny and looked him up and down, letting his eyes linger on his abdominal area. He felt completely exposed.

"Okay, Ronny, let's have you look straight at the camera, serious expression, stand tall." Paul directed Ronny as he continued to take polaroids from different angles. "Great." He moved in to adjust his hair. "I'm shooting a closer shot. Give me a serious expression then let's have a smile." Ronny followed direction and offered a full wide smile to Paul who snapped away. "That's perfect, Ronny. Make sure you buy some underwear briefs like Chad's for castings. Most clients prefer them so they can see your legs."

*I'm sure they do.* Ronny moved to quickly put his clothes back on. *I guess I'll be stripping down a lot?* He had never been ashamed of his body, but for the first time he felt self-conscious about it.

"Looking good, Romeo," joked Chad.

"Thanks, Hulk Hogan."

"Oooh, I like that," Chad laughed, then pulled a face, imitating Hulk Hogan. "Grrrrrrr."

Once dressed he went over to Paul at the desk where he was passing around Ronny's polaroids to each of the bookers; a few of them stopped what they were doing and glanced to look at him again.

"Polaroids okay?" he asked, hoping he looked as good as the guy in the *Italian STYLE* shoot.

"If I had your body, I'd be walking around naked," replied Brett.

"But you don't, Madonna, do you? So keep your shirt on pleeaassse," injected another booker from across the table.

"Talk to the hand, honey," Brett was quick to respond. "I'm sure your good friend Santo Diaz will be looking forward to seeing Ronny again," Brett added as he handed Paul the polaroids.

Ronny suspected Santo's reputation was no secret. He decided he needed to keep Brett on side and offered him a smile. "Sounds like Santo Diaz is pretty popular in the industry," Ronny added, not wanting to sound negative.

"Well, not as popular with a certain *Italian STYLE* editor, but he does manage to get a lot of work," Brett quipped with a snarky expression.

"Don't you have a booking to write up?" snapped Paul. Brett rolled his eyes and turned to face the desk and pick up his phone. After taking copies of Ronny's passport and checking measurements of all his sizes, Paul gave him the information for the test shoot the following afternoon and the address for Foto Aldo.

"The photo shoot tomorrow will be amazing. Francesco is a great photographer. There will also be a hair stylist there to trim and style your hair." Paul turned to include Chad in the conversation. "I'm taking both of you with me to Lorenzo Mancini's party on Thursday night. A lot of important people will be there, so make sure you both dress up. Ronny, you're already booked for the show so it will be good for you to meet Lorenzo and his sister Carlotta."

"Thanks, Paul, sounds great. I'll call you at the end of the day." Ronny smiled as Paul handed him a portfolio that included the tear sheets of him from the magazine and some composite cards inside the back cover. He put it into his backpack. The last few weeks had gone by so fast and now everything was becoming real, he felt a sense of pride seeing his portfolio and his composite card.

"Enjoy Milan. It's great to have you here, Ronny." Paul waved and turned back to his desk and picked up the phone as they walked out of the agency. Ronny felt more confident seeing the reaction of the bookers; they really seemed to like his look, he felt cautiously optimistic.

Chad walked out ahead of him, he reminded Ronny of Milo, taking things one day at a time and going with the flow. He looked back at the framed magazine covers on the wall. He imagined walking into the agency one day and seeing photographs he had taken on display. *One day.*

# CHAPTER 13

Ronny arrived back at the apartment after shopping at the small supermarket around the corner from the Pola for food. Chad was lying shirtless on his bed looking at a sports magazine.

"I bought enough food to keep us going for a few days," declared Ronny as he carried the two shopping bags into the kitchen and started to unpack the groceries.

"Perfect," said Chad as he sat up and put down the magazine.

Once Ronny had unpacked the groceries, he retrieved his box of photographic prints from his bag. "Would it be okay if I put a few of my photographs up on the wall above my bed?"

"Sure, go ahead. Put as many as you like; this room could use some help."

He opened the box and laid out the prints on his bed and started to attach them to the wall. Chad stood up and moved next to him to look at the prints. Ronny held a photograph of a young street kid staring intensely straight into the camera. Then to the next few of a striking young woman standing in the ocean in a summer dress and close-ups of her wet face. Chad was silent as he surveyed them. Ronny hung up more photographs of his friends at the beach volleyball court, the old woman at the fruit stall, the young prostitute with a heavy layer of makeup that he photographed at sunrise.

"They look like they belong in a magazine."

Ronny beamed hearing Chad validate his work. This was the first time anyone outside Brazil had seen his photographs. "Thanks. I love taking photos and it's why I'm really here in Italy. Modeling is a good start, but I really want to be a working photographer." He felt empowered to say that out loud.

"How did you get into photography?" Chad asked.

"Well, I've been taking photographs for a few years now. It started as a hobby and became a passion. I carry my camera almost everywhere I go and take portraits of all kinds of people. These are some of my favorite photos," he said proudly as he continued to put more up on the wall.

"If you're up for taking some test photographs of me, I could use some new pictures and I really like your work."

"For sure," Ronny replied. He couldn't wipe the smile off his face.

"I was about to go up onto the roof and meet some of the other models living in the building for a drink and watch the sunset. You should come up…Ella will be there, too." Chad smirked as he stood up and walked to the kitchen to retrieve some beers. "I saw you looking at her. She shares a room with Camille so that's how I got to know her. She's a bit shy but when you get to know her she has a great sense of humor."

"She seems really cool," Ronny replied. He couldn't deny that he had thought about Ella a few times since he had met her. There was something different about her, something special.

Chad walked toward the door. "Are you coming?"

"I'll see you upstairs. I just have to call my brother to let him know I'm alive." Ronny was excited to update his brother on how things were going.

Chad nodded and headed up to the roof. Ronny finished unpacking his clothes and lay down on his bed, reached for the phone, and pulled out the calling card he bought at the supermarket. He dialed his brother's number.

"Olá," Luiz answered. Hearing his brother's voice made him feel a little homesick.

"How is everything going?" asked Luiz in an excited tone. Ronny spoke quickly, trying to update him on everything that had happened since he left—Milan, the people he had met, and what the agency was like.

"I'm so glad you've landed on your feet," Luiz said. It felt good to talk to him knowing how invested he was in Ronny's success.

"Have you heard from Mom?" Ronny asked, momentarily distracted from the excitement he felt sharing all his news.

"I haven't heard from her. I'm sure she would be missing you, though," Luiz replied. Ronny was silent as he imagined her sitting alone in the kitchen waiting to see what state Diego would be in when he got home.

"I'll try and give her a call when Dad's out," Ronny said.

"Nothing else to update. Besides the fact that Maria and I are trying to have a baby," Luiz added.

"A baby! That's amazing." Ronny knew that his mother would miss being a part of her grandchild's life. She loved children. "You'll make a great dad."

"I remember when Dad was great." There was a reflective sadness in Luiz's voice.

"All those fun trips up the coast we had. So many great summers."

"I miss those trips too. Time to make some new memories," Luiz said. He had inherited the best traits of their father. Hearing Luiz's plans to start a family made him wonder if he'd be back for the birth. He hadn't thought about returning to Rio, but seeing his brothers baby would be a good reason.

"Say hi to Milo if you see him," Ronny said as he hung up the phone. He put his hands behind his head and thought about Milo and what his friends were up to. *I have to give him a call*. His present reality was so different from the one he left behind. He might have been working with Milo at the brothel by now if things had been different. He looked up at the photos above his bed and smiled to himself. As much as he missed his brother and friends, he was excited to be in Italy. He closed his eyes and took a few deep breaths.

He woke up with a jolt when Chad walked in the door.

"Wake up, man. You'll miss the sunset." Announced Chad.

"I must have fallen asleep." Ronny scratched his head as Chad grabbed a few beers and left to go back upstairs.

When Ronny walked out onto the roof deck, he could see the Milan skyline lighting up in the distance. Green plastic chairs were scattered around a few tables near the side wall. The good-looking crowd turned to see him approach.

"Nice of you to join us." Chad called out.

"Sorry, guys, I passed out. I must have been more tired than I thought," Ronny replied as he approached and sat down on an empty chair next to Camille. He quickly scanned the crowd, and when he saw Ella, she offered him a smile and nodded. The look in her eyes wasn't one of a young girl. She had a depth beyond her years and a warmth that made him feel like he had met her before.

"Yeah, jet lag's tough," Ella said softly. "Try flying here from Australia; now that's another level."

"You already met Josh downstairs, and this is Annika from Russia," said Chad, gesturing toward a thin blonde girl sitting with the group.

"Nice to meet you." He smiled and motioned to cheer with his beer. *More beautiful people,* he thought to himself as he looked around at the group. Ronny had never really compared his looks to anyone until now when he knew he would be going up against other guys for jobs based solely on his appearance.

"So how are you enjoying beautiful Milan?" asked Josh with a slightly sarcastic tone. He looked like someone out of an eighties music video in his tank top, training gear and bandana tied around his forehead.

"It's fucking ugly," exclaimed Annika in a thick Russian accent as she went to take a sip of wine with a cigarette in her hand. Annika looked like a skinny blonde doll with a hard striking face, a tight black dress, and heels. Ronny had heard rumors of models that had eating disorders to stay thin. He suspected Annika might have anorexia. He wasn't sure if Annika was with Josh. She appeared to be flirting with Josh so Ronny presumed they might be together but then he told a story about traveling just outside Milan on weekends to 'dance for dollars' in his underwear at a nightclub.

"Hey, if someone's going to cover my hotel and travel and pay me three hundred dollars plus tips to dance around and drink for free, I'm in. Survival of the fittest," said Josh as he raised his beer. *Seems like it's not too different from Rio after all*, thought Ronny as he continued listening. *Everyone's got something to sell.*

"Signore e signori diamo il benvenuto al supermodel Josh," pronounced Annika in her best Italian accent as if she was introducing Josh at the club. Everyone started laughing.

"Josh, if you could have as much success with modeling as you do with the girls dancing for dollars, you will kill it," added Ella.

"Last time Josh danced for dollars he ended up having sex with three girls in one night in the back of the club," Camille discretely told Ronny as she lit up a cigarette. He wondered if Josh was being paid for the sex as well as the dancing. Nobody seemed to care, least of all Josh.

Josh wasn't even defending himself and just laughed. "Hey, what can I say, I'm a good dancer."

"No, darling, it's not your dancing that's good," Annika quickly added before bursting into laughter. This all sounded familiar to Ronny; Brazil wasn't the only place where good looks were worth something to those willing to pay for it. *At least he's not sleeping with Ella,* thought Ronny as he took another sip of his beer, amused by the model banter. Camille turned to Ronny. She had been to Milan before and knew how it operated.

"There's always a way to survive in this town." She told him that hungry broke models were low-hanging fruit for opportunistic party planners and club promoters who were trying to fill their clubs with sexy young people or introduce wealthy Italian businessmen to the hottest young models in town.

"Darling, this is my season, I can feel it," announced Annika with a determined tone. "I don't want to go back to Russia; I'm done with that place."

"What about your family?" inquired Ella.

"My family are poor, and I would rather stay away, make money, and send it to them rather than go back and be poor with them. There's nothing for me in Russia."

"That sucks, babe. I'm sorry," Ella responded.

Annika was stone-faced. Ronny could see in her eyes that she had been hardened by her life in Russia and she was determined to do whatever it took to succeed. *I guess I'm not the only one who came here searching for a better life.* He wondered how many models were in Milan, how many would achieve success and how many would end up having to go home when they didn't get work, ran out of money, and the agency stopped covering their expenses? He tried not to focus too hard on that reality as he knew he only had a certain amount of money. *I guess there's always 'dancing for dollars' with Josh,* he thought with an amused glance at Josh who was flexing in front of Annika. Ronny couldn't see himself dancing in front of a nightclub crowd in his underpants. Then again, he hadn't imagined himself having sex for money either.

Camille got up to go to the bathroom, and Ronny found himself sitting next to Ella. Ronny looked at her and smiled. *Finally.* She was wearing denim shorts, a vintage surf T-shirt, and sandshoes. She turned her body slightly to him and ran her fingers through her sun-bleached hair. Her expression was soft and open, she looked like she was blushing slightly.

"Do you miss the ocean? I heard Brazil has beautiful beaches," asked Ella.

Ronny noticed the freckles on her nose and that she wasn't wearing any makeup. He sat up a little straighter and tried to block out the conversation going on around him. "You know, it's been so busy since I found out I was coming here I hadn't thought much about it. I used to spend a lot of time down at the beach playing volleyball with my friends." He felt a million miles away from Milo and his friends but wasn't missing Brazil.

"Do you surf?" Ella asked. Her face lit up when she mentioned surfing.

"I body surf but spend most of my time on the sand playing volleyball."

"I miss surfing so much. I grew up in a coastal town called Byron Bay. I get withdrawals if I'm away from the ocean for too long."

"I think I'd be too worried about sharks to surf in Australia." Ronny raised his eyebrows.

"You're more likely to get hit by a crazy Italian taxi driver than eaten by a shark in Australia. Give me a surfboard and a perfect wave any day."

"Probably right," Ronny agreed after his close call with the taxi on his morning run. Ella was soft spoken but easy to talk to; she had a dry sense of humor and a quick wit. "So how's work going for you here?" he asked, hoping the question wouldn't change the ease of their conversation.

"It's been pretty good. I've been to Milan a few times. A lot of people come here to try and get discovered. I guess it's like Hollywood for the fashion industry." Ella smiled and took a sip of her wine. "I like coming during the men's show season because I'm not skinny enough to do the women's shows and there's not as much competition with fewer girls in town. You can also get some good pictures for your portfolio here, do a few jobs to pay for your expenses, then head up to Germany or another catalogue market to make some money."

Ronny was beginning to realize there was a whole strategy to success in the modeling business. Until now his focus had really been on photography and how he could make that work, but he realized he needed to put some focus on modeling and try and make a decent go of it.

"It's crazy to think you aren't skinny enough to do the shows." Ronny took a sip of his beer, trying not to speak too loudly knowing Annika was sitting close.

"I always had broad shoulders, and I guess the surfing and swimming competitively in school didn't help. I do get a lot of swimwear shoots, which are usually done near water, so I love that."

"She is the swimsuit queen," exclaimed Camille as she came back from the bathroom and sat back down between them. Ronny regretted not taking the initiative to move closer to Ella and take Camille's seat.

"So has the agency gotten you any tests lined up, Ronny?" asked Josh.

"Yeah, I have one tomorrow with a guy called Francesco. I think he used to assist Santo Diaz."

"At least he's straight, darling," said Annika, who apparently wasn't one to hold back her opinion. Josh moved uncomfortably in his seat, and Annika noticed his reaction. "What? Josh you know what I mean," Annika declared as she turned to Ronny. "He normally shoots women."

Ronny didn't know Josh well, but he sensed that Josh had had a bad experience with a photographer, and like Ronny he didn't appear willing to openly share it with the group. It was the first time he was quiet. Ronny wondered what might have happened to him.

"Okay, Annika, enough with the opinions," Camille said. "Francesco takes great photographs. I'm sure it will be amazing."

Annika rolled her eyes.

"Okay, I need to eat," declared Josh as he stood up and cut the conversation short. Ronny was reminded how tall he was. Now that the sun had set, everyone else got up to leave the roof as Ella flashed Ronny a smile and walked out. Later that evening when Chad left the apartment to go and meet up with Camille, Ronny sat alone on his bed reflecting back to his earlier conversations on the roof and the group of characters living in the Pola. He missed the simple conversations he used to have with Milo when they were together on their bikes. He took his calling card out of his wallet and decided to call Milo to check in on him and give him an update. Hearing his voice was bittersweet; he missed his friend but didn't want to rehash any of the drama that he had left behind. It was good to catch up on simple things even though nothing had really changed for Milo.

"I'm so glad it's working out for you," Milo said after Ronny had filled him in. Ronny could tell he was genuinely happy for him, but he could sense things still weren't great for Milo.

"Are you doing okay?" Ronny asked, feeling guilty for the fact that on some level he was still judging him.

"Just taking it one day at a time." Milo sounded flat. "I'd rather hear about Milan and all the hot girls you've met." Ronny gave him an update but didn't want to make it sound too good.

"Do you miss home?" Milo asked.

Ronny paused. "I miss you guys. I just don't miss all the drama with my family." He glanced up at the photographs on the wall and found the portrait he took of his mother and wondered and if she was okay.

# CHAPTER 14

The following afternoon Ronny arrived at the street where the photographer Francesco lived. He noticed the mix of old and new buildings, all about eight stories high in a wide array of colors. Some parts of Milan reminded him of Rio. As he passed a small fruit stand, an old woman smiled at him, and her blue eyes sparkled. He took his camera out of his backpack and lifted it slightly, nodding toward it indicating he would like to take her photograph. She appeared to blush and nodded. Ronny quickly made some adjustments on the camera and looked through the lens. Her face came into focus, her eyes softened, and she looked thoughtfully into his lens; he quickly took a few frames, lowered the camera, and gave her a big smile. She instantly returned a wide smile as he continued taking more photographs.

"Grazie," Ronny said.

"Signore," she replied. She picked up an apple, and handed it to Ronny with a nod and a warm smile. Like so many of his subjects before he felt a connection to her and could sense that she appreciated the moment. As he continued down the street, he started to feel nervous about the shoot. His only real experience was being photographed on the beach playing volleyball with his friends, something that felt natural to him. Ronny hoped that Francesco would be able to give him some modeling tips—and that watching him work would inspire his own photography. He finally arrived at the address on Paul's note. The beautiful old building was red brick with ornate cream details around the windows and balcony. At the apartment he was greeted by a handsome dark-haired Italian man in his early thirties dressed in ripped jeans, a T-shirt, and bare feet.

"Ciao, Ronny. Nice to meet you. Come in." Several large black and white framed photographic prints hung on the walls of the apartment. Some portraits, a few female nudes, and a beautiful desert landscape. They were stunning images. He wondered if Francesco had taken all of them and if he had slept with any of the women in the photographs, remembering what Annika had said.

"What a great apartment," Ronny said as he put his backpack down on a chair. "Those photographs are beautiful. Are they yours?" He nodded toward the prints on the wall and walked closer to them, appreciating the print quality and the beautiful frames.

"Yes. They are some of the prints I was exhibiting earlier this year," Francesco replied proudly. "You want a coffee?" he asked as he lit a cigarette and walked to the kitchen.

"Sure," Ronny answered.

"Ronny, this is Leo," Francesco motioned to the young hair stylist dressed in overalls sitting at the end of the kitchen counter. "He's going to cut and style your hair."

"Nice to meet you," Ronny said. Leo smiled and motioned for him to sit down on the bar stool at the kitchen counter. It had been quite a while since he had had a haircut. It was usually done by an old guy at the local barber shop that he loved to photograph, he was intrigued to see what a professional hair stylist could do. As a photographer he needed to have an opinion on the hair as well as the makeup and fashion so he wanted to pay close attention to what Leo was doing.

"You've got a great head of hair," Leo commented as he ran his fingers through Ronny's hair. "Let's take your shirt off," he added. Francesco put a cup of coffee down on the counter. He took off his shirt and put it on the back of his chair. Leo pulled out a black cape to put over his shoulders and around his neck and quickly sprayed his hair damp with water and started cutting as clumps slid down the cape, landing on the floor. After twenty minutes Leo was done with the haircut. "Looks so much stronger. Now we can see your face instead of all those curls," he said.

"Perfect, Leo. Grazie," said Francesco as Ronny went to the bathroom to wash his face and rinse the cut hair off his neck. He looked in the mirror. The shape and style of his hair looked so much cleaner and more modern, more like a lot of the models he saw in the fashion magazines.

"Looks really great, Leo. Thank you," Ronny said as he came out of the bathroom. Francesco walked into the room carrying his camera.

"Those photos of you in *Italian STYLE* were beautiful." Francesco said. Ronny tried to get a good look at his camera as he came closer.

"Thanks. Yeah, it was a lucky break to shoot that story. I heard you used to assist Santo Diaz?" Francesco paused, glanced at Leo, then continued.

"Yes, I was his first assistant for two years. Okay, Ronny, let's have you put on this T-shirt with your jeans. Then stand over there against the wall next to the window."

Ronny sensed he had struck a nerve when he asked about Santo. *Maybe they had ended on bad terms?* He decided it was best to not push any further and watched as Francesco adjusted the settings on his camera. He had the same camera as Santo, a Pentax 6x7. Ronny tried to take note of the lens he was using and what the settings were on the camera. He put his shirt on and walked over to the wall as Leo came in for a final check of his hair.

"Ronny, just follow my directions and pay attention to the expressions and positions I direct you into. You'll get a sense for the ones I like when you hear me shooting."

He nodded, feeling a little self-conscious as Francesco stood back and took a moment to look at him.

"Let's have you lean against the wall and relax your shoulders. Great. Open and close your mouth. Look at me more intensely, like you're looking into the sun." Francesco started taking photographs. *Relax. Just breathe.* Ronny closed his eyes momentarily and took a deep breath.

"Okay. Take the shirt off...that's great. Now hold the shirt and slowly bring your eyes up to me, get some tension in your stomach. Okay, now throw your shirt at the camera and laugh." He threw it at Francesco, just missing the camera. Ronny broke out into a laugh with his eyes closed and then just kept smiling as he opened his eyes. *This feels ridiculous.* But he remembered studying the male models in the fashion magazines and their expressions. He listened to the direction that Francesco gave him so he could use it when he started photographing models.

"Perfect," Francesco said as he continued taking more photographs. "Now put the shirt back on then look down at the floor and slowly bring your eyes up to the camera with your chin down and wrinkle your forehead." Ronny took note of what Francesco responded to. "Look past me, over here." Francesco briefly held his hand that wasn't holding the camera out to the side to give him an eyeline. "Let's do some shots in the bedroom. Keep the jeans on for now and take off the shirt." He followed him to the bedroom and stood beside the unmade bed next to the large window. "I want you to slowly take off your jeans and stop when I tell you." Francesco gave quick clear direction. He was impressed at how fast he was able to shoot.

Ronny noticed the great natural light that poured into the room and the reflection back off the white walls. By this stage he was feeling more confident, sensing that Francesco wasn't just asking him to take his clothes off to get a look at his body. He remembered what Annika had said about him being straight. He started removing his jeans, pulling them down a few inches.

"Stop there," Francesco added. "Now look up towards the camera raising your eyebrows. Okay, now try a strong expression, now look past me again."

Eventually Ronny took his pants off and sat on the edge of the bed. Even though he was sitting on Francesco's bed in his underwear he didn't feel like he was being objectified. Francesco had a strong sense of direction that made Ronny feel comfortable. He sensed he was focused on creating a beautiful photograph, like a true artist. Ronny took notice of his direction, the angles, and timing.

"Let's have you stand up next to the window, look back at me over your shoulder. Great, now slowly put your jeans back on," directed Francesco as he quickly shot a few more photographs next to the window. "Run your fingers through your hair and take your hand farther back until you get to your neck." Francesco came in closer for a few headshots and then asked him to move to the old leather couch in the living room.

"Leo, let's change the hair slightly. Ronny, can you get changed into the black suit and light green collared shirt for a final look." Francesco added. He motioned to the clothes hanging in a corner of the living room. Leo pushed back his hair, and Ronny followed

Francesco's direction and lay back on the couch. Francesco retrieved a light on a stand and turned it on close to the couch. Ronny took note of the angle of the light and watched him move into position to continue taking photos.

"If you're wearing clothes, remember that's what you're selling. Make sure you're moving your body so the clothes look good." Francesco added. Nobody had put fashion modeling into such simple terms before. The idea that you were selling clothes rather than posing for a cool photo was an invaluable lesson. Francesco continued to take some more photos until finally putting down his camera.

"Perfect, Ronny, you're done. The agency will love these." Francesco pulled the final roll of exposed film from the back of the camera and put it in a small black canister. "I'm developing some film tonight and making prints tomorrow, so I'll be able to get Paul a few prints for you."

"That would be so amazing." He felt really good about the shoot and added, "I really appreciate you taking the time to do this. These photos will really help my portfolio." He couldn't wait to study the photographs and see the final printed result. "Thanks, Leo, for the cut," Ronny added. Leo smiled and nodded and went to collect his things in the kitchen leaving Ronny and Francesco alone.

"I think your timing is perfect as clients are now asking for more masculine guys and you have a strong look and a great body," Francesco said. "I know this is your first time here in Milan and you're new to the world of modeling, so I'm going to be honest with you because you seem like a nice guy. This can be an exciting business with lots of great perks, but I'm sure people have warned you it can also be challenging at times. I've seen firsthand the way male models are taken advantage of by powerful people who can make or break their career, and nobody really talks about it or warns you."

"Yeah, I've heard some stories," replied Ronny, not wanting to share his own experience with Santo. But he could tell by Francesco's expression that it was a serious warning. He was becoming more aware of the underlying threat of being taken advantage of in the business; he considered what Francesco must have endured working for Santo for two years.

"You're a smart guy, Ronny. Just keep your head on straight and play the game, but just be careful not to get burned." Ronny noticed he was careful not to mention any names or say too much about his recent employer. *I guess Santo's power protects him.*

"I really like your work, Francesco. I'm hoping to become a working photographer one day myself. That's really why I came to Milan." It felt good to share his dream with a professional. It would be amazing to assist someone like Francesco, someone who was just as passionate as he was about photography and whose work he liked.

"What do you like to photograph?" asked Francesco. He seemed genuinely interested, which put Ronny at ease.

"I love to take portraits of interesting-looking people that I meet, everyone from old people to street kids. I'm trying to incorporate more fashion into my work so I can focus on fashion photography. I'm hoping that will allow me to take the photos I love and have a career."

"Good for you. Sounds like you've got a good plan. I'd love to see some of your work sometime. Even when you start working, it's important that you continue to do personal creative projects, that's what clients want to see. I did some modeling before I started assisting and it gave me a chance to learn so much and get lots of practice. Use the modeling to make contacts and cover your expenses while you build up your portfolio. Take inspiration from photographs you love in magazines and try to shoot images like that to help you develop your own style and voice."

Ronny listened intently, trying to absorb as much as he could. It had been an incredible few hours with Francesco. He felt so inspired and excited to try out what he had learned from watching him shoot. The fact that he wanted to see some of Ronny's work was a big deal.

"If you have time you should swing by the Foto di Milano, it's a gallery just around the corner. There's a really cool show there at the moment and I think you'd like it. Milan has a lot more to offer than just beautiful people, fashion, and pizza," said Francesco with a smile. Ronny got changed and collected his things into his backpack and headed to the door.

"Thanks again, Francesco. Hey, if you ever need an extra assistant to work with you, I'm available." Ronny gave him a hug. "I hope to see you soon."

"I'm sure you will soon enough," replied Francesco. "You remind me of me when I started in this crazy business. Hey, hang on a moment." He quickly went to his closet and retrieved a small black camera. "I used to take a lot of photos on this; it has a flash—it's great to carry around with you because it's so small and easy to use. Why don't you borrow it, there's a fresh roll of film inside."

"Seriously? Thanks so much!" Ronny took the small camera and walked out of the photo shoot on a high. He took Francesco's advice and walked around the corner to the gallery located in an old run-down building with a big glass window. As he walked slowly around the room looking at the black and white photographs of street scenes and incredible portraits of old Italian men and women, he could see why Francesco had recommended it. As he stood in the center of the room, he felt a sense of independence maybe for the first time in his life. He smiled to himself, imagining they were his photographs being celebrated on the walls, his work being viewed and appreciated.

# CHAPTER 15

Eventually he made it back to the Pola, and when he walked into his room Chad was in the kitchen with Ella and Camille laughing and playing music.

"Hey, Rio, just in time. Our neighbors are cooking us a delicious meal. Hey, nice haircut." Chad smiled as Ronny put his backpack down on his bed.

"Hi, guys. Sorry I'm late. I decided to walk back, and it took me longer than I thought," he replied as Ella looked up and smiled.

"I love this song!" said Ella as the two girls started dancing together in the kitchen. Ronny took out the small camera that Francesco had given him and popped up the flash. He quickly took a few photographs of the girls and Chad.

"Smells delicious!" said Chad as he helped Camille serve out the food, and as everyone started eating a silence came over the small table.

"Sign of a good meal," Camille said as she took a sip of her wine.

"Hey, how was your test with Francesco?" asked Chad.

"I think we got some really cool shots."

"Ronny takes photos, too," said Chad as he indicated toward the wall of photographs. "We're going to do a photo test together." The two girls turned to look at the wall. Ella stood up and went to get a closer look.

"Your photography is beautiful," she said as she continued looking at the photos. "The portraits feel really intimate. Have you ever thought about doing photography as a career?"

Ronny couldn't hide the smile that appeared across his face. The girl he liked appreciated his art. How could this day get any better.

"You know, that's actually my dream. Photography is my real passion; it's really what brought me here to Milan." Ronny felt proud to say that out loud, affirming why he was there. Inspired by his earlier chat with Francesco, he added, "I'd love to take some photos of you and Camille this weekend with Chad if you're interested and available."

Camille and Ella looked at each other, nodded, and smiled.

"Sure, that would be cool," responded Camille.

"Yeah, sounds great," Ella added as she looked back to the wall of photographs.

The conversation flowed easily between the four friends and so did the wine. Until things at home had become tense between his parents, Ronny had always enjoyed family dinners. Their friends would often join them. He was reminded how much he missed sitting at the dinner table laughing with people.

"Hey, does anyone want to smoke some hash? Josh gave me some and he said it was really good," offered Camille. Ronny was used to people smoking weed and hash around him and he had smoked it on occasion with his friends, so it was no big deal. He just wasn't in the mood and knew it would put him to sleep with his jet lag.

"When in Rome. I mean Milan." Chad smiled as Camille retrieved a small bong made out of a Pepsi can from her bag.

"You're like a French MacGyver," Chad laughed as Camille put some hash on top of the can where there were a group of small holes to light it.

"Hash is the shit," said Camille in a mocked stoned French accent. She took a slow drag on the can bong, and after holding in the smoke she moved her face closer to Chad who came forward as she slowly transferred the smoke from her mouth to his. As she finished blowing smoke into his mouth, she moved closer and slowly open-mouth kissed Chad. *That's pretty hot,* thought Ronny as he watched them making out. He quickly reached into his jacket that was on the back of the chair and retrieved the camera that Francesco had given him. He popped the flash and held the camera up and took a photograph. The flash distracted the couple and as they turned to him laughing, he took another photo.

"Okay, lovebirds," interrupted Ella who sounded a little uncomfortable. She turned to Ronny. "Hey, you want to go out to grab some gelato? I know a cool place close to here."

"Sure," he stammered, caught off guard but excited to get to finally spend some one-on-one time with her.

"Sorry. Hash makes me horny," said Camille. Ronny admired that she was such a confident, no-bullshit kind of girl. Ella stood up as Ronny followed her out onto the street feeling relaxed after the red wine and food.

"Hey, handsome, I see you found a new friend," called out the prostitute that must have remembered him from the other night with Chad.

"G'day, gorgeous," replied Ella in her Australian accent without missing a beat.

"I like her. She knows beauty when she sees it. But if it doesn't work out with her, I'm here if you need me," she called out as they walked down the street.

"I've actually photographed a few street workers in Rio—they always have such incredible stories." Said Ronny, Ella smiled.

"You know, your photographs are really good. They really capture something intimate with the subject. You should definitely keep going."

Ronny looked at Ella; he loved that she understood his perspective as a photographer.

"Here it is!" she announced as he followed her inside the small white storefront.

"Wow, how can you decide?" He glanced down at the glass counter to see at least twenty silver bins of beautifully displayed Italian gelato in all different colors and flavors.

"I'm a chocolate and hazelnut kind of girl. You can taste a few flavors if you like." Ella smiled playfully as he asked for a taste of pistachio and gianduja. "I'll take a scoop of chocolate and a scoop of hazelnut in a cone. Grazie."

"Hmm...incredible," he said as he tasted the pistachio. "I'll take a scoop of that in a cone." After he got his cone, Ella moved forward to pay. "Hang on, let me get it!" Ella elbowed him gently in the stomach.

"It's my treat, don't make me hurt you." She passed the money across the counter. "You have to try this." Ella walked outside the store onto the street and licked her full moist lips. She lifted her cone up to Ronny's mouth; instinctively he did the same with her. Ella took a small taste of pistachio. He was distracted as he watched her lick the gelato, so she moved her cone closer to his face, pushed it into his nose, and burst out laughing.

"You're right, it's pretty tasty," he said as he licked the ice cream off his nose. As they walked and talked, Ronny finished off his gelato and turned to watch her biting around the cone edge in an even circle pattern.

"Hey, crazy lady, how long have you been eating ice cream cones like that?" he asked as he put the final piece of his cone into his mouth. Ella stuck out her tongue.

"Ever since I was a little girl. I've always loved ice cream and I used to eat it really fast. One day my dad told me I needed to slow down and showed me how to savor every bite. So ever since then I've eaten ice cream cones like that, and it reminds me of my dad. That sounded so corny," she laughed, mocking herself. She took the last piece of her sugar cone and brought it up towards his mouth. He opened it, expecting her to put it in; instead she touched his lips with the end of the moist cone then slowly pushed it into his mouth, and before Ronny could chew on it, she moved in to kiss him.

He could taste the incredible mix of pistachio and chocolate with hazelnuts. He savored the feeling of Ella's soft lips. He couldn't deny that he had feelings for this girl. Something about her was so vulnerable, genuine, and real. There was an ease to their connection. She slowly pulled back and licked her lips.

"I think pistachio goes well with chocolate," she said, then playfully pushed him away and laughed, walking ahead down the street looking back at Ronny who stood feeling a little surprised by the kiss. There was an innocence to Ella; she wasn't as aggressive or forward as many of the girls he knew in Rio. She felt more like a friend, a friend who just happened to be attractive and funny as hell.

"All the Australian girls I met in Rio were always so cool,"

"So, you've met a few Aussie girls?" Ella mocked. He rolled his eyes. After the initial nerves he felt when he first saw her, he was enjoying feeling comfortable around her. When they got back to the Pola they walked past the reception desk as Mateo gave them a nod. The unexpected kiss had left him on a high.

"Buona notte," said Ella as the two entered the elevator, and without even missing a beat she pushed the button for Ronny's floor and the floor for her and Camille's room. *Well, I guess I'm going back to my room.* Ronny smiled, impressed that Ella was taking charge. As the elevator door closed, she glanced up and moved in closer. Her mouth met his as she kissed him deeply. Ronny pushed his hips into Ella's and kissed her back. Her lips weren't cold anymore. He could feel himself getting aroused until suddenly the elevator arrived with a jolt. Ella was bumped back and burst out laughing. When the elevator door opened, she playfully pushed him out.

"Buona notte."

"Thanks for dessert," he said as the door closed and he turned back to see her slightly blush.

He felt an unexpected shift inside himself. He had been so focused on getting a break that would help his photography career that he really wasn't anticipating meeting anyone and having feelings for them. *Don't get distracted.*

## CHAPTER 16

After an early training session with Chad and Nick, Ronny set off to visit the photo laboratory that Paul had recommended to him. This was where most of the professional photographers in Milan developed their film and got prints made, so he was excited to check it out and buy some film. Foto Aldo was located on a quiet street on the ground floor of an unassuming brick building located halfway between Residence Pola and BAM model agency. When he entered through the glass doors into the large plain white room, Ronny noticed the series of large framed prints on the walls showcasing a stunning series of dance images. Three customers stood at the glass counter that contained photographic and video equipment for sale, and on the wall behind were shelves with various kinds of Kodak film boxes on display.

He continued admiring the photographs until eventually a friendly looking dark-haired guy in his late twenties working behind the counter spoke to him, "Ciao, posso aiutarti?"

Ronny understood he was asking what he wanted. "Oh, ciao, yes, I'd like to buy twenty rolls of Kodak four-hundred-TX black and white film. Grazie."

"Are you from Brazil?" asked the guy in English. Ronny noticed his Portuguese accent.

"I'm from Rio."

"I'm from Bahia. My name is Jose," he replied with a warm smile and a handshake. Jose told him he that had been living in Italy for ten years since his mother moved there to be with an Italian man she met in Brazil.

"Do you like it here?" asked Ronny.

"You know, I've grown to like it, and learning to speak Italian helped a lot. Are you a photographer?"

Ronny hesitated for a moment then answered, "Yes, I'm a photographer, but I came here on a modeling contract. Photography is my passion."

"Good for you," replied Jose. "My boyfriend is a model booker at a women's model agency, so I'm pretty familiar with that crazy world."

"I'm sure he has some stories."

"Sorry, I'm talking away here. Let me get you your film." Jose turned back to retrieve the film. There were now a few people standing behind Ronny waiting to be served.

"Are all these photographs from the one photographer?" he asked as he nodded toward the wall.

"Yes, we exhibit the works of some of the photographers that use the lab. The owner likes to support new artists. This is a young Dutch photographer called Levi. Really talented." Ronny took another look at the photographs as Jose handed him the film in a small square black carry bag with a Kodak logo on the side of it. "Here, take this film bag. You can keep it in the fridge and store your film in it. I'm here every day except Sunday, so let me know if you need anything. Great to meet you Ronny."

He smiled at Jose as he walked out of The Lab onto the street. Getting to buy and develop his film at the same lab as the biggest photographers in the world was inspiring, and the fact that a fellow

Brazilian worked there was a coincidence that he hoped would come in handy.

Later that afternoon Ronny walked into the model agency and saw Paul waving to him from the model booker desk with a phone held to his ear. After giving a smile and nod to the receptionist, Ronny walked up to the booking desk. He couldn't help but notice a few of the bookers looking up at him. *Must be the new haircut*, thought Ronny as Paul put the phone down.

"Ciao, Ronny. Good to see you. Love the new haircut," said Paul as he moved in to give him a kiss on each cheek. Even though Ronny was used to greeting this way in Brazil, he still felt uncomfortable with Paul. He felt the kisses lingered slightly too long but didn't want to make a scene.

"Thanks for connecting me with Francesco. He was really great."

"He's amazing, right? Here, come check out the photographs that his assistant just dropped off. You're lucky he got them done so fast."

Ronny came around next to his chair. On Paul's desk were ten black and white prints of Ronny as well as a number of contact sheets of all the photo frames that Francesco had taken. Ronny stood in front of the prints and started to pick them up one by one. Staring back at him was his face and body but captured in a way that he didn't initially recognize.

"These photographs are perfect, Francesco was raving about you," Paul continued.

The photographs were different from the ones Santo Diaz had taken. Francesco had a way of capturing him that looked more personal. He studied the crop and angles, remembering the direction that Francesco had given him and how he composed each image. He felt the prints and looked closely at the grain on the paper.

"I really like these photographs, I don't know what else to say."

"You don't need to say anything, just take off your shirt," chimed in Brett. Paul shot him a disgruntled look. "Hey, I'm just saying..."

Ronny wasn't fazed by Brett's comment; he sensed he was harmless.

"I'll be in my office if you need me!" said Brett as he glanced sideways, winked, then stood up and walked toward the bathroom.

"These photos, along with the ones Santo took, are exactly what we need to get you working," Paul continued. "We've made color photocopies of these prints so we can make up a few portfolios for you to send around to clients. A lot of the castings are for fashion shows, have you ever walked in a runway show?"

"Um, that would be a definite no." He had only seen runway models in magazines.

"Okay, I'll have Brett check out your walk and give you a few tips; he's our resident walker."

*This gets better and better...now someone is going to teach me how to walk.*

"Did someone mention my name?" asked Brett as he appeared back from the bathroom as Paul rolled his eyes. "Come with me, or should I say walk this way," Brett continued as he set out walking toward the hallway dragging his right foot like a hunchback. He looked back and laughed as Ronny followed him out into the hallway. The fashion industry was certainly filled with an array of characters, and he found Brett to be amusing. "Okay, I want you to walk down the hall to the end and back for me. Just walk like you're walking on the street."

Ronny had never really thought about his walk before and was now conscious of every step. He turned to see Brett standing there with his hands on his hips and a perplexed expression on his face.

"Take longer steps, look straight ahead, don't be stiff, and don't think about it—just work it, babe. Here watch me." Brett walked to show Ronny what he meant. He instructed Ronny to put on his Walkman headphones and walk to the music as if he was heading down the street to the gym. Nineties dance music filled his head as Ronny strutted down the hallway, focusing on the music; as he turned back to walk toward Brett, he saw him nodding and giving a thumbs up.

"Well, look at you, John Travolta—you got some Saturday night fever going on." Brett snapped his finger into the air. Ronny could feel the difference. "Now try it again without the headphones but think of the music in your head. Remember, longer strides on the street and when you get to the end of the runway, pause for a moment so the photographers can take photos of what you're wearing. Pose like this, or this. Make it flow from your walk to the pose. Make it seem natural and confident." Brett demonstrated. "Looking good, Rio. I think you'll give Tiana Taylor a run for her money," Brett added after he walked another four laps of the hallway.

Ronny had heard that Tiana had a reputation of being the strongest runway model in the business. As surreal as all of this was, this was now his world, his new reality.

"Look at you walking like a pro," said Chad as he appeared at the end of the hallway and came forward to give Ronny a high five. They followed Brett back into the agency to where Paul was sitting.

"Ciao, Chad." Said Paul as he stood up. "I just spoke to Santo Diaz, and he loved the polaroids I took the other day. He is going to Paris for a shoot but wants you to go by his house when he gets back to meet with him in person." Paul put his hand on Chad's shoulder and walked him away from the table. Paul lowered his voice, but Ronny managed to overhear him. "As you know, Santo

Diaz is a huge deal. He can honestly make or break your career, so you have to make a good impression with him, and if he likes you, he will work with you all the time. Just do what he asks and don't let me down," Paul said as he looked Chad firmly in the eye and held his arm. Ronny figured Santo hadn't requested to see him again because of their last encounter. He wondered if he should say something to warn Chad.

Paul moved back near the table to include Ronny in the conversation. "Oh, and don't forget, guys, tomorrow night is the party for Lorenzo Mancini. Why don't you both come to my place first and we can all go together, I have a car picking us up. Here's the address, so I will see you guys there at six." Paul handed Ronny a piece of paper with his address on it.

"Thanks again, Paul. I won't let you down," Chad said before he and Ronny walked out of the agency and onto the street.

"Hey, did you get your new photos?" asked Chad as they sat down on the subway heading back to the Pola. Ronny reached in his backpack and handed Chad his new portfolio filled with color copies.

"Francesco is an amazing photographer—he made me look half decent," he replied as he looked over Chad's shoulder at his new photographs. Ronny could appreciate the way Francesco had composed and directed the shots, the way he worked the light, and the expressions and angles he captured.

"These photos are awesome, man, seriously. Wow." Chad seemed really impressed.

"Thanks, man. So, you're meeting with Santo Diaz. That's a big deal."

"Yeah, definitely. Are you seeing him as well? I'm sure he would like your new photos." Chad's question caught Ronnie off guard. It sounded like he was unaware of Santo's reputation. He had to at least warn him.

"Well, to be honest, the last time I saw him was at the wrap party in Rio, the night after that shoot we did with Tiana Taylor. He was pretty messed up on drugs, and when I went to the toilet, he followed me in and tried to grab me so I pushed him back and almost put him through a wall. I told him to fuck off and left." Talking about what happened made it real again, but Chad needed to know about Santo.

"Sorry, dude, that's messed up. You should have knocked him out."

"Well, if I had knocked him out, I'm sure I wouldn't be here in Milan. I get the sense that he likes the challenge. I'm sorry I didn't tell you earlier."

"That's cool. Maybe the drugs had something to do with it. I just hope he doesn't try that on me." Chad handed back his portfolio. Ronny was glad he had told Chad. Maybe he was right and he wouldn't try anything, but he doubted it. When they made it back to their room, Ronny put his bag away and retrieved a box containing more of his own prints.

"Are these more of your photos?" Chad nodded toward the photographs as Ronny opened the print box.

"Yeah, I wanted to edit some down to create an actual portfolio of my work. If I'm going to start test shooting more models and building up my book, I want to have something I can show people. When I got my first camera, I went out and took photographs every day. I was assisting a local photographer in Rio who knew my mother, and he gave me a secondhand camera. He taught me a lot of the technical stuff and how to develop film. I started taking photos of my friends and people I met on the street."

"Your work is amazing, dude," said Chad as he started to lay the photographs out on his bed.

"Thanks, man. Milan will give me the chance to start shooting more models and include more fashion in my work. The photos I took in Brazil were more focused on people than fashion." Meeting Francesco had opened his eyes. He would love to have a career like that and make decent money doing what he loved.

"Oh, before I forget," said Chad, "the agency called. We have a bunch of show castings tomorrow." Chad passed Ronny a piece of paper with the information on it. He recognized the designer's names from his fashion magazines: Russo, Lorenzo Mancini... "Fuck." He stopped suddenly when he saw the next name.

"Fuck what?"

"I think the stylist Flavio on this list is the same one that I worked with on the shoot with Santo in Brazil. When I was getting dressed, he tried to adjust my dick in my speedo, and I pushed him away and called him an asshole. "Fuck!"

"Shit! Paul told me that he was one of the biggest fashion stylists in the world who works with all the designers and clients. He has a lot of influence over who gets selected for the shows and campaigns. He likes to see all the new guys before the show castings," Chad said as Ronny shook his head.

"I bet he does." Ronny packed away his photographs, coming to terms with the fact that there was no escaping these appointments. It felt pointless to even make a plan—best to just see how it went, try to not piss anyone off, and not get in over his head.

# CHAPTER 17

When Chad and Ronny arrived at Flavio's address, they entered the rustic old sandstone building with ornate balconies and large arched windows. Once inside they made their way up to the third floor where there were about fifteen male models sitting in the hallway on the wooden floor outside his apartment.

"Glad we got here early." Chad smiled as they sat down on the floor at the end of the group. Looking around, Ronny started to get a sense of the modeling competition. It was amazing to see the variety of different looks and body types of the guys that were in town from all over the world—skinny, young guys; beautiful, almost feminine-looking men with longer hair; and more athletic masculine types. Ronny noticed that the skinny models that entered Flavio's apartment came back out a lot faster than the more athletic types. He wondered if that was because the market had changed, and now athletic guys were getting more work, or because they were more Flavio's type. Ronny started to feel nervous and uncomfortable as the line got shorter and he thought about seeing Flavio again.

He tried to listen in on what the models around him were talking about. Some of them were discussing jobs, some of them girls, and a few were debating the best way to put on muscle and bulk up. Ronny sat silent until Flavio's assistant let him know it was his turn to go in for the appointment. He stood up and took a deep breath, trying to calm his nerves. The apartment had high ceilings, walls covered with abstract art, and modern furnishings. Flavio appeared to greet him.

"Well, hello, Ronny. So nice to see you again," said Flavio as he walked toward him.

"Nice to see you, too" he replied. It was the same short creepy guy that he remembered from Rio, this time wearing blue silk pajamas. His oily brown hair was tied back in a short ponytail, and his face reminded Ronny of a rat with his beady eyes and tight small mouth. He smelled of cigarettes as he came forward and offered him two slow kisses on his cheek that lingered long enough to make him uncomfortable.

"So the photos from the shoot we did with Santo in Brazil look like they were well received. I know you were direct booked for the Mancini show that I'm styling."

"Um, yeah, thanks. The photos definitely helped me get started. I have some new photographs from Francesco as well." He pulled his new portfolio out of his bag and passed it to Flavio.

"Ah yes. I love Francesco's work." Flavio slowly turned the pages of the portfolio, taking in each photograph. When he finally came to the photographs of Ronny in his underwear, he paused then looked up. Ronny could feel sweat starting to form on his lower back as he took a slow deep breath. "Let me see you try on an outfit. It's from the designer Trusso." Flavio sounded as if Ronny was supposed to be impressed. He passed him a pair of briefs, pants, and a shirt as his assistant disappeared into another room.

Ronny looked around and moved toward the nearest wall to get changed and turned away from Flavio. He quickly put on the white briefs and pulled up the black pants that were tight across his butt. It was challenging to button up the front, but he made it work. The shirt was a printed silk fabric that he thought was probably the most expensive thing he had ever worn on his body. He tucked in the shirt and turned around. Flavio was watching him as he leaned on his desk. His eyes slowly traveled up his body. Ronny averted his eyes and hoped this would be over soon enough. Even though he thought the clothes were too tight, Flavio seemed to think otherwise.

"This style works well on your body; all we need are a few minor adjustments." He moved in closer to stand in front of Ronny. "This could be a very successful season for you this year," he said softly as he undid all but the lowest button of his shirt revealing Ronny's almost hairless defined chest. He swallowed the lump in his throat and wondered if Flavio had heard the gulp. Flavio moved in closer and ran his hands across the back of Ronny's pants. "These feel a little tight. This material may be better with no underwear; let's take them off."

"Um, okay." He was a bit taken aback by the request but went back to the wall and removed his briefs. He tried as best he could to position himself so he wasn't creating a distracting crotch situation in the already tight pants. When he came back out Flavio asked him to walk back and forth before him. *Fuck!* Surely Flavio knew walking would cause more crotch issues. Ronny felt trapped and angry.

"That's better." Flavio moved closer and put his hands on his hips and turned him around. Ronny felt his hand run over his behind. "Yes, much better without the briefs."

*Is this guy smoothing out wrinkles or feeling me up? Fuck!* He just wanted the ordeal to be over as Flavio turned him back around to face him. He pulled slightly on the waistband of his pants. Ronny felt his fingers brush through his pubic hair. He held his breath and closed his eyes. Then without warning Flavio pulled open his pants and put his hand in to reposition him. He tried not to flinch or react to the groping touch. He remembered what Paul had told him about making a good impression. He bit down hard on the inside of his cheek.

"I think a G-string will help," said Flavio. Despite the stakes and trying to make a good impression, he couldn't take it any longer and pulled back abruptly from Flavio's hand. *Enough!*

Flavio stood up, obviously sensing he had pushed him to the limit. "You can get changed back into your own clothes," he snapped as he moved back to his desk and lit up a cigarette.

Blood continued to rush to Ronny's head as his anger rose. *I thought I was escaping this bullshit, and here I am back on the front line.* He changed back into his own clothes, his stomach turning. He pulled his pants up, stood up, as much as he wanted to punch Flavio in the face, he remembered why he was there. Flavio's assistant magically appeared as he took a final look at Flavio with contempt. He saw a skinny creep with a small frame, knowing that he could easily snap his neck and rip his head off. He needed to focus on the big picture and control his anger.

Flavio must have sensed it wouldn't be wise to push him any further. "Next!" he snapped as he cleared his throat and took a long drag on his cigarette. Ronny walked quickly out of the office into the hallway. He nodded as he passed Chad and continued downstairs back out onto the street. Ronny walked halfway down the block then back to sit outside the building next door on the ground. He shook his head. *I guess the only difference between selling yourself in Brazil compared to Milan is that you have the potential to make more money here. Either way, you're fucked.* Chad eventually appeared outside the building.

"You okay, bud?" asked Ronny.

"Yeah," Chad replied.

He could tell he wasn't. "Sorry, man, that guy's a total creep."

"That's the same stylist that groped me before on that job. I should have knocked him out, fucking asshole!" Chad said as he sat down. "He put me in a pair of shorts and thought it was okay to just go ahead and rearrange my dick. I couldn't deal and pushed his hand away. I know that's probably ruined my chances of getting a job, but the agency should warn us about creeps like that," Chad vented.

"They don't because they know that's what happens. These guys hold the power and make the decisions on who gets the breaks, who gets the jobs, who makes the money. So the agency has to play the game, too."

"That's bullshit, man," Chad declared. Ronny felt a combination of anger and helplessness, trying to rid his mind of Flavio's touch. A minute passed as they sat together. He knew that Chad felt the same frustrated anger that he did. Finally, Chad stood up and slapped his own face a few times.

"Okay, we need to shake this shit off and get back to business."

"Hey, how about a slice of pizza?" asked Ronny as he stood up.

"My dad always asked me if I wanted slice after I lost a wrestling match to make me feel better, and it always worked."

Ronny knew that Chad had come from a much more sheltered upbringing than he did and imagined this must be affecting him on a deeper level.

"I might need a whole pizza," Chad continued as he pretended to clip Ronny behind the head.

After stopping for pizza, they made their way to their next appointment. Ronny knew he had to refocus himself; he needed to put what just happened in the back of his mind. When Chad and

Ronny arrived at the Trusso fashion show casting, there was a group of models smoking outside on the street standing in front of the modern glass building. He started to feel nervous, hoping this casting wasn't going to be as traumatic as the last one. He tried to distract himself by studying the faces of the models, imagining how he would light their face to take their portrait.

To his relief the casting went well and eased his nerves. An hour later they arrived at their last casting for the Mancini show. "You know Flavio will be here at this casting," reminded Chad.

*Really? Ugh!*

"Fortunately, he will be with a bunch of people from Mancini, and Paul told me the designer's sister Carlotta will be there, and I heard she doesn't like him so hopefully he will be on his best behavior," Chad added.

"Can you guarantee that?" Ronny asked.

"Brett told me that he got really drunk at a party and started groping Carlotta's husband. Eventually her husband punched him in the face."

*That Brett certainly does love the gossip.* "Glad someone finally punched the little creep. Why the hell do they still use him to work on the show?"

"Fashion politics. Paul told me that Flavio is one of the most sought-after stylists in the world. He contributes to the biggest magazines and styles a lot of the big ad campaigns. Mancini always wants to work with the best in the business, even if they're a pain in the ass."

"Or grabbing your ass," Ronny added.

"Fuck him. I wish I was successful enough to get him kicked off a job," said Chad as he stared forward with a serious look on his face. Ronny knew Chad was trying to make a joke of the situation, but the truth was they were both traumatized. "That's the first time

I've heard you talk like that. Maybe getting your crotch grabbed was what you needed to light the fire."

"I know I seem pretty relaxed about the whole modeling thing, but I'm not just here to eat pizza and hook up with hot girls. I want to catch a break, make some money, and get to travel. I'm not going back to work on the farm." Ronny saw the competitive athlete come out in him, and for the first time he sounded serious about modeling. As they walked into the beautiful Mancini design building, Josh was just coming out.

"Hi, guys!" he said.

"Hey, man, how's it look in there? Busy?" asked Chad.

"There are about twenty guys waiting. It's not as bad as it was earlier when I got here; there were close to forty guys—it took a while."

Ronny was already booked for the Mancini show, but the casting people wanted to meet him in person and see him walk. They approached the slick modern foyer, and the woman behind the reception desk motioned for them to sit on the large black leather couch under two large framed photographs of Tiana Taylor from last season's Mancini fashion campaign. Chad gave a friendly nod to the other guys sitting in the reception area. Ronny was feeling more relaxed than the last casting and eventually was ushered into the main casting studio. The large contemporary white space with black painted floorboards overlooking an internal garden was an impressive room. In front of the windows was a long table with four people behind it: Flavio, Carlotta Mancini, and two other casting people dressed in black.

"So nice to see you again, Ronny," said Flavio in a condescending tone as he walked up to the table. He took a deep breath as his heart started to race a little faster; he was trying to stop his face from going red as he felt the anger built up inside him.

He ignored Flavio and looked across to Carlotta and the other two casting people.

"Ciao," Ronny smiled politely as he placed his composite card and portfolio on the table away from Flavio. *Don't mess this up because of that little creep.* He put on the charm as Carlotta looked back at him with a smile. She was a stylish woman in her mid-forties with kind eyes, sharp features and platinum blonde hair. She wore white jeans and a fitted white leather jacket and gold jewellery. She seemed impressed with Ronny's confidence and sat up to look more closely at his portfolio as they made small talk.

"Now you know, Carlotta, that Ronny was direct booked from Brazil for this show by Lorenzo when he saw the photographs I styled in Rio."

"Yes, thank you. I am well aware he is already confirmed for the show; my brother and I discuss all the decisions about casting," Carlotta quickly responded. Ronny sensed the tension between them. "Lorenzo and I loved the photographs you shot with Santo and Tiana," Carlotta added. "You have a strong look that works perfectly for the new Mancini collection."

"Why don't you take off your shirt for us, Ronny," said Flavio quickly, almost cutting Carlotta off. He sat back in his chair looking like the cat who got the cream. Ronny made a concerted effort to not lose his smile and removed his shirt, placing it on his backpack before running his fingers through his hair then bringing his eyes back to Carlotta.

"Could you walk for us please," asked Carlotta politely.

He nodded, turned, and walked away from the table to the end of the room, trying to focus on the music track playing in the background. After doing two laps of the room, he walked back to the table feeling all eyes in the room on him. He felt relieved he didn't have to be alone again with Flavio; as hard as it was to face his abuser, he couldn't afford to mess up this appointment. When he got back to the table he reached down to his backpack and grabbed his shirt and put it on.

"Thank you, that was perfect. I look forward to seeing you and Paul at the party this evening," said Carlotta, holding his eye contact. He didn't look at Flavio, and as he turned to walk away. Ronny felt a sense of relief; he liked Carlotta and hoped Lorenzo Mancini was just as professional.

Chad stood up as Ronny walked back into the reception area. "I'll wait for you outside," said Ronny, sensing that Chad was a little anxious about seeing Flavio. "You'll be fine, bro. Carlotta is great." Chad fist-pumped him as they passed.

## CHAPTER 18

Ronny sat on a bench outside of the Mancini offices waiting for Chad to finish his appointment; after about fifteen minutes Chad walked out with a blank expression.

"What happened?" asked Ronny with a concerned tone.

"I got Flavio in a headlock and choked him out!"

"What! Is he okay?" After the words left his mouth, Ronny immediately regretted asking about Flavio. "I mean are you okay?"

"Well, that didn't actually happen, I just imagined choking him out to get me through the casting." Chad added. Ronny was relieved that he hadn't done something that stupid, although the thought of seeing Flavio in a headlock was somewhat gratifying.

"I used to do that the night before an important wrestling match. I would imagine choking my opponent out. Sometimes I even choked my pillow…one night I got really into it and all of a sudden the pillow popped open and feathers went everywhere. My mother came into the room and I looked like I'd killed a chicken." Both guys started laughing, breaking the day's tension.

"How did the casting go?" Ronny asked.

"Carlotta was great; she told me I had a body like Michelangelo's David."

"Good for you, man. I hope we get to walk the show together."

"Yeah!" Chad gave Ronny a high five. "Let's go and have some fun at this party tonight. I could really use a night out."

"I'm with you." Ronny needed to let off some steam. His body felt tense and tight, like he had been holding his breath.

Later back at The Pola they got ready for the Mancini party. Ronny put on a black suit and a crisp white shirt that he had brought with him from Brazil. His mother had originally bought the suit for him to wear to his uncle's funeral.

"Looking sharp, Rio," said Chad as he came out of the bathroom wearing an open purple shirt that was almost see through and a pair of black jeans. Chad put on his leather jacket, and they headed out to grab a taxi.

"Double trouble!" said the prostitute as they walked down the street past her standing under the lamplight with two other girls. Her voice was deep, and Ronny recognized her from the other evening with Ella. "Buona sera, signore."

Ronny smiled and nodded.

"Hold on, you two," she added, speaking English with a thick Italian accent. "Now where would you two be going so dressed up?"

"Off to a fancy party," replied Ronny as they paused in front of the girls.

"My name is Chanel. Beauty by design, baby." She slowly moved toward them. "I run things around here, and if you ever need anything you let me know, okay?" She moved closer to Ronny. "Anything," she emphasized as she ran her hand up his arm. He slowly pulled away releasing his arm. Even though Ronny sensed she was just playing around, he was becoming more sensitive to people's touch and what their intentions were. He had definitely had his fair share of inappropriate touching this week.

"I'm Ronny, and this is Chad." Chanel was wearing a blonde wig, and a heavy layer of makeup on her hard face couldn't hide the deep scar that ran across her cheek. She was wearing fishnet stockings, a few colored tank tops layered over one another, and a short skirt with chunky high heels. He presumed the Chanel bag on her shoulder was a fake. Chanel looked like she had endured a lot in life. "Grazie, Chanel. Nice to meet you. We need to go or we'll be late. Have a good night." He moved back toward the curb to hail an approaching taxi. Paul lived in the Isola area of Milan, which was a lot quieter than where the Pola was located. Chad rang the doorbell of the beautiful brownstone building, and Paul buzzed them up to his apartment on the second floor.

"Buonasera. Come in. You look great," Paul said as he opened the door, he was dressed in a black shirt and suit. Black seemed to be the color of choice for people in the fashion industry who wanted to avoid any scrutiny of what they were wearing, especially attending a designer's party.

"Thanks for having us over," replied Ronny. Paul's apartment was filled with an eclectic mix of vintage furniture. Even though it wasn't a huge apartment, there was so much to look at.

"Allo, fellas, all right then?" Nick announced in a strong British accent as he entered the room from the kitchen carrying some glasses. "What are we drinking, lads?"

It was a surprise to see Nick. "Hey, bro, good to see you," Chad said as they stepped forward to greet Nick.

"Nick's coming with us tonight," Paul said as he took the glasses. "Have you guys ever tried a Campari? It's a favorite Italian drink."

"I'll try one," Chad responded. "It's so cool to be in a place where the drinking age isn't twenty-one."

"When in Italy," Paul said as he prepared the popular Italian drink at a small bar cart in the corner. "Guys, grab a seat and make yourselves at home. Ronny, I'll make you one too so you can try it."

Ronny nodded politely. The room was dimly lit and cluttered, and it was hard to know where to look. "You've got so many amazing things in here, Paul. It must have taken you a while to collect everything," said Ronny as they grabbed a seat on the velvet couch in front of the glass and brass coffee table that had books piled high on it and a vase of wilting roses. There were old portrait paintings on the walls with heavy gold frames mixed in with black and white photographs of naked men. In the corner was a huge plant that almost touched the ceiling. The floors were covered in colorful rugs, and Italian music played in the background. A vanilla scented candle flickered on a side table helping to disguise the smell of cigarettes.

"I've always liked to collect things more than I like getting rid of things. I think I'll need a bigger place soon," answered Paul as he took a moment to look around the room. "Nick mentioned you've all been training together."

"Yeah. Nick, I know you told us you lived in this area. Is it close?" Ronny asked.

"I'm staying here with Paul," replied Nick as Paul joined them, balancing four bright red drinks with slices of orange twisted into the ice. Ronny was glad he was staying at the Pola with Chad. As friendly as Paul tried to be, he still made him feel uncomfortable.

"Here's to a fun night and a successful season. Cheers!" said Paul as he handed out the drinks and clinked glasses with all of them. Ronny took a sip of the bittersweet drink and wished he'd asked for a beer. "So, I heard the Mancini casting went well," Paul continued. "Chad, I spoke to Carlotta and she kept telling me you have a body like the statue of David." Chad glanced over at Ronny and winked. "She wants you to be in the show and will be putting a good word in with her brother. If all goes well, you will both be walking in the show together."

"Yes!" exclaimed Ronny as he gave Chad a high five. Finally, some good news after all the bullshit.

"Really? That would be awesome," Chad said, and he slapped Ronny on the shoulder.

"I'd do anything to get to walk in that show," added Nick.

"I'll know soon who the final lineup is," Paul said as he put his hand on Nick's shoulder and for a moment started to massage him before removing his hand. Ronny noticed that Nick didn't react.

After some more small talk they finished their drinks and Paul stood up. "Sorry to break up the party, but the car will be here in a few minutes, and I want to make sure we get there early before it gets too busy."

"I just need to use the bathroom before we leave." Chad asked.

"Down the end of the hall," replied Paul who was collecting the empty glasses on the table and blowing out the candles around the room. Once Chad reappeared, they walked out onto the street. A handsome young driver got out of a black car and walked around to the passenger side to open the car doors.

"Buonasera, Mr. Paul." He waved as they approached.

"Buonasera, Mattia. Thank you." Paul smiled. It was obvious this was Paul's regular driver.

"Ohh fancy," said Chad only loud enough so Ronny and Nick could hear. "I could get used to this." The three models sat in the back, and Paul took the front seat.

"Heading to the Mancini party, correct?" Mattia inquired.

"Si," replied Paul as he turned back around to face them. "You will love Mancini's house—it's on the outskirts of the city but it's worth the drive." The car sped off as Ronny watched out the window. The crowded streets of Milan slowly gave way to more open spaces and larger houses. The crazy new lifestyle he was experiencing was so far away from his family drama and the world he once knew. He smiled to himself, buzzed from the cocktail and excited about the night ahead.

"Lorenzo Mancini is Italy's most celebrated designer known for his sexy, chic clothes and campaigns that feature only the top models in the world," Paul said with a serious tone. "He is the one who started paying the highest day rates for his models and is credited with launching the supermodels. His designs are favored by rock stars and celebrities alike who wear his clothes and enjoy being a part of his lavish lifestyle. Mancini always throws the best parties at his many houses around the world and tonight will be no exception with his kick-off to fashion week."

"Will he be in Italy for long?" asked Ronny. He was looking forward to meeting Mancini and thanking him personally for booking him for his fashion show. He would never know the lifeline he had given Ronny and what he had saved him from.

"No, he travels constantly. He just arrived in town from Miami after opening his latest store there, and he's here to do final checks on the spring/summer collection and oversee the final casting of the models walking the runway. Following the show, he will attend the campaign shoot for the collection and then take off for his vacation home in Lake Como. His sister Carlotta is really the driving force behind the brand's identity and publicity; she oversees everything and makes sure the right people attend the shows and are seen wearing his clothes. There will be a lot of very influential people here tonight. Unfortunately, Santo Diaz, who shoots the Mancini campaign, is away shooting an editorial in Africa. Lucia, the editor of *Italian STYLE*, will be there and so will Flavio, the stylist for the show."

Chad let out an audible disgruntled sigh.

"That's right—you met him earlier today. How did the appointment go?" asked Paul as he turned back to face them.

"Well, aside from the fact that he felt me up, it went really well," Chad responded as the smile quickly left his face. Ronny could sense that he was trying to make light of a situation that had been traumatic for both of them. He was surprised he said that out loud to Paul and wondered how he would respond.

"Yes, I've heard he can be very hands on. But he is also one of the most powerful stylists in the business," replied Paul without any sympathy in his voice. Ronny processed what Paul was saying and gave Chad a sideways glance. *Sometimes there's a price to pay to get what you want.* Eventually their car pulled up behind a line of cars in front of the home and a gathering crowd that could be seen in the distance.

"Have a good time tonight, guys, but be on your best behavior," instructed Paul as he looked back at them. Finally, Mattia pulled up in front of the villa and got out to open the door for them. Nick got out of the car first.

"Holy shit, now that's a house! Buckle up, lads."

# CHAPTER 19

As Ronny got out of the car, he looked up the steps at the six-story building that towered above them. It was lit up from below, and he could see the walls were faded yellow stone and the bottom half of the building was covered in thick green hanging vines. It looked like something out of a fairytale. He felt butterflies in his stomach.

"Looks more like a hotel than a house," said Ronny as Chad got out of the car behind him and paused for a moment with his mouth slightly open staring up at the villa.

"Come on, follow me," said Paul as he ushered the guys up to the entry gate where a tall, stylish black woman with a clipboard and a walkie-talkie stood next to a huge security guard in a black suit. Paul gave her their names. The crowd noise increased behind them as Ronny turned around to see a flurry of flashbulbs going off.

"Tiana is here," the host said into the walkie-talkie, as she looked past Paul and focused on the models coming in behind them.

"The supermodels have arrived," muttered Paul as the crowd parted and Tiana Taylor appeared looking incredible in a silver Mancini dress and high heels; her long hair fell perfectly down her back. She was accompanied by two other tall striking models—one blonde, and the other had short red hair. The three girls looked incredible in their short, sexy, flashy dresses. Ronny watched them pose together for the paparazzi and understood why they were the top models in the world and in many ways celebrities themselves. Ronny hoped Tiana would remember him. He thought about the shoot day in Rio and how incredible it was to watch her work. Now that he was here in Milan maybe there was a chance they would work together again, especially after the response to the photo spread in *Italian STYLE* magazine. His dream, however, would be to photograph her himself.

"Are they here for the men's shows?" Chad asked Paul.

"Mancini had them all flown in for the party and a campaign shoot for the upcoming season. Publicity is always an important part of the game with Mancini," Paul answered as Tiana led the other two girls to the entrance near where the guys were standing. She looked at Ronny out of the corner of her eye.

"Olá, Tiana," said Ronny as she stopped briefly at the entrance.

"Oh, ciao," Tiana replied vaguely, looking like she was trying to remember his face and where she had met him.

"Everyone loved the photos we did together in Brazil for *Italian STYLE*," he added, hoping to jog her memory.

"Yes, of course." She smiled politely enough as she walked past him into the party holding hands with another hot supermodel.

Finally, they were ushered past the host through the large iron gates, and they walked up the stone steps. Ronny had never been in a house like this, to calm his nerves he eagerly took the welcome drink that was handed to them by one of the twelve good-looking male waiters standing in a line with trays of drinks. They continued through the entrance and into the large reception area. He looked around the room in silence taking in the opulence of the space: the art on the walls, the high ornate hand-painted ceilings, and the massive chandelier hanging above the sexy crowd of people gathering in the foyer.

He was surrounded by stylish, eccentric people from all walks of life. Ronny recognized many of the faces from the social pages he had seen in *Italian STYLE*. The biggest names in fashion, the club scene, athletes, musicians, and celebrities were all there on show, and most were wearing Mancini. It was impossible not to be impressed and want to be a part of this world. He felt like he was in a place with so many opportunities. Food was being passed around, and Ronny was reminded just how hungry he was. He wasn't shy about helping himself to the fancy appetizers.

"Let me introduce you to Lorenzo," Paul said as he moved his hand from Ronny's shoulder to his lower back and led the guys over to where he was standing.

"Always surrounded by the most handsome men, Paul," said Lorenzo Mancini as they approached.

"Ciao, Lorenzo. So good to see you, my friend. What a fabulous night. It's always great to have you back in Milan," replied Paul as he moved to kiss Lorenzo on his cheeks. "Let me introduce you. This is Nick from London, Chad from America, and Ronny from Brazil, who you booked for your show from the *Italian STYLE* shoot with Tiana."

"Ciao. Welcome to the party," Lorenzo said as they all shook the designer's hand. He was a handsome, tanned man in his forties wearing a bright patterned Mancini shirt, gold chains and black pants with black studs running up the outside of the leg. There was an undeniable magnetic charm about him. He looked as stylish as Ronny had imagined, and it was hard not to be starstruck by the man.

"Thanks for having us. Your home is incredible," said Nick.

"This old building covered in weeds? My sister loves it and won't let me sell it," replied Lorenzo with a smile as he turned to Ronny. "I loved the story you shot with Tiana and can't wait to see how you look in my clothes this season. We are bringing sexy back in a big way. Thank God that grunge look is over."

Ronny beamed. He was thankful the trend toward athletic-looking models was working in his favor.

"You are bringing sexy back and the glamour, darling," added Carlotta as she walked up and took Lorenzo's arm. "Nice to see you, Paul." She looked striking in a tight body-hugging dress made of a shimmering green fabric that clung to her body and accentuated her every curve. She seemed high on something. *Probably cocaine,* Ronny suspected.

"Ciao, Carlotta. You look stunning," Paul replied and stepped back to make sure she saw the guys.

"Ciao, Chad." She recognized his face as he smiled at her. "Lorenzo, Chad is the model I told you about from the casting."

"Ah yes, the statue of David," Lorenzo said. "My sister has an eye for talent. I look forward to seeing you walk next week."

"Nice to see you again, Carlotta," replied Chad as Carlotta flashed him a smile.

"Ronny, did you enjoy shooting with Tiana? She is stunning," Lorenzo asked.

"She was amazing."

"The photos of you two were so sexy. Amazing chemistry. I loved them," Lorenzo continued.

"Grazie. I'm so excited to be here to be a part of your show. I can't thank you enough, Mr. Mancini." Ronny smiled, trying to express how he felt without sounding overly zealous.

"I think you will love the collection," replied Lorenzo as he put his hand on his shoulder. Ronny felt his body stiffen slightly. *Relax.*

At this stage he was still trying to work out where he stood with the big players in the industry, hoping Lorenzo wouldn't turn out to be like Santo.

"Have a fabulous time. Enjoy, enjoy," Lorenzo said before turning to his sister. "Carlotta, come say hi to Lucia—she just arrived."

"I just have to use the bathroom, darling. See you in a minute," she replied as she blew an air-kiss to the group and headed down the hall where Tiana and another model were standing waiting for her. The three then proceeded to disappear into a side room together. He suspected they were going to do more cocaine. It seemed like it was the drug of choice for the fashion industry. What surprised him was how openly accepted it was.

"I will come find you in a little bit to meet Lucia," added Paul as he headed off to network.

"Thanks, Paul," replied Chad as he turned around. "Hey, you want to find some more food? I need to eat something before I get too drunk."

"Sounds like a plan," Nick said as they headed off to find some food. The next room was as opulent and over the top as the foyer. Huge bowls of flowers adorned the tables, and the couches were covered with rich fabrics and cushions similar to the pattern on Lorenzo's shirt. Nick asked a passing waiter if there was a buffet, and they were directed onto the patio where there was a table overflowing with seafood, caviar, meats, pasta, cheese, and breads. *Doesn't get much more decadent than this*, thought Ronny as they proceeded to fill plates of food and sat at one of the many round bistro tables set up outside for guests.

"How's this fucking house?!" Nick said as he picked up a shrimp and put it in his mouth.

"Insane," replied Chad, who couldn't get the food into his mouth quick enough.

Ronny looked up to admire the interior windows of the courtyard. He was trying to eat some food and take everything in at the same time. There was so much to look at.

"Everyone knows Mancini hosts the wildest parties," said Nick.

"Dude, there's Bon Jovi," exclaimed Chad as he sat starstruck in his chair. "I love his music. My dad will freak out when I tell him I saw him."

"Get ready, lads, this party is going to go off." Nick added.

He liked Nick and the sound of his strong British accent. "Hey, man, how did you end up living at Paul's place?" Ronny inquired.

"Well, I have a girlfriend and kid back in London, so when I was scouted by Paul, I told him I didn't have the cash to make the trip, so he told me he would advance my flight and I could stay with him for free. I know it's a bit weird but, fuck, I look at this as an opportunity and I didn't have a lot of options. I was a boxer in London, and after getting hit in the head too many times I ended up with a severe concussion, so my doctor says I can't fight anymore. The way I see it is, I'm here to have some fun, make some cash, and look after my kid." Nick finished off his drink. Ronny considered the similarities between Chad's and Nick's stories. Both athletes that had their careers cut short.

"Good for you, man," he acknowledged Nick as Chad stayed silent.

"Hey, you guys want another drink?" asked Nick, his smile revealed the wide gap between his two front teeth. Ronny studied his face with the scar and his piercing eyes.

"I'll have a beer," replied Chad as Ronny nodded.

Nick walked inside to the bar, Chad turned back to Ronny and said quietly, "I have to tell you something. When I went to go to the toilet in Paul's apartment before we left, I walked down the hall and noticed there was only one bedroom. The door was half open and as I walked past, I could see on the floor in the corner was an open bag with clothes in it and a pair of boxing gloves sitting on top that could only have belonged to Nick." Chad paused. "I think Nick might be sleeping in Paul's bed."

"I think you might be right," Ronny answered discreetly without even missing a beat. He suspected that was the case after his brief conversation with Nick. "Unfortunately, in this business the name of the game is how to get through the fire without getting burned. Nick's a survivor." Milo came to mind. He had been so quick to judge his decision to work at the brothel until he himself had almost fallen to the same fate. "I know it's hard for you to understand where he's at. You're lucky to have a family that supports you." When Ronny thought about Nick and his boxing scars, he remembered Chanel, the sex worker on the streets out the front of the Pola and the scars he saw on her face. She was a survivor, too.

Chad sat silently for a moment. "I just couldn't imagine having to deal with that to get ahead," he said softly.

"But we just did with Flavio," said Ronny. He was realizing that his own moral line was becoming more flexible as he continued down this path to try and catch a break. He wasn't proud of what he had done, but he knew in order to get ahead he had to play the game.

# CHAPTER 20

Nick appeared carrying three shots of tequila and three beers. "Okay, lads, this will get the night going for us," Nick said, breaking up the serious conversation Chad and Ronny were having. He put down the drinks and passed out the shots.

"Up ya bum then!" Nick added as he threw back the shot and the guys followed suit. When they entered the main room again, Paul was standing next to an attractive well-dressed woman in a cream suit, yellow blouse, and styled blonde hair; Ronny recognized her as the editor of *Italian STYLE* from the social pages of the magazine. Ronny was more starstruck by her than Bon Jovi. Paul waved them over.

"This is Lucia Romano, fashion editor of *Italian STYLE*," Paul announced. "Lucia, this is Nick, Chad, and Ronny, who was featured in your last issue with Tiana. Lorenzo direct booked him for the Mancini show after seeing the story."

"Buonasera, gentlemen. I hope you are enjoying your time in Milan," Lucia said as they all nodded and smiled. She looked at Ronny. "Those photos of you and Tiana have been so popular. She has never looked better. I think you had something to do with that. Bravo."

The only thing that would have made Ronny feel more proud would be if he had taken the photographs himself.

"Grazie, Lucia. I'm a big fan of your magazine. That issue you did for the environment last fall was my favorite. So powerful!" Ronny said as Lucia looked at him with an impressed expression.

"I'm glad you liked it. Unfortunately, not everyone felt the same." Lucia smiled politely at the guys. "I look forward to seeing you in the Mancini show, Ronny. If it's as fabulous as this party, I'm sure it will be a hit." She kissed Paul goodbye. "Paul, it's good to see you. I'm on deadline so I can't stay long. It's nice to meet you all. Ciao, ciao."

Lucia left the group and headed back into the party to say her farewells. Meeting the editor behind his favorite magazine had left Ronny on a high. These were the moments that made being here all worth it. The room was now full of people, the DJ in the corner started playing louder dance music and the lighting changed to highlight a mirror ball that was suspended above the crowd with laser lights. Ronny could see Tiana and her two sexy supermodel friends starting to dance in front of the DJ. The floor around the supermodels cleared as Carlotta joined them. *They must have some good cocaine,* thought Ronny as he watched them move. Suddenly the room was filled with the sexy crowd of people dancing, laughing, and partying. Ronny had done drugs in Rio with his friends at a few big parties and Mardi Gras. From his limited experience he preferred the way ecstasy made him feel over cocaine. Nick was right, this party was going off. Ronny turned around and saw Jose, the Brazilian guy who worked at Foto Aldo.

"Ciao, Ronny," said Jose.

"Nice to see you, Jose. What a great party, eh!" Ronny replied.

"Mancini parties are always the best. Hey, this is my boyfriend Antonio." Jose turned to introduce Ronny to a lean, dark-haired man in his late twenties. Ronny shook his hand and smiled.

"Congratulations on the shoot for *Italian STYLE*," said Antonio as he moved closer to Ronny.

"Yeah, that's what got me here to Milan. Mancini booked me for his show after seeing that shoot."

"A photo can make or break you in this business," said Antonio.

"Ronny is a photographer as well," Jose said.

"What do you like to shoot?" asked Antonio.

"Portraits of people mostly. To be honest I'm inspired by beauty in all forms. Lately I've been focusing on including more fashion into my work."

"You must be a Libra," said Antonio.

"How did you know?" replied Ronny, surprised.

"Ha! I'm a Libra too, and I can totally relate to your obsession with beauty. You should bring your photography portfolio into the agency so I can see your work. I've always got young girls who need new photos; they are the rising stars of the business, and you want to shoot them before they get too busy and become famous."

"Antonio discovered Tiana Taylor and Claudia," Jose added.

"Honestly, that would be incredible! Thanks, Antonio," Ronny replied. His smile couldn't hide his excitement at the prospect of getting to shoot some young new faces that would help him build up a strong portfolio and get more tests.

"I'll give you all his information when I see you next. We are going to get some food. Great to see you, Ronny," said Jose.

"Obrigado, Jose." Ronny patted Jose on the shoulder before they moved on toward the buffet. It was reassuring to meet good people in the industry; it gave him faith that not everyone was out to take advantage of him. The DJ started playing a Grace Jones remix as the crowd erupted. Grace Jones herself burst through the crowd onto the dance floor wearing huge gold sunglasses and a serpent muumuu over a gold bikini. She looked wild and definitely high on something. She commanded the space as she danced with Carlotta and Tiana. Ronny's eyes widened as he acknowledged how completely surreal this moment was.

"This party is insane!" declared Chad as Ronny looked around the room watching the cocaine-, ecstasy-, and alcohol-fueled crowd revel in all their fashion week glory. Being right next to celebrities like Grace Jones, Bon Jovi, and the top models in the world partying together at the world's top designer's house may have been the most incredible experience he had ever had. As dark as the business could be, there was also the other side: the glamor, the celebrities, the fashion. It was hard not to be impressed and want to be a part of it. Nick turned to Ronny and Chad and motioned them to him to join him on the dance floor.

"Come on. Let's get amongst it, lads!" said Nick as he nudged Chad forward.

Ronny had left his jacket on a chair near where they were standing and laughed as he saw Nick get Chad in a headlock trying to encourage him to dance. He could tell Nick got a little out of hand when he partied. The British tourists who came to Rio for Carnival were always the loudest drunks in the crowd and often ended up in fights. As he closed his eyes, he felt the beat of the music and started to move. Ronny had always loved to dance. He had a nice buzz going and felt removed from the drama of the day. He danced next to Chad who was now out of the headlock. Ronny could sense people were starting to notice them and slowly he started to get more into the moment and dance with Chad. *I bet Chad would never dance with a guy in Iowa.* Ronny laughed to himself. The tequila shots were definitely helping Chad's confidence.

As the three danced, Ronny moved closer to Chad. "Nice to see you loosening up, Iowa." As he moved back away from Chad, he bumped into Tiana who was dancing behind him with Carlotta.

"Scusa," said Ronny as Tiana turned to look at him. She looked incredible with her slinky body-hugging dress, lean tight body, and long straight black hair. She offered Ronny a brief smile as the light bounced off her skin that was covered in a light sweat. "You look incredible," he added as Tiana put out her hand and ran it over his exposed chest casting her eyeline down to look at him. Ronny felt the sexual chemistry between them. Her touch aroused him. It was hard not to stare at her incredible feline features. Her dark eyes surveyed his body until she finally spoke.

"People who saw that story of us in Rio thought we must have been fucking."

"Funny, I thought we were too," Ronny joked as she pulled her hand away and smiled. Her eyes traveled up from his chest to his face. He could tell that she was high. For a moment Tiana started dancing with Ronny, offering flirtatious expressions that he remembered from the photo shoot in Rio. She was an incredible-looking girl—so sexy and so magnetic. It was hard to keep your eyes off her. He couldn't quite believe this was all happening. A hand appeared on Tiana's shoulder, and then Carlotta put her arms around Tiana's waist and started to dance with her. Carlotta smiled at Ronny and saw Chad standing behind him; she motioned for him to come closer. She leaned forward so they could hear her.

"You are a star, Chad. I told Lorenzo I want you for the show." She touched his cheek then turned to Tiana. "Darling, I want to introduce you to someone. Come, come." With that she smiled and they left the dance floor.

"That's amazing, man," Ronny said as he high-fived Chad. He imagined Tiana, like the other handful of supermodels, was living a dream. Genetically gifted, their looks had them destined for fame and fortune.

"Tiana wants to fuck you, bro," said Chad.

"I think Carlotta is hooking her up with a rockstar or a billionaire. She knows how to play the game, and so does Tiana. I'm sure supermodels would be the ultimate status symbol for a powerful guy who could buy anything he wanted, not to mention investing in good genes for his kids. Carlotta is no fool."

They continued to dance for a few more songs then moved to the bar. Ronny felt a hand around his waist and turned to see Paul smiling and Nick standing behind him. Paul's touch made his body stiffen as he turned around to free himself. It was that time of the night when the alcohol and drugs kicked in and people were loosening up. Ronny felt like he needed to be on guard.

"Allo, lads!" said Nick as he put his hand up on Chad's shoulder and started massaging it. "Told you this party was going to go off." Nick's pupils were dilated, he couldn't stop chewing, and it became obvious to Ronny he was high on drugs. He moved closer to Ronny to whisper in his ear. "Hey, Ronny, you want some ecstasy, man? One of Carlotta's assistants gave me a bunch and told me to hand them out to my friends. They're fucking amazing."

"I'm good, bro. Thanks, though," Ronny replied. He wanted to stay focused on the possibility of meeting more people who may turn out to be contacts for photography. He wasn't there just to party.

"Then keep them for later," Nick handed Ronny four white tablets, and Ronny put them in the small pocket of his pants and nodded to thank Nick. "Back in a minute," Nick added turning away.

"So what do you think of the party?" asked Paul as he stepped closer to Ronny.

"It's awesome."

Paul placed his hand on his back again. Ronny's body instantly stiffened as he considered Paul's intentions. "Carlotta has taken a liking to you and Chad, and now they want him for the show too. This is the start of great things for you guys this season." Paul added as he stood close to Ronny. He noticed Paul was starting to slur his words as he moved his hand down to rest on the top of his butt. Ronny quickly sobered up. He felt conflicted, unable to move away or think of a conversation that would distract Paul away from feeling him up.

"Thanks, Paul. I really want to do a great job for you," he replied as he started to feel his heart race and his face getting warmer. Here he was right back where he started with Santo. *Breathe.* He turned to see Chad speaking to Nick who had returned. He felt trapped and started to feel a cramp in his stomach.

Paul ran his hand down slowly over the top of Ronny's ass. "Ronny, I'm here to take you as far as you want to go."

He started to bite the inside of his mouth trying to distract himself, trying not to react. He froze until something snapped inside. He grabbed Paul's hand with a firm tightening grip, pushed it quickly away, and looked him in the eye.

"I'm not Nick, Paul!"

Paul pulled his hand free and bumped into Chad who turned to face Ronny. He must have sensed something had happened; his smile dropped away when he saw Ronny's expression. Paul turned away, sheepishly took a sip of his drink, and walked off into the crowd as Ronny rubbed his face. *Fuck! Maybe that was a bad idea.* His patience for people touching him inappropriately was waning and it was getting harder for him to control his reactions.

"Hey, Chad, do you still want to do the test photo shoot tomorrow? I'm kind of spent and was going to leave unless you want to hang?" The faint taste of his own blood lingered in his mouth. He needed some fresh air and space.

"Sounds like a plan, man. I want to be fresh for the shoot, so let's get out of here," replied Chad.

"Nick, see you at training," said Chad. They made their way out, and as they rode back in the taxi together, he told Chad about what happened with Paul.

"What did he say when you told him you weren't Nick?" Chad asked.

"Nothing. I think it caught him off guard. I know it puts me in a weird position since I need him to promote me for jobs. I just don't want to pimp myself out," Ronny replied. Chad shook his head and remained silent as he continued. "I grew up next to the favellas, what you would call the slums. Young, good-looking girls and guys were targeted and taken advantage of. Struggling against poverty is a harsh reality for many people where I come from. I knew guys that ended up working with gangs, and my best friend started working at a gay brothel having sex with tourists for money to support his family. I've been through hard times, and if I didn't have my brother to take me in when I was kicked out of home who knows what would have happened. Survival is survival."

"I'm sorry, man. I can't imagine how tough things must have been for your friend."

Ronny saw by Chad's expression that it was hard for him to relate to Milo's story. He reflected back to his own reaction when he first found out about Milo and how hard it had been for him to accept it. In many ways it still was. "I guess you and I have a choice—to work the system and win, or fight against it and risk losing." Ronny looked out the window. He considered young hungry models like Nick who would get to a point of desperation and do whatever it took to catch a break. Ronny had seen so many fashion advertising campaigns in magazines; there would always be the top male models of the moment, then some unknown random guy. Ronny now knew that unknown model was the one who must have done whatever it took to get his place in the campaign.

It wasn't right, but it's the way the fashion business worked. An undisclosed part of the business that people are aware of but turned a blind eye to. His desire to be a working photographer, however, was greater than his distaste for what he was uncovering. He didn't see another option for himself. They rode the rest of the way to the Pola in silence. Ronny tried to block out what had just happened with Paul and focus on tomorrow's test shoot. Photography was always the best distraction.

## CHAPTER 21

As Ronny and Chad were walking out of the Pola the next morning on the way to the gym to clear their heads, Josh came bounding out behind them followed by Annika.

"Hey, guys, let's do this!" he cheered as he got them both in a headlock. Josh didn't seem to know his own strength and could have easily snapped their necks if he wasn't careful.

"Dude, you're like Lenny from *Mice and Men*," exclaimed Chad.

"Darling, how was the Mancini party?" asked Annika. "I'm sure it was fabulous."

"Where do you start," replied Chad. "It was an incredible over-the-top night in an insane house with everyone there from Grace Jones to Bon Jovi. Mancini sure knows how to throw a party."

"How late did you guys stay?" asked Josh.

"We left before it started getting too weird," replied Ronny.

"Before people started trying to have sex with you," said Annika with a laugh as they continued walking. "Welcome to fashion week, darling. Now you know what it's like for women in every industry, not just this one. Success often comes at a price until you become big enough to call the shots. But fuck it, I'm here to work and if I need to sleep with Tony Santiago to get a big campaign, I will. Actually, he's pretty hot."

Ronny looked at Annika, taken aback by her brutal honesty and attitude. He knew Tony Santiago from *Italian STYLE* magazine; he was a successful fashion photographer, known for his beautiful, sensual portraits of women and his ability to charm them.

"That guy has banged all the supermodels," said Josh. "After he finishes a photo shoot in a studio, cleaners have to come in and deal with everything from used condoms, to cocaine lines on the glass coffee tables." It sounded like Tony was making porn, not art. Ronny glanced at Chad, who was listening intently. Ronny couldn't tell by his expression if he was shocked or impressed.

Annika continued, "It must be the ultimate fantasy for them when you think about it. When a photographer is shooting you, directing you into positions and expressions that please them, telling you what to wear and when to take it off. Capturing your image, the way they want to see it. But imagine when they can interact with you, smell you, touch you, taste you."

"Fuck you," added Josh as Annika pushed him in the shoulder and continued.

"They are inside their fantasy, experiencing all of it, controlling everything and using drugs and alcohol to take it to another level. That must be the ultimate high for them. Photographers hold the power, but when you become a supermodel and people want to use your image for their campaigns and fashion shows, the power shifts and you get to call the shots. Unfortunately for male models in this business, you will never be as famous as the girls so you will always have to deal with more bullshit for less return."

Ronny could relate to some of what Annika was saying. He thought about the rush he got from directing his subjects to capture their beauty the way that he wanted. The intimate relationship as he encouraged them to let him in and be vulnerable and trust his eye. Sure, he had slept with a few of the girls he had photographed, but it was consensual and he always respected his subjects.

"Annika, are you sure you're not a dude?" asked Chad. Ronny studied the hard sharp features on Annika's face. Russia must have raised her tough and left her with a ruthless ambition that would see her do whatever it took to get a new life. In many ways they had walked a similar path.

"Well, I was born a guy until I cut my dick off and started modeling," she replied with a straight face as Josh shot her a shocked expression until she burst out laughing. "Don't worry, darling, this Russian pussycat is all real." It was obvious Josh was sleeping with Annika. Unlike so many people in the business, Ronny found it refreshing that Annika was so straight-up and told it exactly how it was.

"So how's your appointments going?" asked Josh after he finished laughing at Annika.

"I think it's going pretty well. Some good castings, some crotch grabbing, and people really seem to love my butt," replied Chad. Ronny noticed that Chad tended to mask any uncomfortable situation with humor. *Whatever it takes to deal with it.*

"Hmm. Yes, nice butt," said Annika as she looked at Chad's behind.

"How about you, bud?" Chad asked Josh.

"Well, I just found out that a test shoot I did with Santo Diaz has been picked up for an international jeans campaign."

"That's so cool, man," said Ronny as he slapped Josh on the back. "So what was the photograph?"

"Well, it's a shot of me in a shower holding a pair of jeans," replied Josh, not offering a lot of details about the shoot.

Annika burst back into the conversation. "Naked, darling. Just a shot of his hot body naked with jeans to cover himself. Naked. Very sexy."

"Hey, I got paid. At least I don't need to dance for dollars for a while," Josh added.

"So how was the shoot? I'm supposed to meet with Santo next week for an appointment," asked Chad. Josh paused for a moment. Ronny sensed that there was more to the story.

"Must be cool to see yourself in a big campaign," he added, thinking that may help Josh feel more comfortable talking about what happened.

"Um, yeah." Josh appeared shaken. "I just went to his house for an appointment. He said he wanted to do some test shots. I started off in his studio wearing no shirt, just the jeans he gave me. Then he started taking me through a breathing exercise that was meant to help me relax." Again, Josh paused, seeming lost for words. Finally, he stopped walking down the street, stood with his hands on his hips looking at the ground. Ronny felt sorry for Josh knowing how hard this must have been for him to talk about.

"He loves those breathing exercises," said Annika.

"Fuck," said Josh as he took a deep breath.

"Tell them what happened," Annika encouraged him in the nicest tone the cold Russian could muster. Ronny felt a wave of anxiety start to build in his stomach.

"Annika already knows about this and it's no secret what Santo is like. I know you're going to meet him, Chad, so I'd rather warn you so you can be prepared for something that may or may not happen."

"Thanks, man, I appreciate the heads up. So what happened?" asked Chad, sounding concerned.

"Well, he asked me to start breathing slowly and deeply. He

then started touching me between my eyebrows telling me to 'relax this' and then he would let his hand go down to touch my stomach and said, 'Tense this.' He did this a few times, then he asked me to move into the shower in the studio bathroom and take off my jeans. There was a studio light set up in there and he turned it on as I stood in front of him in the shower."

"He reached out and touched my hand and said to touch myself where I felt my 'energy' was. I freaked out and didn't move so he then took my hand and guided it to my chest. He asked me, 'Can you feel the energy?'"

Ronny knew where this was going and tried to swallow the lump in the back of his throat.

"Then he put his hand on my hand and guided it down below my stomach. He paused there and told me to 'just breathe.' Slowly he guided my hand down further, and I knew he was encouraging me to touch myself."

Ronny listened intently, shocked by what he was hearing, feeling his anger build toward Santo and this fucked-up reality of the business.

Josh continued, "He stood back, watching me and then turned the water on in the shower so I was wet. After a while he handed me the jeans and I covered myself with them. He took some photos with the jeans covering me and then told me to drop the jeans. He asked me to get some soap on my hands and wash myself. He told me to touch myself and when I looked up, I think I saw him undoing his pants. It was hard to see as the lights were bright in my eyes. I looked back down and didn't look up at him again, but I think he was jacking off. He told me I was going to be a star. Eventually he stopped talking and as he was leaving the room, he told me we were done and to get dressed. I got out of the shower, got dressed, and left."

Everyone was silent, shocked by the story. They were all aware that this kind of thing was happening, but nobody really talked openly about it.

Chad stood shaking his head. "Fuck, man, sorry that's intense."

Ronny looked at the ground. The abuse was all around him, like an inescapable virus that at some point was going to infect each of them. It seemed it was just a matter of time, and Chad was next. Ronny wondered when his time would come. It had become obvious that Milan was no better than Brazil when it came to being taken advantage of. Again, he weighed the idea of going back home, trying to get a break there first, but he knew he'd eventually have to leave Brazil to be successful.

"Well, at least I got a bunch of cash out of it when they bought the photo for the jeans campaign. Fucking asshole."

Ronny was standing next to Josh and put his hand on his back trying to distract him.

"I hate jacking off with soap; it hurts like a mother fucker," Chad joked, trying to lighten the mood. Josh faux-punched him and managed an awkward laugh.

"I'm glad you can make jokes about it," said Josh. It was obvious to Ronny that the agencies were using the guys as negotiating tools with Santo to score the big campaigns and shows.

"Sorry to freak you out, Chad. Hopefully he won't try anything with you," Josh added.

Annika was quick to comment. "Yes, why would he try anything like that on Chad with his hot body, perfect ass, and a face like that."

Chad finally spoke. "Thanks for the heads-up, man. I'll try not to rip his head off if he grabs my dick." Chad winked and continued, "Now let's get our beautiful butts to the gym."

Ronny could tell that Chad was doing his best to mask his nerves. As he went through his stretch routine after his workout, he tried to process what Josh had told them about his test with Santo. He acknowledged the fact that a fashion model's success was based on their ability to incite desire as he'd heard and seen in so many photo shoots in magazines. He knew nudity and looking seductive was what a lot of clients and photographers wanted to see. It was almost what was expected of you in order to get the success you wanted. Ronny had no issue being naked; he was proud of his body, he just wasn't that comfortable with the idea of giving away his power for the sake of work.

"That was crazy what happened to Josh," said Chad as he came and sat down next to Ronny as he finished up his stretch.

"Yeah, that wasn't cool, but I guess at some point he knew what was happening and he stayed." Ronny heard the words leave his mouth and realized it sounded unsympathetic. "Sorry, man. I know I sound cold about it, but remember I come from a place where people are poor and do whatever it takes to feed their families and have a better life. I'm not going to judge anyone for doing what they need to survive." Ronny felt guilty saying that. He regretted the way he had judged Milo and his mother. "Is it an ideal situation? No. It makes me angry as hell. I know this is how it is and that pisses me off. I'm not angry at Josh, I'm just angry that we have to deal with this bullshit." Ronny paused to take a breath and try and calm himself down then continued to speak. "To survive you need money, and to get money you have to have something to sell. If you don't have a degree or a business, sometimes you're forced to sell yourself. In the past I had sex with someone for money. I'm not proud of it, but it was offered to me and I took it." He was disillusioned with the industry he so badly wanted to be a part of. He had hoped things would have been better. The unfortunate reality was it was worse.

"You okay?" Chad asked.

"Yeah, I'm okay. Sorry. It just sucks that this is the way this works. I was trying to escape this bullshit in Brazil and here I am dealing with it again. You grew up in a different world than I did. I understand who Chanel the street prostitute is. I understand who Annika, Nick, and Josh are because I can relate to the decisions they've had to make in order to get ahead and get a better life. Having nothing and living in a shitty situation is a great motivator." Ronny realized he was probably freaking Chad out. "You have so much potential here, Chad, and I'm not telling you to let Santo grab your dick, but unfortunately we both need to play the game to a point if we are going to succeed and try not to get burned in the process."

Chad looked at him. "You remind me of one of my early coaches who didn't sugarcoat anything. I just wish there was a way that we could get ahead without having to deal with this bullshit," Chad said then looked away.

## CHAPTER 22

Ella and Camille walked into Chad and Ronny's apartment that afternoon to get ready for their photo shoot. It was so good to see Ella again.

They laughed as Camille tried to teach Ella to speak some French. Ronny had been excited about the shoot ever since they had agreed to do it, and now that they had arrived, he felt a little nervous. He was ready to put some of what he had learned into practice.

Ella smiled. "I'm trying to learn how to introduce myself in French and order steak and chips. Salut. Je m'appelle Ella et je vais prendre un steak frites." Her Australian accent was thick.

Camille burst out laughing. "Oh my God, your French accent is parfait."

"I like the way it sounds. Very sexy," added Chad in a mock French accent.

"Okay, enough with my terrible French. Ronny, what's the plan?" asked Ella as Camille tried to contain herself. "We brought our portfolios down in case you wanted to see them."

He took the portfolios and sat down at the small dining table next to Chad and opened Ella's portfolio and started to turn the pages; some photos were moody, and some were playful and showed off her personality. There was also a series of photographs showing her dancing. "Were you a dancer?"

"Yes, I studied modern dance and ballet," she replied. "I preferred surfing, though, so I didn't continue with dancing."

"I love these, they're amazing." He made a mental note to get some movement photographs of Ella. Ronny hadn't seen too many portfolios of models he knew. He was amazed at how different each photograph looked. He made note of the angles that worked well and the poses he liked for their bodies. He then looked at Camille's portfolio. In one photo she looked innocent and young, and in another she looked seductive and sexy. Camille had a face structure that could handle more dramatic makeup, but personally Ronny preferred Ella's look. She was such a natural beauty. He looked up at Ella standing there in her shorts and T-shirt with no makeup on. You could see she had a few freckles on her nose, and her unwashed hair fell perfectly around her face. He felt the chemistry between them, and it was hard not to want to flirt with her.

"Your books are beautiful," he said. "I love the way you both look right now. I want to shoot something raw and natural up on the roof. Can you grab some jeans, a white T-shirt, some briefs, and I have a white collared men's shirt we can use. I want to shoot something that's classic. Just put on some light natural makeup and keep your hair down."

"Sounds like a plan," Ella replied as Ronny handed back their portfolios.

"Both your books are amazing," added Chad, who looked up at Ella as she screwed up her face and made fun to deflect the attention away from herself.

"We'll go and grab our things and meet you up on the roof," said Camille.

As the girls left the room, Ronny turned to Chad. "You will look incredible together." He collected his camera gear, small round reflector, water spray bottle, and film. "Just wear your white briefs under your jeans. Oh, and bring your white tank top and a towel." His tone changed as he became focused and excited about the photographs he was going to take. The girls made their way up onto the roof where Chad and Ronny were already setting up. It was a warm afternoon with a light cloud cover.

"Perfect light for a photoshoot," said Ronny. On the back of the entrance structure to the stairwell there were two painted walls, one white and one black. Camille told Ronny that they had been created by other young photographers that had stayed at the Pola and done test shoots of models living there on the roof. The test shots would help both parties to build up their portfolios.

"Hey, I brought up my boombox," Camille said. She plugged it into a nearby power outlet, put in a cassette tape, and pushed play. A David Bowie song rang out as Ella started dancing around Camille. Ronny loved to watch her move. She turned to look at him and smiled. He noticed the warmth in her eyes, the mischievous glint he remembered from that night in the elevator. He had thought about the kiss they shared many times, and despite trying to play down the attraction he felt, he couldn't deny his feelings for her. Was she flirting? He looked away from her gaze. Right now his focus was on the shoot.

"Okay, guys, let's do this. Chad, you can wear your jeans and take your shirt off. Ella, if you could wear the tank top and briefs, that would be great, and Camille, can you put on that white men's shirt," Ronny said as he started to load film into his camera. He pulled out the small water spray bottle and once Chad stood up, he proceeded to lightly spray Chad's hair and style it with his hands.

"Should I do any push-ups?" Chad asked quietly.

Ronny touched him on the arm. "You look great, bud. I'll guide you through. Don't worry about it. Trust me." After being photographed by Francesco and Santo, he took inspiration from the way they directed models, he was excited to try out what he had learned.

"Chad, let's put on your white tank top and stand in front of the white wall." Ronny came in to adjust his hair and spray his body with a little water. "Let's have you start to take off the tank top. Okay, great, hold it there." He started shooting. "Chin down, Chad, and bring your eyes up to me as you start to pull up your shirt. Great!" Ronny offered direction and Chad followed it. He was in the zone, focused solely on capturing Chad's masculine strong features, and intensity of his expression. "Great, man, really great! Camille, let's do some singles of you."

Camille changed places with Chad. Ronny stood back and started giving Camille some direction. He considered the crop, the angles, and the expression.

"Perfect. Let's bring your eyes to camera, turn your face away three quarters. That's it. Perfect, eyes away, stronger expression, now back to me. Let's have you move off the wall." Ronny moved back and forth with her capturing more photographs as she began a dance with his lens. He was totally present in the moment; this was when he felt most alive. He had Camille change into the men's white shirt and continued shooting and moved closer to get some beauty shots. "Amazing," said Ronny as he high-five Camille.

"Superbe, Camille!" called out Ella who had been watching from the side.

"Ella and Chad, can I see you together in front of the black wall. Chad, wear the jeans and keep the shirt off," Ronny directed. "Stand in profile, and Ella, stand behind him. I want you to push yourself into his back and put your hands under his arms and up onto his chest. Chad, take your hands back onto her hips. Bend the leg closest to me and take the knee up higher. Ella, just work your body into his body. Great." Ronny came in and quickly sprayed the couple with water and continued to offer direction and shoot as the two created beautiful shapes together. "Chad, just relax your body and tense your abdominals."

Suddenly Chad farted, and Ella burst out laughing.

"Wait, what?" Chad

"Maybe not that much tensing." Ronny tried to keep them focused. They looked incredible together as Ella worked her body around Chad's. He came in closer to get some different angles. "Ella, bring your hand up to his face. Just there. Beautiful."

Their faces were a perfect combination of strong jawlines, moist luminous skin, intense eyes, and full lips. The sun was setting, so Ronny pulled back to get some wider crops. The ambient light that occurred just after the sun set was his favorite. He looked through the lens as Ella and Chad worked together, moving as one, reacting to each other's touch and bodies as Ronny captured this raw sensual moment. Ella's leg came forward and she ran her hand down over Chad's stomach to sit above the waistband of his jeans.

"You guys look incredible! Ella, let's do some singles of you. Chad, that's a wrap. Man, you were amazing." Chad moved forward and high-fived Ronny.

"Ella, I want you to keep exploring different emotions. Give me some standing shots and then some dance movement with a variety of expressions," said Ronny as she started moving like a dancer, using her body and her face to express a wide range of emotions. She was incredible to watch. He photographed her with a wider crop then moved in closer to capture some beauty close-ups. Ronny felt so passionate in the moment. As hard as he tried to stay focused on the photograph, he kept being distracted by Ella—her free spirit, her features, and the vulnerability in her eyes. When she looked at him through the lens, Ronny felt like she was showing him who she was, letting him in. His breathing grew deeper, and for that moment it was just the two of them. Ronny stopped speaking as he moved closer to her and momentarily put down the camera so she could see his face. They looked at each other in silence as time seemed to stand still. Ronny then continued to photograph Ella until his roll of film ran out.

He put down his camera and called out, "That's a wrap, guys! Wow!" He came forward to hug Ella. She embraced him tightly and softly kissed his neck. "This was how I had imagined you being photographed. Raw and natural," he added as her eyes met his for a moment and Camille as Chad started applauding. He had never felt such a connection to someone he had photographed.

"Amazing!" said Camille as she stepped forward. "Tellement chaud."

"I haven't danced like that in a while," replied Ella as she turned to high-five Chad. "Next time can you book a taller guy with a better body?" she joked as she laughed and pushed Chad away in jest. He stumbled into Ronny and caught himself.

"These Aussie girls are so rough," Chad said.

As Ronny was packing up his camera, he smiled to himself. Working with professional models was a whole new experience that allowed him to not have to offer as much direction and focus on the composition and image. He was on a high and knew these would be some of the best photographs he had taken. He felt someone touch his back and stood up to see Ella standing next to him.

"Thank you," she said softly as she moved closer and kissed him. Ronny didn't have his lens to hide behind now. She pulled back and looked at him with those same vulnerable eyes. He felt the connection they shared. *I'm in trouble,* he thought as she smiled and moved to collect her things.

# CHAPTER 23

When Ronny and Chad returned to the apartment, they found Nick sitting outside in the hall on the floor next to the door. As they approached Nick looked up; his eyes were red and he looked disheveled. *Something's not right*, thought Ronny.

"Hi, guys. Sorry to come by. I just needed to get some air and wanted to see if you were home." Nick slurred his words as Chad and Ronny quickly looked at each other trying wondering what had caused Nick to be like this. It was obvious he was drunk or still high from the night before.

"That's cool. Let's get you inside," Chad said as he helped Nick to his feet. Ronny opened the door, and the trio went inside. Nick slumped onto a chair at the small dining table as Ronny went to get him a glass of water.

"What's going on? Are you okay?" Chad asked.

"I'm sorry, guys. I couldn't stay at Paul's tonight. I was hoping I could sleep on your floor?"

"Don't apologize. What happened?" Ronny asked as he passed Nick the water.

After a long gulp Nick continued. "Paul was pretty out of it last night after the party, and I didn't know how to deal with being there. When I first moved in, I was sleeping on his couch to save some money. Shortly after, he offered for me to share his bed, and in the beginning he didn't try anything. Then one night we got drunk at a restaurant nearby and slowly things changed." Nick wiped his face mid-sentence and took another gulp of water. "Then last night we both took drugs, so I was fine to hang out but I didn't want to do anything else so I had to leave. I spent the last few hours drinking at a bar near here," Nick slurred his words. His eyes were bloodshot and the dark circles under his eyes stood out against his white complexion.

"Sorry, man. Of course you can stay here." Ronny went to ask Mama Pola for a fold-out bed.

When Ronny got back, Chad started to make some food, and Nick continued to share his story—his hopes for work in Milan so he could send money back to his girlfriend and son. In many ways Nick's situation reminded him of Milo; they had both been forced into abusive situations because they wanted to support their family. Nick had come to Milan with nothing and was reliant on Paul and the agency to allow him to stay and get work. Ronny sensed he had done things with Paul, but this time Paul had gone too far.

"I'll be fine to go back there tomorrow, but I just couldn't stay there tonight," Nick continued.

Ronny watched Nick quickly eat the pasta that Chad had prepared; it seemed like he hadn't eaten in a while. After dinner Nick had a shower and lay down on the fold-out bed. They talked for another half hour before he put his arm up over his head and soon fell asleep. It was obvious he was exhausted. Ronny sat in bed looking through a few fashion magazines to distract himself before trying to sleep. Nick's light snoring kept him awake as he thought about Nick and Milo. He considered his own journey and how close he had come to following the same fate as Milo. *When things get desperate your only option is to hustle.* Ronny had already sacrificed so much for his photography, and despite being confronted with all the challenges and abuse, he was still committed to seeing it through. Ronny got out of bed as quietly as he could, grabbed his wallet, and headed down to the reception where Mateo, Mama Pola's son, was working the night shift.

"Buona serata," said Mateo as Ronny walked up to the desk.

"Ciao, Mateo. Would it be okay to make a call with a calling card on the reception phone?" Ronny noticed that Mateo was watching what looked like an Italian soap opera on a small old television set sitting on a side table behind the reception desk.

"No problem. You can make it on the chair in the corner."

"Grazie," Ronny replied with a smile. He sat down and opened his wallet to retrieve his calling card. Behind the card was the photo Milo gave him before he left Rio. He looked at the photo before dialing Milo's number, hoping he would pick up.

"Olá" Milo answered.

"Olá, Milo." As soon as he heard Milo's voice, Ronny felt a wave of emotion wash over him. For the first time he felt alone in Milan, like nobody really knew who he was and where he came from.

"Ronny? Hey, man, it's good to hear your voice. Where are you? Still in Italy?"

"Yeah, I'm still in Milan. Things are okay. How are you doing?"

"I'm good, bro. You know, still dealing with the usual stuff, but things are good. If I didn't have my kid, man, I would be up there to visit you for sure. I'm sure we could have some fun with those model girls." Milo reminded him of Chad. "Hey, how's the modeling going?"

"It seems to be going well, and I've met some cool people. It's good to hear your voice, I miss you, man." Ronny paused as he looked up to make sure Mateo was engrossed in his TV sitcom and wouldn't be able to hear him. An image of Nick's face came to mind, his expression unable to hide the trauma of his abuse. He cleared his throat to continue. "Hey, I wanted to tell you I was sorry about the way I reacted when you told me about working at the club. I shouldn't have reacted like that. I know you're doing what you're doing for your family." His eyes started welling up with tears as he remembered hearing Milo's baby crying in the background at his apartment.

"I know it's not an ideal situation, but it's a means to an end. I'm actually trying to get a daytime job so I don't need to work there anymore, but the extra money is helpful." Like Nick, he continued on as if everything was okay.

"I shouldn't have judged you. I was at that point myself. If Milan hadn't come up, I would have been there with you. I didn't have many options." Ronny felt the emotion building and the regret of not completely resolving this with Milo before he left. "You've been my best friend since we were kids and you've never judged and always supported me."

"You're like a brother to me. I'm sorry I didn't tell you about the club and everything that was going on earlier. I was embarrassed," Milo said.

"You can tell me anything. I'm sorry I wasn't there for you. I'm really sorry." There was a moment of silence on the phone before Milo spoke.

"Met any girls?"

Ronny smiled. *It always came back to girls with Milo.*

"Actually, I have met someone." The words came easily out of Ronny's mouth. "It's early days, and I know this whole fashion world here is far from reality, but she is so incredibly real and down to earth. I wasn't expecting to meet anyone." Ronny felt a sense of pride talking about Ella.

"Good for you, man. Just don't get her pregnant." Milo laughed. Their conversation flowed easily as if nothing had changed between them. The sound of Milo's voice made Ronny miss his friends and Brazil. "Have you spoken to your mom?" Milo asked.

"Not yet. I've been thinking about her but didn't want to call in case my dad answered," Ronny replied.

"You should try," Milo said. Ronny knew he was right. "I'll go by and check on her," Milo added.

"Please," Ronny responded. He rubbed his eyes after he finished the call. It was late but he felt a sense of relief after speaking to Milo. Back in bed he tried to distract himself by focusing on the photo shoot earlier that day on the roof. Every time he closed his eyes, he saw Ella's face and the vulnerable open look in her eye as she modeled for him, letting him in, letting him see her.

## CHAPTER 24

The following morning Nick left their apartment after Chad made some coffee. Aside from a hangover he seemed in good spirits.

"I'm worried about him," Ronny said as he joined Chad back in the kitchen after he left.

"He seemed better this morning," Chad replied.

"Just because he didn't talk about it today doesn't mean it's not affecting him."

"I'm going to head to the gym. You want to join?" Chad asked, seemingly trying to change the subject.

"No, I'm going to take the film from yesterday to the lab," Ronny answered, not wanting to push his opinion further. He was excited to get the film developed as soon as possible. As he left the Pola and headed off to Foto Aldo, he savored the feeling of independence, acknowledging the fact that he was in Milan on the way to develop the film from his first test shoot there with real models.

"Olá, Jose," said Ronny when he entered Foto Aldo and walked up to the counter. Jose was standing near the back shelves looking into the eyepiece of a small black video camcorder. He had a natural ease and warmth about him that reminded Ronny of his friends from home.

"Hey, Ronny, nice to see you. Looks like you were having fun at the Mancini party," said Jose.

"Yeah, that was a fun night. That house was incredible."

"Carlotta Mancini sure knows how to throw a party."

"Is that a new video camera?" asked Ronny as he nodded toward the camera in Jose's hand. He had seen catalogues for the camcorder in Danilo's studio but never used one.

"It just came in from Sony, it's their latest model."

"Is it hard to use?"

"I've just started playing with it and its seems pretty easy. It records to a tape and its so compact.

"Is that one expensive?"

"They're becoming less expensive as other brands launch their own versions. We're actually doing a promotion and are loaning this one out to our regular customers for a few days to try them out. All you need is to leave a credit card for security." Jose added as he passed Ronny the camcorder. He felt the weight in his hand and turned it around to look at the controls and where the tape was located.

"I'd love to learn how to use it some time," Ronny said, feeling disappointed he didn't have a credit card to put down to borrow the camera and try it out. "For now I just have some black and white film to be developed that I shot over the weekend. I'll need two sets of contact sheets. Thankyou." Ronny handed back the camcorder and gave Jose the film rolls.

They spoke in Portuguese for a while about life in Brazil and what had changed since Jose had left so many years ago. Jose shared his hopes of one day returning to reconnect with some friends from his childhood. Ronny felt nostalgic when he shared what he missed about Brazil—his friends, the locals, and the beach. Jose spoke fondly of his mother. Ronny thought back to when he was younger and remembered his mother's laugh, her beautiful smile. He looked down at his hands, noticing how much they looked like his mother's and touched his palm. He may have inherited his father's looks, but his hands were definitely his mother's.

"Did you get to meet Lorenzo at the party?" Jose asked, bringing Ronny's attention back to the conversation.

"I met him briefly. He was with Carlotta, who I'd met at a casting. He seemed really nice. Your boyfriend Antonio seems cool."

"Yeah, he's great. Oh, before I forget let me give you his contact info so you guys can connect and take your photography portfolio into the agency." Jose wrote down Antonio's information on a piece of paper and handed it to Ronny.

"Thanks, Jose. I should have my portfolio together to show him soon." As Ronny left Foto Aldo, he glanced up at the framed prints on the wall and admired the series of beautiful landscapes that were now exhibited there. *One day my work will be seen.* He was excited to see how the photographs from the test turned out. In his head he started to put together his portfolio, considering the order and which prints would go side by side. A taxi driver yelled out of his taxi as Ronny took a step out onto the street to cross without looking. He was lost in his thoughts, imagining which of his photographs he would put in an exhibition. When he arrived back at the Pola and walked through the foyer, Ella was walking out of the elevator.

"Hey there, Mr. Photographer," Ella announced with a smile. She walked toward him wearing shorts and a vintage T-shirt. She ran her fingers through her sun-kissed hair.

"Well, hi there, Miss Aussie supermodel," Ronny replied. Ella flicked her hair and did a 360-degree spin and broke out laughing. She embraced him.

"I just dropped off the film from yesterday's shoot," Ronny said.

"I can't wait to see how they turn out. I'm sure there's at least one good one of me in there."

"I think there's more than one." Ronny smiled. She had a natural way of deflecting attention away from herself. He studied her face, noticing the freckles that ran across her nose. "I loved seeing you dance. You have incredible movement." He felt his smile widen.

"It felt really good to dance on set, and your direction helped a lot. Speaking of dancing, we're going to Club Hollywood this weekend. You and Chad should come with us. I'm sure a bunch of the models you know will be there too. Do you like to dance?"

"I love to dance," Ronny replied, and he thought he saw Ella blushing slightly.

"Sounds like a plan. I have to run; I'm supposed to meet a friend for yoga. I'll be up on the roof for sunset later if you want to join me." Ella put her backpack over her shoulder and gave Ronny a kiss before walking out the door. As Ronny stood waiting for the elevator, he turned to watch her walk out on the street and briefly look back at him and smile. When he got back upstairs to his room, Chad was sitting on his bead reading a magazine.

"How was the gym," Ronny asked.

"The usual. Nick turned up; he seemed in better spirits. He said to pass on thanks for letting him stay here."

"How did he look? Did you ask about Paul?" Ronny sat down on the bed next to Chad.

"He looked much better. I think he's having a tough time here with everything going on. I asked about Paul and he said it was fine," Chad replied, not sounding convinced.

"Let's hang out with him this week. I want to make sure he's okay," Ronny added. Seeing Nick in the state he was in was haunting. He kept seeing Milo and his mother. Chad put down the magazine and turned to sit on the bed next to Ronny.

"I honestly don't know if I could deal with someone doing that shit to me. I had a creepy gymnastics physiotherapist who tried to touch me a few times." Chad paused and didn't look up at Ronny. "I told my dad, and he almost killed the guy."

"You okay?" Ronny asked. He suspected Chad had never shared that with anyone. He looked at Chad slightly slumped over; his usual bravado was gone, and he sat there as a vulnerable young man.

"Yeah. It just freaks me out. I know I want to get work, but Flavio was enough."

"I know what you mean. I've been thinking about it as well." It was only a matter of time before he would be confronted with the situation when he'd have to make a choice to either let it happen or not. *Was there another way?* "Francesco told me to play the game but not get burned," Ronny continued.

"What does that mean, though, when the biggest photographer in the world is trying to grab your dick and you're naked?" Chad asked.

He had a point. Milo slept with men for money, and somehow he made peace with that and was able to go home at night and live his life. Surely Ronny could do that a few times to get what he really wanted. In time he would forget. If he were guaranteed success with his photography, would he let Santo have his way with him. He wondered if that's what Francesco had to do.

"You know, I never told anyone about that physiotherapist." Chad looked up. Ronny felt a deeper connection to Chad knowing he had trusted him with something that personal.

"I wish I could have warned you about Flavio, but I didn't know it was going to be him at the appointment," Ronny said.

Chad took a deep breath. "Maybe I can talk to Paul and tell him I will only see Santo if I can be assured that he won't try anything." He sounded unsure.

"Honestly, I don't think that will help the situation. There's too many models out there who would do anything to be in a big campaign."

"Well, then I guess I will miss out on the chance to work with him."

"Chad, I think you've got a lot of potential to land some great campaigns here. This is just starting for you, so just play the game as far as you're comfortable. At least you know what you're dealing with." Ronny touched Chad on the arm; he was unsure his advice would help.

Chad went to have a shower as Ronny went into the kitchen to make some food. Ronny was lost as to what to do or what to even say to Chad. He knew it was ultimately Chad's decision how far he wanted to go with Santo Diaz or any of the other people who wanted to take advantage of him in the industry. The situation was so messed up, and there didn't seem to be anything they could do about it if they wanted to stay and get work. Chad appeared from the bathroom, his hair still wet from the shower.

"Hey, you want something to eat?" Ronny asked.

"Sure." Chad stood in the doorway in his towel. "I'm sorry I lost it. I guess I have had that bottled up for so long. I feel much better, but to be honest I'm nervous to meet with Santo. I guess I will take your advice and just play the game as far as I can until I get kicked off the field."

"Or score a goal and win," Ronny added. He tried to sound upbeat for Chad's sake and mask his frustration and anger. He felt trapped by the reality of what was unfolding for Chad and inevitably for himself; it was only a matter of time before he would need to face Santo again.

# CHAPTER 25

Chad was already at the agency when Ronny arrived. As he walked up to the bookers' table, he could see Chad was talking to Paul.

"Ciao, Paul," said Ronny as he nodded in Paul's direction. Paul didn't respond; he continued speaking to Chad, moving closer to him, but Ronny could hear their conversation.

"Chad, this is way too important to miss. I'm sure Santo will be fine, and I know he is considering you for the Mancini campaign. The meeting is going to be at his house." Paul handed Chad a piece of paper with the time and address for Santo on it. "Carlotta already wants you for the Mancini show, so you'll just go to the fitting for the show on Thursday morning with Ronny, Lorenzo will be there as well." Paul looked up at Ronny to include him in the conversation. "You and Ronny have also got two castings tomorrow for two magazines and another show casting for the designer Vita Rona."

"Sounds good, Paul," answered Chad.

Ronny could tell that Chad sounded despondent. He knew Paul was pressuring him, reassuring him everything would be fine. This was his playbook and in many ways his job. If he gets models to these appointments and they get booked for the job, the agency gets its commission.

Paul smiled quickly at Ronny and collected the sports catalogue photos on his desk that had just come in for Chad. It felt strange seeing Paul after all that had gone on with Nick and the last time he saw him at the Mancini party. There were two contrasting realities playing out at the same time in this business—the smiles and the glamour and the dark side nobody seemed to acknowledge.

"Well, Ronny, looks like you have some competition in the body department," Brett said as he looked across at Chad's photographs and headed for the kitchen. Ronny excused himself to get a glass of water and headed to the kitchen where Brett was busy making himself a salad for lunch.

"That looks pretty healthy," said Ronny as he grabbed a glass and started to fill it with water from the tap.

"Babe, how do you think I have this figure? Not from eating pasta and pizza," snapped Brett as he continued making his salad.

"It's so hard not to eat it when it's all around you, and it's so good." Ronny gave Brett a warm smile.

"Honey, I deal with that every day on the street and at work." Brett laughed. Ronny continued some small talk with Brett, getting him more comfortable until finally asking his intended question.

"Hey, you know when you mentioned that the person that dislikes Santo Diaz the most was Lucia, the *Italian STYLE* editor? What did you mean?" Ronny asked as Brett stepped closer to him and took a quick glance to the side to ensure nobody was around.

"Well, not a lot of people know this because it's rather embarrassing for poor Lucia, but she has been really screwed over and humiliated several times by Santo. On one occasion Lucia had the idea to shoot an iconic cover with the actress Sahara Johnson because she was about to star in a huge movie role. This was the first time a celebrity would be featured on the cover of *STYLE* magazine. She knew she had to use Santo because he is under contract, so she had a call with him to discuss the idea and start to organize the shoot. Santo was in New York at the time, and apparently that evening he was having dinner with Liz Kirby, the editor of *American STYLE*. It's the larger magazine title from the same family." Brett paused briefly and moved closer to Ronny, signaling he was sharing something confidential.

"Well, after a few drinks he apparently told Liz what he was planning to shoot for Lucia. Liz rang him the next day and told him that she had booked Sahara to shoot the cover for *American STYLE* magazine even though Lucia had organized the shoot for the following month." Brett paused to eat another mouthful of salad then looked back up to Ronny and continued with his mouth half full of food. "Santo sided with Liz and shot the cover story but denied to Lucia that he had said anything to her. Well, she found out that he had and despite not wanting to work with him again she is forced to by the publisher who Liz Kirby has a lot of influence with. That cover became iconic because it was the first time a celebrity had been featured on such a high-profile fashion magazine, and Liz took all the credit. Lucia was pissed."

"Wow, that sounds intense. Now I understand why she isn't a fan of Santo." Ronny's mind raced as he considered that maybe Lucia could be an ally for him in some way against Santo. *But how?*

"That's only one of many times he has betrayed her trust, and let's get real, Lucia is from Sicily so you don't want to get on her bad side." Brett finally took a breath and another mouthful of salad. He seemed to be the sort of guy who lived for gossip, and as much as he tried to keep things to himself, he just couldn't. "You want some salad?" Brett asked as he smiled at Ronny.

"I'm good, man. Thanks." Ronny touched Brett on his arm and left the kitchen and headed back to Paul's desk.

"German catalogue clients are going to love these shots," Paul said to Chad as he organized the photographs on his desk.

"How's Nick doing?" Ronny asked, hoping that Paul knew he was keeping an eye on him and watching out for Nick. Paul paused for a moment then continued to collect the catalogues and spoke without turning to face him.

"He's fine. I think he just needs to focus more on his modeling instead of partying and he will be doing great. He has an appointment today with Santo, so I hope he makes a good impression."

Ronny watched Paul closely; he appeared to show little remorse or concern for Nick. He knew Santo would be using the Mancini show and campaign as bait.

"Thanks again for the new photos," said Chad as he put them in his backpack.

"Grazie, Paul," said Ronny as he walked away from Paul's desk, encouraging Chad to do the same. Chad followed Ronny out the door and back out onto the street. He knew that Paul was pressuring Chad. *I wonder how many models are being optioned for the Mancini campaign?*

"I saw that you and Ella had a connection on the shoot. I think she really likes you," Chad said as the two walked down the street.

"I didn't expect to meet someone like that here. Honestly, I haven't thought about dating anyone for a while. She is an incredible girl with such a wicked sense of humor. I don't know what's going to happen. I think I'm just going to enjoy it and take it one day at a time. If anything is meant to come from it, it will," Ronny said, trying to downplay how much he connected with Ella despite the reservations he had around relationships. He was really attracted to her and hoped for something more, but the idea of getting close to her and taking his eyes off his photography goals made him nervous.

He had been distracted by relationships in the past and couldn't afford to have that happen with all that was at stake.

"I'm in a similar situation with Camille. We're both aware this is a temporary thing, but we're enjoying it while we have it. Ella's a down-to-earth girl and she's been modeling for a while, so I'm sure she's smart enough to knows what's up." Chad was right that she was smart; it just felt like there was a deeper connection between them.

Back at the apartment, as the sun was getting low, Ronny grabbed a bottle of wine he had bought earlier and headed up to the roof to see if Ella was there. When he opened the door to the roof, he was relieved that she was alone.

"Want some company?" Ronny asked as Ella turned and flashed him a perfect smile. It was good to see her.

"It would be rude not to share this sunset with someone," Ella replied. She stood up and kissed him on the cheek.

"I brought us some wine." Ronny removed the cork and poured two glasses.

"To Milan," said Ella as she toasted Ronny and took a sip. "I sometimes come up here at sunrise when I can't sleep and meditate. The sunrise always reminds me of being home and going for an early surf."

"I always loved those photographs of surfers surfing with dolphins," Ronny added. "I've done that," Ella added. "There really isn't anything that compares to that feeling of freedom. Being in the ocean surfing and seeing a dolphin swim up beside you."

As much as Ronny tried to keep the conversation light with Ella, it was difficult not to want to open up to her. He remembered those vulnerable eyes through his lens. This naturally beautiful girl on the outside was showing him who she was, the painful parts of herself she was protecting. *We all have pain from our past,* thought

Ronny. He knew how guarded he was with his and felt so moved by Ella for letting him see her pain. Letting him see her inner beauty. For trusting him.

"It's really good to see you." She paused then continued, "Well, not 'really' good." She laughed her infectious natural laugh.

Ronny watched her, studying her face, smiling to himself. As she talked about her family, Ronny got distracted by the train of thought that raced through his head. There was so much going on for him right now. *What do I really have to offer such an incredible girl? I'm broke, and I come from a broken home.* Ella stopped talking.

"Where's your head at?" she said as she touched his forearm.

"Sorry, I've got a bit on my mind at the moment."

"Everything okay?"

"Before I left Rio things weren't good with my parents and I'm just dealing with a few dramas here. Nothing I can't handle," Ronny replied, not wanting to give too much away.

"Sometimes you have to live your life for *you*," Ella replied and then paused. She spoke like she had made some of those decisions for herself.

"You sound like you're talking from experience."

"If I did everything everyone else wanted me to do, I probably wouldn't have left Australia. I want to experience as much as this life has to offer me. Sometimes it's tough to leave your family and your friends behind and take a chance to follow your dreams. I try not to have regrets and I don't wonder what could have been or should have been. Don't get me wrong, I've made some decisions that didn't work out well for me, but they've all led me to this moment." Ella's expression was serious as she took a sip of her wine.

"I'm glad they did," Ronny said. "I hope that didn't sound too corny."

"Maybe a little corny, but I'll let it slide." Ella looked out at the sun as it set behind the buildings on the horizon. She was so authentic and easy to be around. "Sometimes when the sun sets over the ocean, you can see a flash of green just as the sun goes below the horizon."

"I've only ever seen it rise on the ocean." Ronny added.

The two sat in silence watching the sun disappear.

"This is my favorite light," Ronny said after the sun had gone.

"Mine too." Ella leaned in and kissed him slowly, passionately. Everything else in Ronny's world went quiet for that moment. Ronny adjusted his body on his seat, moved his leg and knocked over his wine glass that was sitting next to his foot. Ella pulled back, and he picked up the glass.

"Taxi!" Ella joked.

"Glad it was empty," Ronny said. He wanted the kiss to continue.

"I better head down. I've got to get organized for a big shoot tomorrow. I'm looking forward to seeing some of your dance moves."

Ronny helped her collect her things, and they left the roof. *Live my life for me.* Her words stayed with him after he said goodbye at the elevator. The memory of her kiss lingered, and he looked forward to seeing her again.

## CHAPTER 26

Ronny woke up the next day excited knowing the contact sheets from the test shoot would be ready that afternoon. The appointment for the Mancini fashion show fitting was at 11 a.m., and Lorenzo Mancini himself would be there. Ronny and Chad arrived together at the modern glass building and made their way to the waiting area of the impressive Mancini showroom to see a number of models already there who had also been confirmed for the show.

"You okay?" Ronny asked Chad. Ever since he had confronted Paul about Santo, Chad had been quieter than usual.

"I'm fine. I just want this to go well so I can nail this show. I guess I'm just nervous."

Ronny sensed that he was more nervous about the upcoming appointment with Santo Diaz than the fitting. He couldn't deny he was worried about him and what might happen.

"Hey!" called out Josh, who was sitting on the floor against a wall, waiting his turn. They walked up to greet him and sat down to talk for a while until Flavio's assistant came into the waiting area.

"Josh, Flavio is ready for you." Josh nodded and got up, leaving Chad and Ronny sitting on the floor.

"Tighten your belt, Tarzan," said one of the other male models in the room as Josh walked past, and a few guys started laughing. Flavio clearly had a reputation, but in Ronny's eyes it wasn't a laughing matter.

"What a loser," Chad muttered, nodding toward the model who called out. He was visibly agitated. "So are you ready to see Flavio?"

"I'm just keeping my eyes on the prize," Ronny replied.

Finally, it was time for his fitting. As he walked into the main studio, the light was pouring in the large windows, casting shadows on the wooden floorboards as a Prince song played in the background. Two models were already in the room; one standing in front of a long white table that Lorenzo was seated behind with his assistant, and another walking down the room toward a large mirror on the far wall. Lorenzo was wearing a patterned collared shirt with his sleeves rolled up.

"Ciao, Ronaldo, thanks for being here," Lorenzo announced as Ronny made his way past the model who was leaving to stand in front of the table.

"Nice to see you again, Mr. Mancini. I'm excited to be here," replied Ronny. He liked the sound of 'Ronaldo' when he heard it. That was his name at birth, but everyone had always called him Ronny. "Ciao, Carlotta. Nice to see you as well." He acknowledged Lorenzo's sister, who walked in front of the table in a tight black dress smoking a cigarette and playing with her long platinum-blonde hair.

She smiled at Ronny as she took a drag on her cigarette and leaned on the edge of the table. "We are so excited to have you be a part of the show."

"Well, hello. Nice to see you again so soon," said Flavio as he appeared creeping up behind Ronny and put his hand on his lower back. Ronny instantly got a chill and had to stop himself from pulling away from his touch. He was wearing a green kimono, slippers, and his trademark ponytail. "Come with me so we can try your first outfit."

He followed Flavio to the private change area off to the side of the larger studio. He pointed to a rack of clothes that he had positioned in the far corner of the dressing room that was crowded with racks of colorful clothes. On Ronny's rack hung a few pairs of swimwear, some pants and two patterned shirts.

"Let's have you try these on," he said as he handed Ronny a pair of swimmers. He took off his shirt and started to undo his pants. Flavio stood shamelessly in front of him while he undressed. He watched him remove his clothes and when it came time to remove his briefs Ronny turned his body away so all Flavio could see was his backside.

"I'll check the fit," said Flavio as he came in and stood in front of Ronny. He pulled the swimwear down lower on his hips and reached around to smooth out the wrinkles on his butt. He stood up and moved in front to take another look at his body. He reached down to the swimwear and again pulled them open, reaching in to reposition Ronny's package. He flinched back slightly in response to his grope, momentarily closing his eyes.

*Deal with it, Ronny. Fuck! I can do this. I need this job.* He tried to think of anything other than what was happening to him in that moment. Images raced through his mind. His brother who gave him the money to help him stay in Milan and achieve success. The photography career he wanted so badly that depended on his modeling success. Milo who managed to put up with so much more than this. He stood there for as long as he could before finally opening his eyes.

"I can do that for you if you tell me how you want it positioned," said Ronny. The anger inside him was boiling up as he tried to control his temper.

"I would rather do it; that's what I'm here for. I can have you canceled from this show if you keep up the attitude. Don't forget that," snapped Flavio. Ronny looked down at the floor, speechless and ashamed at what he was subjecting himself to.

"Let's try on these pants," Flavio said as he passed Ronny a pair of pants. "Let's see how they fit without underwear," he added.

*Fuck you!* Ronny removed the swimwear and turned to take the pants from Flavio who held the pants in his hands, slowly unbuttoning the fly as he stared down at his crotch. Flavio stood looking at Ronny standing there naked before slowly handing him the pants.

"Thanks," replied Ronny sarcastically as he took the pants and got dressed. Again, Flavio didn't waste any time coming in to check the fit of the pants, cupping Ronny's crotch and adjusting the shape of his package. Again, Ronny held his breath and tried not to flinch. He bit down and clenched his jaw, trying to focus on why he was allowing this to happen. *Fuck! I'm going to get you back for this somehow, you little creep.*

"Okay, let's get you out there."

Ronny walked out again in front of Lorenzo and Carlotta.

"Let's see you walk please," said Carlotta. Ronny walked away and back to the table. "Hmm…those pants seem a little tight across the back. Can I check the waistband?" Carlotta asked. Ronny nodded before she lifted the shirt and put her fingers down the back of Ronny's pants and pulled the waistband. As annoyed as he was about Flavio's assault and being manhandled, he appreciated that she asked and felt that as he was at a fitting, her touch was justified.

"Lorenzo, I think the waistband should be in stretch fabric, so they move with the body, and they could be a little longer, no?" Carlotta continued as she looked to Lorenzo.

"How do they feel, Ronaldo?" asked Lorenzo.

"They do feel a little tight when I walk, and when I have underwear on, they would be tighter," replied Ronny.

"I agree, they do look a bit tight," said Lorenzo. Carlotta gave Flavio a sideways glance. Ronny could sense the tension between them and hoped he stirred the pot with his comment.

"I think it would make more sense to have the models wear underwear or a G-string with pants for a fitting don't you think?" Carlotta stated, seemingly aware of Flavio's tricks and calling him out. "Make sure to do so." She seemed to reprimand Flavio.

"They can be adjusted, and the waistband can be changed," snapped Flavio as he dodged the eyeline of Carlotta and walked off back to the changing area. Ronny waited for a moment then followed him. As he entered, he overheard an unsuspecting Flavio and his assistant talking behind a rack of clothes.

"That bitch wouldn't know the first thing about fashion. I should have blown her gay husband while I had the chance," Flavio said. Ronny stood with his mouth open in shock. *I wish I recorded that.*

"I'm just going to change and leave," announced Ronny after a brief pause; then he made his way back to the rack.

"Just leave the clothes on the rack," Flavio replied in a sharp tone as Ronny changed quickly and walked back out across the studio.

"Grazie, Ronny. See you at the show," called out Carlotta. Ronny walked toward the door just as Chad was entering. He felt excited knowing he was confirmed for the show but was also reeling from hearing what he had just heard.

"Ah, the statue of David," Carlotta said when she saw Chad.

"I'll wait for you outside, man." Ronny walked past Chad and left the room, relieved that the fitting with Flavio was over. He was nervous for Chad, but at least Carlotta appeared to be onto Flavio and his antics.

As he was walking back into the foyer, he heard someone yelling, then saw Nick being escorted outside by two security guards. He looked disheveled. *What now?* thought Ronny as he passed the guys still waiting for the fitting.

"I was supposed to get this job!" Nick yelled out, struggling with security who tried to hold him back.

"Hey, Nick, calm down. What's going on?" Ronny asked as he went outside, Nick stopped struggling when he saw Ronny.

"I was getting booked for this job. That's what Santo told me at our meeting," Nick added. Ronny touched him on the arm, he could smell alcohol on his breath. He tried to deflate the situation to not cause a scene.

"Man, this isn't helping." He was shocked to see him in such a state. Ronny tried to help usher Nick away from the front door onto the street away from the building. The security guard gripped his arm tightly. Nick struggled to free it and swung around to punch the guard who ducked, and Nick fell forward and put his fist right through the glass entry door. As he pulled it back out, he cut his forearm and blood started rushing out. Ronny gasped. He saw the whole accident unfold almost in slow motion.

"No, Nick. Stop!" Ronny exclaimed as the glass smashed down around their feet. He acted quickly and took off his shirt, wrapped it around his cut forearm, and sat down with Nick on the step. "Don't move; this will stop the bleeding," Ronny added as Nick stopped struggling and put his head against Ronny's chest and started crying. "Call an ambulance," Ronny called out as a few of the other models appeared at the door to see what was going on. Seeing Nick in this state was a disturbing reality check. Not everyone could handle the heat of this business, and Nick had definitely been burned by it. A wave of sympathy came over Ronny as he sat there comforting Nick. *Who knows exactly what he was promised by Santo and what he had been subject to in the process*. He felt the resentment growing again towards Santo.

"Is he okay?" Chad asked when he finally appeared and crouched down next to Ronny. Chad looked white in the face. Ronny wondered if it was from seeing Nick in this state or from the fitting with Flavio.

"The ambulance is on its way. I managed to stop the bleeding," he replied. Ronny didn't go into detail as to what happened. Chad looked on with concern as they sat in silence. Moments later Paul appeared at the same time the ambulance arrived.

"I came as soon as I heard," Paul said as he stood next to the paramedics attending to Nick. "Are you two okay?" he asked Ronny and Chad.

Chad nodded, but Ronny just sat there. He looked slowly up at Paul with resentment in his eyes. "Nick's not okay. But you knew that." The paramedics moved quickly to move Nick onto a stretcher as Paul talked to them in Italian. Ronny wasn't sure if Paul had heard him.

"They said he will be fine," Paul said. "I'll go with him. I will need to make sure he's okay and handle the paperwork." Paul got into the ambulance with Nick and it drove away. Ronny sat back down on the step shirtless. His chest still had spots of Nick's blood on it.

## CHAPTER 27

One of the security guards brought Ronny out a wet towel to wipe the blood off his skin.

"Grazie," Ronny said as he cleaned himself up. "I think Santo had told him he had the Mancini show when he was at his house for the test shoot," he said to Chad, who looked visibly shaken.

"How bad was the cut on his arm?" Chad finally asked.

"He won't be boxing for a while." It was a deep gash in Nick's forearm, and he knew it would be a long road to recovery. "I'll call Paul when we get back to the Pola to make sure he's okay."

"I just realized I had this. It's clean," Chad said as he pulled a T-shirt out of his backpack.

"Thanks." Ronny put it on and started to walk down the street with Chad, still in shock.

"What are you doing now?" Chad asked. Ronny took a second to refocus and remembered he needed to head to Foto Aldo to collect the proof sheets. He welcomed a distraction and was still shaking when he left Chad.

"You okay?" Jose asked when he saw Ronny.

"Yeah. Just been a crazy day with castings," he answered, not wanting to have to rehash the day's events. Jose handed him his box of black and white contact sheets and left him to look through them. When he opened the box, he noticed how much better the quality of the proofs were compared to the ones he had printed in Brazil. He picked up the magnifying glass on the counter and moved to the end to take took a closer look at the images. This was his first real shoot in Milan and straight away he could see the difference. The light, crops, and composition of the photographs looked so much more professional. Shooting real models elevated his work and left him with so many strong options to choose from. He could see the influence after shooting with Francesco and knew these photographs were exactly what he needed for his portfolio. He came across the contact sheets of Ella by herself and took a moment to look closely at her expressions. He enjoyed the distraction as he slowly looked over the contact sheets and marked some of his favorites.

"Looks like a great shoot. May I have a look?" asked Jose.

Ronny nodded and passed him the contact sheets. He felt nervous as Jose looked through the magnifying glass.

"You have a great eye, Ronny. These are really strong. I love your portraits and the ones with movement. Great composition."

"Thanks. I really love them too," Ronny said, proud of what he had created.

"I'd love to see some more of your work. I know Antonio would too."

For the first time Ronny felt confident that it was time to start sharing his work with agents. He had been waiting for the right time and now he felt ready. He remembered he had a box of prints in his backpack from his earlier work in Brazil that he had brought to show Jose.

"I brought some more of my work to show you," he said, and he handed Jose the box of prints.

Jose took his time to look at the photos. "You can tell your subjects trusted you. Really intimate."

"I try to encourage them to reveal their inner beauty that not everyone can see," Ronny added. Whenever he talked about his subjects, he was reminded how much he loved photography. He turned back to the contact sheets and took time to select twelve images to be printed. Jose helped him make some final choices and suggested some crops that made them stronger as prints.

"Let me give you my home number as well in case you ever need anything," Jose said.

Ronny left Foto Aldo, despite his concerns about Nick's well-being, he was excited to get back to the Pola and show Chad and the girls the contact sheets. When he opened the door to his room, Chad was hanging up the phone.

"That was Paul. Nick's going to be okay," said Chad.

"That's a relief." But Ronny knew that Nick wasn't really okay. He had unanswered questions, but for now he wanted to celebrate his new photographs. "I just collected the test shoot contact sheets. Can you call Camille and Ella to come down to have a look?" Ronny asked, then headed to take a shower and wash off the day. By the time he got out, the girls were there.

"Have you guys had a busy day?" asked Ella. Ronny and Chad looked at each other, and Chad took a sip of his beer.

"It's definitely been a busy one," replied Ronny. He decided not to tell them about Nick. He imagined Nick wouldn't want people knowing about the incident. "So, I just picked up the proofs from our test shoot. I got you girls a copy so you can take them to your agent to order prints." Ronny reached down into his backpack and pulled out two boxes of proof sheets and a magnified loop to look at the images. He passed one set to Ella and Camille and one to Chad before standing up and turning on the light so they could see the contact sheets more clearly.

"I hope you like them," Ronny said nervously, not wanting to upsell his work.

"I love the emotion and movement," Ella commented. Ronny looked at her expression, trying to gauge if she was being serious. Her opinion mattered; they all did.

"These are so raw and natural, Ronny. The agency is going to love them," Camille added. "How the hell are you ever going to choose? They all look beautiful."

Ronny sat there soaking in the positive reaction to his work. He felt a sense of pride and affirmed that he could do this. It was worth all this effort. *This is a turning point. I can feel it.*

"They look awesome, man. Great job. Wow," Chad said. "I know I'm looking at a photo of myself, but it looks better than I think I look. Does that make sense?" Everyone laughed as Chad shook his head. "You know what I mean."

"Now remind me, was Chad on an apple box because he doesn't look that short in these photos." Ella added and laughed at Chad. Ronny looked again at the photographs of Ella dancing, taking time to study her expression and the freedom of her movement. They were his favorites. He glanced over at her, and she looked up as if she knew he was looking at her photographs.

"I love the ones of you dancing," he said.

"Me too," Ella replied as he saw that same open expression he had captured.

"Okay, you two. We are still here." Camille nudged Ella. "We should celebrate tonight at Club Hollywood."

"What time are you heading to the club?" asked Chad.

"We'll get there around ten thirty. We need to go to an agency dinner before so let's meet there."

"Sounds like a plan. I love that club. I'll do some push-ups and wear some lifts in my shoes." He winked at Ella and stood up on his toes. The girls gathered their things and went to get ready for their dinner.

"See you on the dance floor," said Ronny as the girls left. Despite all the drama going on with Nick, there was a lot to celebrate.

# CHAPTER 28

Club Hollywood was located on the Corso Combo in downtown Milan in a building with an underwhelming façade. Most of the walls were dark except for the glowing red fluorescent 'Hollywood' sign. When they arrived in a taxi just after 10:30, the crowd was already ten people deep at the door. Ronny got out of the taxi and adjusted his black collared shirt that was tucked tight into his jeans. Chad walked up behind him; he was wearing one of Ronny's vintage black sleeveless T-shirts with the iconic Rolling Stones lips on the front.

"You look like a young Marlon Brando, man," Ronny said and smiled at Chad.

"That's the look I was going for." Chad wrinkled his brow and put his hand up to his chin in jest. As the two approached the velvet roped area, the hostess spotted them and immediately called them forward past the pressing crowd. She was wearing black leather shorts, high heels, a red leather jacket with spikes on the shoulders, and a black admiral hat with chains on it.

"Nice to see you boys again," she said. Ronny recognized her as the same hostess from the Mancini party. "You two are fine. Enjoy," she said as she discreetly handed Chad a handful of tickets and gave him a wink.

"Thanks, bella," replied Chad with a mischievous glance and turned to Ronny. "The Club gives out free drink coupons to all the models who come here. You have to love Milan." Chad led the way down the tiled hallway lit with purple lights. The dance music got louder as they entered the main room. "Welcome to Hollywood," announced Chad. There was scaffolding over the large sunken dance floor filled with colored lights and mirror balls. A lot of people were already dancing to the music with more standing around the bar—sexy, stylish, cool people. The club was dark, Ronny's eyes adjusted so he could make out the leather booths and seating around the outer walls and the lit-up bar area in the corner. Beyond that, above the DJ booth, was the raised VIP room overlooking the dance floor that was roped off with a security guard standing at the entrance. Chad led Ronny to the bar area where Ella and Camille were already standing with a few other models. Chad snuck up behind Camille and put his hands on her hips and pulled her towards him. "Ciao, bella."

"You scared me," she replied as she turned around and playfully slapped him. Both girls looked incredible. Ella was dressed in a short body-hugging green dress with shoestring straps, smokey eye makeup, and Camille wore a short, black, sequined skirt and white halter top under a black jacket.

"Wow, you look incredible," said Ronny. It was the first time he had seen Ella all dressed up.

"Not bad yourself, Rio." She quickly looked him up and down. "You guys want a drink? My shout." She held up four drink tickets and winked.

"I loved those photos you took of us," said Camille to Ronny as she touched him on the arm and came close to his ear.

"I think it would be hard to take a bad photo of you two." *I could get used to these compliments.* It was the first time she had touched him like that.

"You've obviously never seen me in the morning," said Ella with her usual dry wit as she turned to the bar to retrieve a round of four drinks and handed them out. Camille slowly pulled back from Ronny.

"I think I know someone who would like to," said Chad as Ella rolled her eyes.

Ronny felt a little embarrassed. "So how was your agency dinner?" he asked.

"Um, well, it was okay," replied Ella.

"Doesn't sound okay," Ronny continued.

Camille chimed in. "There were about six models, two agents, and four men there who are some of the main investors in the agency. They're wealthy Italian guys who are pretty creepy and somehow think they invested in an escort service instead of a model agency."

"We were told to be nice to them. One of them looked like a serious gangster. I think he must be connected to the mafia," Ella added.

"Fortunately, a few of the Russian girls responded to their advances and so we got off the hook. I think they are in the VIP section up there." Camille nodded toward the back of the club. Ronny was reminded that in this game the girls are preyed upon just as much as, if not more than, the guys. He thought about Carlotta Mancini and the roster of supermodels she was able to introduce to a rockstar or billionaire. *Valuable assets.*

Ronny raised his drink up to make a toast. "So after what's been a pretty crazy week, are you guys ready to have some fun tonight?"

"Bloody oath!" cheered Ella as Camille burst out laughing after taking a sip, spitting out her drink.

"You are so Australian!" Camille wiped her mouth, and everyone took a sip of their drinks. Ronny reached into his pocket and pulled out four white tablets that Nick had given him at the Mancini party.

"What are they?" asked Camille.

"They're ecstasy tablets that came from Carlotta Mancini's assistant." Ronny added. Camille looked back up at the group and then back down at the tablets in Ronny's hand.

"You had me at hello," she said as she took one of the tablets. "If these are from Carlotta Mancini, you know they will be good. Who's in?"

"I'm game if you are," said Ella as she took one of the tablets from his hand and looked at him. Ronny had done ecstasy a few times with friends and had always enjoyed it, especially when music and dancing were involved.

"How strong are they?" Chad asked.

"Have you tried ecstasy before?" Ronny asked.

"Not really. I have never tried anything except alcohol and weed."

"Nobody is pressuring you, but if you want to try it, we are here to look after you."

Chad nodded and looked up at Camille. "Well, I am a team player and I guess if we are in, we are all in." He took the last tablet from Ronny's hand, and they all swallowed the pills.

"Oh, before I forget—" said Ronny.

"What?!" snapped Camille. "Now you forget to tell us something!"

"Make sure you have a good time," laughed Ronny.

"Bloody wanker!" exclaimed Ella.

The crowd at Club Hollywood now almost filled the space as the beat of the music got louder. The DJ and sound system were incredible; you could feel the energy in the room. Ronny took a moment to look at the variety of people in the club—artistic-looking guys and girls with shaved heads, wigs, makeup, leather, and fishnets; hot, sexy Europeans; club kids; as well as stylish businessmen wearing suits who paid big money to buy tables at the club. He had been to a few big clubs in Rio, but the crowd was nowhere near as edgy and fashionable. As they finished their drinks, Josh and Annika appeared with several other models.

"Well hello, darlings. Looks like this is the place to be," said Annika, looking as sexy as her skinny, hard Russian self would allow in a slinky, short gold dress.

"I'm dancing for free tonight," said Josh as he started some mock dance moves in black pants and a black tank top that revealed his chiseled arms.

Annika turned to look at him. "Of course you are. Now where's my vodka?" Josh headed to the bar to get some drinks.

"Does he always do what you want?" asked Ronny.

"If he wants to keep his Austrian balls he will." Annika didn't miss a beat.

The DJ played a remix of Robin S.'s "Show Me Love," and Ella screamed, "I love this song. Come dance." She grabbed Camille's hand and led her to the dance floor where the two girls started dancing. Ronny loved to watch Ella light up, he envied her carefree outlook.

"So I heard you took some hot photos on the roof?" Annika said to Ronny.

"They did most of the work. I just clicked the camera." Even though he deflected attention away from himself, he was so excited by the result.

"Hey, I have some good cocaine if you guys want any," Annika offered.

"We're good. Thanks, though." Ronny smiled. He knew it wasn't a good idea to mix cocaine with ecstasy, and the few times he had tried cocaine in the past it had always made him feel anxious. *It's probably what keeps Annika so thin.*

Josh arrived back with Annika's drink. "Here you go, babe."

"Thank you, darling," she replied as she took a sip.

"So are we going to hit the dance floor?" Chad asked as he struck a Saturday Night Fever pose with one hand pointing to the air. He must have been starting to feel the effects of the X.

"Well, you've certainly loosened up, Captain America," Annika commented as she glanced at Chad with raised eyebrows.

"Let's do this!" Chad cheered, and they made their way onto the dance floor. The beat of the music vibrated right through Ronny's chest. He could feel the ecstasy starting to take effect. In the center of the dance floor the girls playfully danced with each other as the surrounding crowd cleared a space to watch them move. The four friends danced in a circle. It was a euphoric moment, a feeling that Ronny wanted to last. He couldn't help letting his eyes wander to look at Ella. Watching her move. Watching her live.

He looked up at the lights and mirror ball realizing he had a huge smile on his face. He could feel his face getting hotter and the music getting louder. Ronny took a deep breath, and the air felt like the most incredible oxygen he had ever breathed. The X was coming on strong as Ronny closed his eyes; the feeling was a little intense, he looked over to see if Chad was okay. He was dancing slowly with his eyes closed and a huge smile on his face. Chad slowly opened his eyes; he was rolling pretty hard, so Ronny put his hand on his shoulder and started massaging the back of his neck. Chad reached up and held his forearms, still slowly shuffling his feet.

"So, are we having fun yet?" Camille said, moving with the music.

"You're pretty," Chad said to Camille as he lifted his head.

"Thanks, Iowa. You hanging in there?"

"Living my best life. I love you guys," Chad responded without opening his eyes.

"We love you too, Iowa," replied Ella. "This music is incredible," she added as she danced around them.

"This is one of my favorite DJs, Frankie Knuckles. He's in town from New York," said Camille. Ronny moved in to dance closer to Ella. He loved to dance. He touched her arm, and her skin felt amazing. They danced together for what felt like hours. It felt great to let go, laugh, and get lost in the music. Sweat covered their bodies as the ecstasy heightened the euphoric moment.

"You're driving me nuts, you know that," said Ella as she put her hand on his chest and let her hand slide down.

"Is that right?" replied Ronny in a playful tone as Ella turned her back to him and started to move her body back against his. *What is it about this girl?* She moved with the music and pressed her body into his, and let her hands wander back onto his hips. Ronny pulled her back to him; her body felt incredible as she leaned her head back on his shoulder. She took her hand up into the back of his hair and pulled his face down toward her and open-mouth kissed him deeply. Ronny closed his eyes as her tongue entered his mouth; her full lips felt soft as his tongue explored her warm mouth. *I can't control myself.*

He let his hands travel farther around her waist and pulled her hips toward him. Ella slowly pulled away from his mouth and lifted her head up and opened her eyes, becoming aware that people were watching them.

"You two might want to get a room," said Chad.

Ronny laughed. Meeting Ella had caught him off guard. Was it the ecstasy or was this someone he was having a deep connection with? This was the most fun he had allowed himself to have in a long time. He held her hand, unable to deny his feelings for her. They went and sat down on one of the booths on the side of the dance floor to drink some water and have a break.

"Not a bad dancer yourself, Rio," Ella said as she finished taking a drink of water.

"I learned a few things from watching you," Ronny flirted.

"I've been watching you, too." She came in close to whisper in his ear. "I know you have a lot going on in that handsome head of yours. It's nice to see you let go and have some fun." Ella ran her fingers through his hair and pushed back his curls.

"You're right. Thanks for reminding me." Ronny smiled at her. This was the start of the life he wanted for himself. A new beginning. "I was dealing with a lot at home and, honestly, if it wasn't for this trip to Milan, I don't know what I would have done. I came here to follow my dream of becoming a photographer, and modeling was a way to help me get there. I never expected to meet anyone."

Ella squeezed his hand. "I'm scared, too, you know." She moved in and kissed him again.

# CHAPTER 29

"Sorry to interrupt, but it's time for us to leave. Josh just got his tooth punched out, and they will ban him from the club if we don't take him home. Chad is helping him outside," Camille declared. Ronny shook his head, frustrated that his conversation with Ella had been cut short. Apparently, Josh got into a fight at the bar with two Italian guys who he claimed were flirting with Annika, and one of them knocked Josh's tooth out.

Everyone was still pretty wired when they got back to the Pola. They all headed up to the roof to watch the sunrise except Annika who stayed at the club after their fight. Ronny could still feel the effects of the ecstasy as the sun lit up the horizon. The ambient light was beautiful. Josh turned around holding a can bong, exhaled hash smoke, and asked if anyone wanted some. Everyone burst out laughing at the sight of Josh with a fat lip, missing a tooth and now talking with a lisp.

"Fuck you." Josh gave them the finger. "My agency is going to freak. Whatever! At least I got one good hit in before they jumped me. Assholes."

"I'm good, man," replied Chad as he took a sip of his beer. "I've had enough drugs for one night."

"Hash isn't drugs, man. It's a game changer," said Josh.

"I'll have some," said Camille as Ella moved closer to Josh.

"You feeling okay, Josh?" she asked.

"My lip's thore, but it's not too bad. I think I swallowed my tooff!" Josh added. Everyone erupted in laughter as Josh continued speaking with a lisp. Ella came and stood next to Ronny and looked out over the city skyline.

"I haven't seen the sunrise since last New Year's. Milan looks so beautiful in this light."

Ella added. Ronny put his arm around her. He wished it was just the two of them there enjoying the light, taking in the moment.

"I'm waiting for Annika to appear and tell us it's still fucking ugly,'" laughed Camille after she took a hit of hash. Josh rolled his eyes at the mention of Annika's name. He turned to Chad.

"Hey, thanks for getting me out of there. I'm sure they would have put me in jail or cut off one of my fingers or something." Chad put his hand on Josh's shoulder.

"All good, man." The sun slowly broke the horizon at 5:30 a.m.

"It's a new dawn, a new day, and I'm feeling good," said Josh.

Camille walked over to Ronny and Ella. "I'm going to go back down to Chad's place if you guys want to go to our room to chill out. Is that okay?"

"Okay, sure," replied Ella as she took a hold of Ronny's hand. "Hey, you want to come downstairs to our place to chill?"

"Chill, eh?" replied Ronny with a smirk as he glanced over to see Chad wink at him. The thought of being alone with Ella in her room excited him. The kiss on the dance floor at the club was still fresh in his memory.

"Yo, Josh, we are going to head downstairs. Why don't you take some painkillers and try and get some sleep," Chad said to Josh as the group headed downstairs.

As Ronny walked down the stairs with Ella, he started to feel nervous. It had been a long time since he had been intimate with someone he had feelings for. *Breathe. Just breathe.*

When Ronny entered Ella and Camille's room, the soft warm morning light was creeping in the window through a patterned scarf that was hanging there. He noticed the vintage posters on the walls and the crystals next to a scented candle on the side table. Ella took a moment to light a few candles around the room.

"I told you my parents were hippies," she acknowledged as she touched the crystal. "Do I need to sage you?" She laughed as she turned around and headed to the kitchen. "Want something to drink? I have some fresh OJ or tea?"

"OJ would be great. Thanks. Can I use your bathroom?"

"Sure."

Ronny felt a chill as he walked to the bathroom. He always got a chill when he was nervous. He closed the door and rubbed his arms trying to warm himself up. He splashed some warm water on his face and looked up in the mirror. His pupils were dilated from the ecstasy. *Get it together, man. Why am I so nervous?* He hadn't gone looking for sex, but here he was in Ella's room. He slapped himself in the face trying to get focused. The last time he had casual sex, he had committed to not doing it again until he met someone who was worth it. *Maybe that's why I'm so nervous.* Ronny knew by being there he was opening himself up. This wasn't just sex with Ella. *It means so much more than that.* When Ronny came out of the bathroom, Ella had put on some jazz music and was walking out of the kitchen with a cold glass of orange juice for him.

"Ah thanks, just what I needed." Ronny took two gulps of the cold juice. It tasted delicious. They sat down on the small couch and Ronny drank the rest.

"Thirsty?" Ella asked as she raised her eyebrows.

"I haven't danced like that for ages. That club was amazing." He put the glass down on the table as Ella leaned down to remove her shoes.

"It was nice to see you let go and enjoy the music."

"I know I need to let go more." Ella ran her fingers through his thick hair. "You're amazing, you know that," he added as he looked at her and touched her forearm.

"Thank you. You're pretty incredible yourself. You know you don't need to carry it all by yourself. It's okay sometimes to let someone in and get some support."

Ronny paused for a moment then looked down at his hands. The hands that always reminded him of his mother's. "After I was thrown out of my home by my father, I would have been on the street if my brother hadn't given me a couch to sleep on. My brother Luiz, his wife, and my friend Milo are really the ones that are there for me." It felt good to share that with Ella.

"What happened with your mum?"

"I love my mom. Unfortunately, she stayed with my dad in an abusive relationship. I remember when they were in love, before he had the affair. They were so happy." It was easy to talk to Ella, but it felt odd to summarize so many years of pain and trauma in a sentence. It almost took the power away from it.

"I'm sorry." Ella paused. "You're not your dad, Ronny."

Ronny looked at her. He thought about what she said. She was right.

"I'm not going to lie—things got desperate there for a minute. I was just lucky enough to get scouted to come here to Milan for fashion week." Ronny leaned forward as their lips met softly; his hand cradled her face. Her hand traveled up his body to rest on his chest, and her tongue entered his mouth as his soft stubble brushed against her lips. Their breathing intensified as she turned her body to face his.

"I might be sweaty," he said as he took a moment away from her mouth and removed his shirt.

"I like it," Ella whispered. She stood up and without losing eye contact with Ronny, she pushed one of the straps of her dress off her shoulder. He stood up in front of her and removed her other strap. Her dress fell to the floor as she stepped out of it. She stood there wearing light pink briefs. He took a moment to look at Ella. Her dirty blonde hair falling around her shoulders and cascading down toward her breasts. Her skin glowing in the ambient morning light.

"I wish I had my camera," he said as he slowly pulled his shirt up over his head and moved in closer. He touched her arms and kissed her deeply, passionately pulling her closer so her soft breasts pressed against his chest. His tongue explored her mouth as her hands moved up his back. Ronny felt the strength of her body as he moved his hands down to her hips to pull her closer. She was right; he wasn't his father. He was able to be vulnerable and open with Ella. She inspired him to look forward and imagine what might be possible. He took his time exploring her body before Ella reached into her side table drawer and pulled out a condom.

"You never cease to surprise me," he said as he took the rubber and kissed her softly.

"My parents taught me well," Ella replied as they lay down on her bed next to each other. He took his time to kiss her body and slowly took off her underwear and then his own. She reacted to his touch and ran her fingers through his hair then caressed his face.

"Thank you," he whispered. He was grateful for the many insights that she had inspired in him. He started kissing her again then moved on top of her. Ella positioned herself as he slowly entered her, pulling back momentarily before sliding in deeper again. He took his time and savored the moment. This felt so right.

When his pace quickened, she touched his back to slow him down. He slowly pulled out of her and paused before thrusting deep into her again and deeper again. She adjusted to his rhythm then gasped as he thrust deep inside her. Ronny felt her warmth engulf him. The sensation was intense as his mouth opened to let out a deep sigh. He used his arms to push himself up on his knees so he could watch himself entering Ella, teasing her, arousing her, and feeling connected to her completely.

The warm morning light played perfectly on her face and body as he savored the moment, watching her move underneath him. Ella looked up at Ronny as he continued teasing, watching her react, increasing his pace, moving in and out of her until he could sense that she was getting close. Ronny felt Ella tightening herself around him as she let out a deep moan. Unable to resist any longer, she exploded into an orgasm. His pace quickened as he slid deeply into her, feeling a deep pleasure rise in his body, gasping out a deep cry, unable to hold back his own release.

He lay down next to her on the bed, and his arms fell over his head as he breathed deeply. His eyes closed as he smiled and let the euphoric feeling surge through his body.

"I knew when I looked at you through my lens on the roof that I really saw you and you let me in. Ever since that moment I haven't been able to stop thinking about you," Ronny said as he looked across at Ella and moved her hair back from her face, she took his hand and kissed it.

"I wanted to show you who I was," Ella replied softly as she moved closer to Ronny and lay her head on his chest.

Around lunchtime Ronny slowly opened his eyes and saw a small post-it note on the ceiling. He rubbed his eyes and focused on the note. 'You got this,' was all it said. He smiled knowing that's what Ella saw each morning when she woke up.

"Morning, sleeping beauty. I wasn't sure if you were going to ever wake up." Ella appeared from the kitchen wearing a vintage T-shirt. Ronny smiled and scratched his head. "You want some breakfast? I'm making eggs."

"Is there anything you can't do?" Ronny replied. He could hear the eggs in the frypan.

"River dancing. I couldn't get into it," Ella replied as Ronny laughed.

"I'd love some eggs." He got up to put on his pants and went to the bathroom. When he came out he sat down with Ella at the small dining table and shared eggs and coffee, it felt natural to wake up with her.

"How's everything been going with your castings and work?" Ella asked. Ronny was silent as he considered what to tell her. "What's on your mind?"

Ronny wasn't sure what to say but decided to tell her the truth. "It's been pretty crazy. I was hoping things here would be different." Ronny took a sip of his coffee. "When I went to the wrap party in Rio at Santo Diaz's hotel, he followed me into the bathroom. He was high on cocaine and tried to pay me for sex. I tried to get away, but he started grabbing me, so I slammed him into a wall and almost knocked him out. Now I'm here dealing with the stylist Flavio that keeps touching me up and Santo has been taking advantage of guys from our agency, and it's only a matter of time before I have to see him again. Our friend Nick just cut his arm open boxing out a glass door because he didn't get the Mancini show after Santo promised it to him." It felt good to tell someone all of it.

"I'm sorry, Ronny. I could tell something was up," Ella said as she touched his arm. "Have you told your agency?"

"My agent is in on it. He's aware of what's happening, but the jobs that Santo Diaz and Flavio brings the agency are too valuable." He felt a wave of anger wash over him.

She looked away for a moment, then continued. "I know I would be so much more successful in this business if I had done certain things that were asked of me. Things I said no to." She paused and glanced down at the table, searching for a point of focus. "I was one of the finalists in the Argenta international model competition that was being held in Europe." She spoke slowly and softly. "Pedro Argenta owns the agency, and the competition is a really big deal," a distant, lost expression came across her face, "I got down to the final six models, and the night before the winner was announced, I ended up sleeping with him. I was sixteen years old." She nervously clenched her hands on her thigh as she shuffled her feet. "I'm not proud of what I did. I was naïve enough to believe what he had told me, that I would win if I slept with him. The next day, I didn't win. I lost. I lost myself," Ella continued as he watched her struggling to tell the story. He could tell she was still traumatized by what had happened.

"Did you tell anyone?" asked Ronny as he touched her arm.

"I told the organizers of the competition what happened. They told me they would do something about it, but nothing happened. I didn't have any evidence. I threatened to go to the press, but they kept giving me excuses, and they twisted it around, trying to convince me to believe it was somehow my fault and that I was just being a sore loser. Turns out Mr. Argenta had a lot of powerful friends, and I was virtually blacklisted in the industry, I struggled to get an agent, and rumors were spread that I had a bad reputation and I liked to party and do drugs. It was really tough for me to catch a break and get work for a long time." She wiped away the tears pooling up in her eyes, and he could see that the lost expression had been replaced by anger and frustration.

Ronny admired her courage and imagined how hard it must have been to come back from what she had dealt with. In the past, he may have judged her for selling herself for success. But after all he had now been through with his mother, Milo, and the models he had met in Milan, he understood why she had done it and what it took to do so.

"I was young and stupid. I thought that was what I had to do to get ahead. I was lied to and taken advantage of." Ella looked down, avoiding eye contact as Ronny reached down and lifted her face to his.

"Thank you for sharing that with me. I'm sorry you had to go through that. I can't imagine how you dealt with that at such a young age." He thought about Tiana Taylor and the other supermodels and wondered if they all had similar stories. There was a dark undercurrent that ran through the business. You could only go so deep into the water before you got swept away.

"I'm sorry for telling you all that and dragging you back into my past. I haven't shared that story for a long time." Ella took a deep breath and forced a smile. "Well, I guess now you'll go on to become a famous photographer and start dating supermodels," she joked.

"Well, of course that's why I got into this game in the first place. To bag myself a supermodel. I really need to return Tiana Taylor's phone calls." Ronny smiled. He welcomed the distraction of her humor.

"Bloody wanker." Ella playfully pushed him away. After she had opened up and shared her story, he felt even closer to her. Ronny had no idea what the future held for them, but right now, this felt right. He kissed her softly. After Ronny helped Ella clean up, Camille rang the room to check if it was okay to come up. Ronny put his shirt on and collected the rest of his things.

"I have to fly out tonight for a catalog shoot in Germany. I'd like to see you when I get back," said Ella as she reached out and touched his face.

"I'd like that too. I had such an incredible time with you." He hugged and kissed her as she tried to playfully pull away.

"I've got to clean this room up and get myself organized. You're too much of a distraction."

"You got this," Ronny said as he winked and opened the door to leave. Ella smiled widely as he shut the door and headed downstairs.

# CHAPTER 30

"Now that was an insane night," said Chad as Ronny entered their room. "Did you have a good time with Ella?"

"You could say that," Ronny answered, not wanting to give too much away.

"Playing it cool, eh? I get it."

"Not too cool. She's the most amazing girl. I'm just enjoying it and seeing where it goes." Ella was the best thing that had happened to him in a long time, but he didn't want to put any pressure on it. Chad and Ronny ordered in pizza that evening and had a quiet night. They were both exhausted and fell asleep early. The following morning they were drinking coffee in the kitchen when the phone rang. Ronny answered it.

"It's Paul. I'm downstairs, I need to come up and talk to you and Chad." He sounded serious.

"Paul's here. He's coming up," Ronny said. *Something's happened to Nick.* He started to feel sick to his stomach. There was a knock at the door. Ronny let Paul in. He looked washed out in the face, and his confident demeanor was gone.

"Can we sit down," he asked anxiously as he walked toward the small table, and they all sat down. "There's been an accident. It's

Nick," Paul said as he took a breath. He brought his hand up to his face and started to scratch his forehead, momentarily closing his eyes as if he had a headache. Ronny had sensed the worst, and now it was becoming real. He couldn't speak.

"Is he okay?" asked Chad with a sense of urgency.

"He killed himself after he got home from the hospital last night."

"What?" Ronny stood up and put his hand over his mouth. It was like a nightmare that had just become real. "No!" He couldn't accept it. *How could this be?* "No," he said again softly as he tried to make sense of what he had just heard.

"What happened?" asked Chad in disbelief.

"I woke up this morning and found him in the bathroom. He had hung himself."

The words were like a knife going into Ronny's chest. He sat back down at the table in shock.

"I already let his family know. They told me that he was in rehab in London and when he came down here to Milan he started drinking and doing drugs again. We didn't know he had been in rehab." Paul looked shaken. Chad was speechless. Nick must have reached a breaking point after injuring his arm; he must have felt there was nowhere to go. Ronny slumped back down in his chair.

"I'm sorry. I know you were close. I didn't want you to hear this from anyone else." Paul stood up. "I need to go deal with the authorities. I'm so sorry," he said before leaving the apartment.

In the sobering light of day, the two friends sat for a moment in silence. The traffic and street sounds outside the window became louder as Chad wiped the tears from his eyes. Ronny felt sick, almost unable to breathe. *What if that was Milo? Or my mother?* Tears welled up in his eyes as he put his hands up to rub his face.

He noticed a plastic bag on the back of the chair that Paul had been sitting in. He opened the bag and pulled out Nick's boxing gloves.

"I guess Paul was going to give these to us," Ronny said as he moved them around in his hands.

"He loved boxing," said Chad as he shook his head slowly. *I wonder if Paul told Santo Diaz that Nick is dead*. The sadness and anger rose as Ronny squeezed the gloves tightly. Chad put his hand on top of Ronny's forearm. He let the pressure on the gloves go.

"Why would Nick do that?" Chad asked.

"Because he couldn't see a way out. It all got to be too much for him." Ronny felt overwhelmed with emotion. He closed his eyes as warm tears ran down his cheeks. This didn't need to happen. For a moment he thought he might throw up. He went to the bathroom and splashed some cold water on his face trying to wake himself up out of the nightmare that was once again his reality. Nick couldn't fight anymore. Ronny felt guilty for not acting sooner to help Nick. That could have been Milo. Tears mixed with the cold water as he splashed his face again. He reached for a towel and put it against his face; he pushed his face hard into it and let out a muffled scream.

"You okay, man?" asked Chad who was still sitting at the table.

"No, I'm not." Ronny opened his eyes with a focused clarity. "I can't just sit back anymore and do nothing. It's not right. I need to do something about Santo so he can't do this to anyone else," exclaimed Ronny.

"He's untouchable. How the hell do you think you can stop him."

"This has happened to so many guys, and the agency is aware of it and lets it continue." He thought about Ella and what had happened with Pedro Argenta. 'I didn't have any evidence,' he remembered she said. *How can I get evidence?*

"You said it yourself; sometimes you need to do things to survive, or in this case get work," Chad said in a frustrated tone.

"I know I said that, but is it really the way it has to be? Getting harassed to get to where you want to go. Are you cool with that?" Ronny exclaimed in an aggravated tone as he looked at Chad. "Because I'm not. Not anymore." He stopped himself, realizing he was taking his frustration out on Chad. "Sorry, man." Ronny sat on his bed and put his head in his hands. Slowly he lifted his head and looked at his photographs on the wall. "I might have an idea."

"How do you feel about your appointment with Santo?" Ronny asked.

"I'm trying not to think about it." Chad sounded despondent. Ronny looked at him. He looked broken.

"I have a plan to help us blackmail Santo Diaz for good so he can never touch anyone like that ever again."

"How the hell are you going to do that? Hold him at gun point?" Chad replied sarcastically.

"Not exactly at gunpoint." Chad looked at Ronny with a perplexed expression as he continued. "I know this guy, Jose, who works at the photo lab I go to. He's a real camera buff and he just got this new video camcorder in. My plan is simple. Before your appointment with Santo, I'm going to call Paul and tell him you've got food poisoning and won't stop throwing up and that you can't make it. I'll convince him to let me go in your place so I can apologize to Santo for our last meeting when I pushed him into the bathroom wall in Rio." Ronny was talking quickly. Chad sat listening with a bewildered look on his face.

"You're sounding crazy, man." Chad replied.

"I heard from Josh that whenever a new male model is requested to meet Santo at his studio, he asks to do a naked test shoot to see if he wants to continue working with them. He will push you as far as you will go, and depending on how far that is it will impact the jobs you do or don't get. He does it to everyone, and the agents are aware but don't say anything because of the commission money they get from the models' jobs. Santo is too powerful."

Chad shook his head and listened in silence to Ronny's words. He shuffled uncomfortably in his seat then stood up and moved to sit next to him. Ronny continued.

"So what I'm thinking is I'm going to have the video camcorder hidden in my backpack with a hole cut in the side so the camera can get a clear shot of whatever is going on. When he says he wants to take some photographs of me, I'll excuse myself, go to the toilet, and come back out with the video camcorder turned on. I'll then place the backpack facing in a direction where it will record everything that he does to me. I heard that Lucia, the *Italian STYLE* editor was betrayed by him several times. I can go to her with a copy of the tape and ask if she would help me blackmail Santo."

"How do you know that she will want to meet you? You realize that she works with Santo and could destroy you. You're putting everything at risk. This sounds insane!" Chad said in a frustrated tone. His face was red, and his eyes were bloodshot. Ronny looked up breathing heavily, then covered his face as he started sobbing. Finally, he took a breath and wiped his eyes as Chad put his hand on his shoulder. He struggled to get his words out.

"I can't sit back anymore and watch this. I need to do this to try and stop Santo and in turn hopefully other people who are doing the same thing. I know what I am risking and I'm not asking you to be involved. Just help me get the camcorder and let me take your place for the appointment. It's all on me. I need to do this for Nick." *For Milo. For my mother.* "Please help me."

Chad shook his head. "I'm worried about you. You're taking a huge risk. You've never used a video camcorder before, and you're going to try and film the biggest photographer in the world abusing you from a hole in your backpack." Chad sounding frustrated, and he looked shattered. When Ronny heard Chad describe his plan in a sentence, he had to admit it did sound insane.

"I know it sounds nuts, but that's why we are meeting my friend Jose, so I can learn how to use the camcorder. He said it was easy to use and works automatically."

"What if Santo discovers it? You will be in so much shit. He would have you kicked out of Milan, and you would be blacklisted and never have a chance to work in the industry again."

"I know the risk. I know. You have to ask yourself how many times you're going to be taken advantage of. Paul isn't going to protect us; he has an arrangement with Santo and turns a blind eye to what's happening. Look at what happened to Nick. It's bullshit."

"Fuck, man. I don't know. You seem to have a real vendetta against Santo."

Ronny paused for a moment. "I'm just done with what we are expected to deal with. I know it's part of it, but honestly it shouldn't be this fucking hard to get ahead." Ronny reflected back on his life realizing that abuse and being taken advantage of had been something he had always witnessed in his community and life. The harsh reality was for him to achieve success he had to be abused himself, just like Nick. Ronny was on the front-line witnessing people like him being harassed from all angles. *Am I taking all my frustrations out on Santo because of all the shit I've had to deal with? Is he the scapegoat for my life?*

"Ronny, I've never done anything illegal in my life."

"Don't think of this as illegal; think of it as insurance against the shit we would have to deal with working with him. You heard what Josh said happened to him. Are you ok with that?" Chad looked shellshocked. "Just come meet Jose and let's check out the video camcorder then see how you feel."

"This is making me really feel uncomfortable."

"Trust me, please trust me." Ronny squeezed Chad's tense shoulder.

## CHAPTER 31

When they arrived at Foto Aldo later that morning, Chad reluctantly handed over his credit card, and he and Ronny followed Jose to the park to learn how to use the camcorder. After he explained the basic workings of the camera, Jose pointed to the auto settings on the side of it.

"Once you have it set on automatic, you push this button here to start recording. The lens is set to the standard setting, but you can zoom in if you need to. It will always focus automatically if it's set on auto."

"So you can hand hold it or put it on a tripod or some other surface and it will keep recording until you turn off that record button?" asked Ronny.

"Correct," Jose replied. "Let me show you." Jose placed the camcorder on the bench and stepped back to prove that it kept recording. "It will keep recording video and sound until you push stop or the tape runs out."

Jose passed the camera to Ronny, and he went through the steps to turn the camcorder on and start recording.

"Here's where you eject the tape," added Jose.

"So how can we play the video back?" asked Ronny as Chad stood back watching.

"I can take you back and show you the footage we just shot now on a monitor in my office."

"You can copy the tapes, right?" Ronny asked.

"Yep, just takes a few days, and the quality is the same."

Ronny was trying not to focus on things going wrong. Chad was right. If this didn't work and he was found out, he would never be able to work again in the business, either as a model or a photographer. In the same way Ella was blacklisted, Santo would destroy him. The reality set in, and he tried to drown out the voices in his head telling him not to do it.

When they got back to Jose's desk, he inserted the video tape, and the moving images they had just recorded came up clearly on the screen, and the sound was crystal clear.

"You're all set. See you on Tuesday," said Jose as they left to head back to the Pola.

"What did you think?" asked Ronny as he and Chad walked together.

"It's easier to use than I thought, but I'm still not convinced about your plan. I feel sick just thinking about it." Chad added.

The weight of the situation left Ronny feeling sick as well. That evening they sat together with a couple of beers and went over the gameplan for Ronny's meeting with Santo.

"Are you nervous?" Chad asked.

Ronny paused for a moment. "Yes. I'm nervous. Nervous about something going wrong, nervous about being found out and losing everything I came here for. But honestly, I couldn't live with myself if I didn't try. I have to do this," Ronny replied as he squeezed Nick's boxing gloves that sat on the table. "I know I need to play along with the test shoot. I know it's not going to be easy, but I have to let him go through with the shoot and see how far he tries to push me." Ronny heard the words come out of his mouth, almost affirming to himself what the plan was. "The worse he looks and sounds, the better it is for us." He considered just how much abuse he would be able to deal with. The thought made his stomach turn.

Chad took a long swig on his beer. "You know, I have competed in some pretty intense wrestling matches, but nothing has got me as nervous as this plan of yours. I just feel like so many things can go wrong."

"Chad, you need to help me focus!" Ronny replied with a stern tone.

"You sound like one of my old coaches." Chad shook his head, took a swig of his beer, and looked back at Ronny. "You're like a crazed dog with a bone. I'm not happy about this plan of yours, but okay. I'm in. Now let's get this backpack and camera ready and consider anything that could go wrong."

Ronny and Chad sat talking at the table as Ronny cut open one side of the backpack he had bought at the small market down the road. He stitched the fabric around a bent wire coat hanger on the sides and bottom and left a piece of material hanging down from the top so the hole was concealed while he was wearing it on his back. Once inside Santo's bathroom he would be able to lift the flap and tape it up so the hole would be large enough for the lens and microphone to record what was happening.

"Nobody can know what we are doing," Ronny emphasized as Chad nodded his agreement. "If I get caught, just deny that you knew anything about it." He looked at the backpack. He could see the hole clearly and worried that Santo would as well. He wished Ella was there to give him some reassurance. *You got this…You got this.* Ronny spent most of the night lying on his bed watching the light reflections from the cars driving past on the street below dance across the ceiling. He could hear Chad occasionally tossing in his bed. *Am I doing the right thing? Maybe Chad's right and this plan is crazy.* So many scenarios played out in his head. What if he got caught? What if he had to go home to Brazil because BAM Models canceled his contract? What if Chad was guilty by association and lost his contract, too?

He wished there was someone he could speak to about all this, but then he thought of Brett and how fast gossip traveled in this industry. Ella was someone he trusted, but he worried she may try and talk him out of it after her experience with Pedro Argenta. He felt small. *Who am I to think I could change something about this business?* Then he thought about Milo and wondered what he would do if he were in Ronny's shoes. He got out of bed as quietly as he could, put on a T-shirt, and grabbed his wallet and headed down to the reception to call Milo.

"Buona serata," said Mateo as Ronny walked up to the reception desk.

He sat down near the phone in the corner and dialed Milo's number.

"Olá," Milo answered. Ronny felt relief hearing his voice. Milo always seemed to be there when he needed him.

"Ronny? Hey, man."

"How are you doing? It's so good to hear your voice."

"I'm good, bro. You okay? You sound distracted." Milo could always tell when Ronny had something on his mind.

"You remember that photographer Santo Diaz?" Ronny's tone was serious.

"The guy that shot the photos of us on the beach that day."

"Yeah, well, that night when I left the wrap party it was because he tried to assault me in the bathroom and offered me money for sex. I almost put him through a wall."

"Now I understand why you left so suddenly. The guys I knew that came along from the club said he always rents a few guys when he is in town to be on call."

"Yeah, well, it turns out he takes advantage of most of the guys he photographs for the big jobs. He shoots them naked and sees how far he can push them. If you let him have his way with you, then you stand a chance of being booked for the job. I will be seeing him this week and chances are he will want to shoot me naked and try to take advantage of me as well."

"Can't you tell the model agency that brought you to Milan so you don't need to deal with that?"

"They know this goes on and they just accept it. If their model gets the jobs, they make the commission. A guy I know just went through this with him and ended up committing suicide." Ronny paused.

"That's fucked up. I'm sorry to hear that. What are you going to do?"

"I came up with a crazy plan to put an end to this bullshit." Milo was quiet, and Ronny could tell he was listening. "I was going to use a hidden video camera to record him abusing me and use that to blackmail him. But I know there's a risk of getting caught."

"That's brave, man. Are you going to be okay to put yourself through that?" Milo asked as Ronny went silent as he considered what he was doing.

"I can't just sit back and do nothing. Do you think I'm crazy?"

"I think we are both a little crazy. But I know you wouldn't do this if you didn't believe it could work. Trust yourself."

In the back of his mind, he knew he would get Milo's support. He was a survivor and a hustler and a good reminder for Ronny of where he came from and what was at stake. He came to Milan to make this work, but what he discovered here wasn't something he could deal with in silence anymore. He had reached a tipping point, and something had to change. His latest photographs gave him a new confidence to consider that maybe Milan wasn't the only market for him, so if he got kicked out, he had options.

"I just needed to hear someone I trust tell me I wasn't nuts," Ronny continued.

"You left Rio to find a better life for yourself and to follow your passion. You need to go for what you believe in."

He knew Milo was right; he understood the risks and knew what he had to do. "I love you, bro. Wish me luck, man.

"You don't need luck, just balls. Ciao, my friend."

Ronny hung up the phone and headed up to his room and got back into bed. He felt nervous about the day ahead, but speaking to Milo had helped give him the courage to see his plan through. *I need to do this.*

# CHAPTER 32

When he woke up and opened his eyes he paused for a moment, wondering if it was all a dream, until he sat up and saw Chad staring at the ceiling with a serious expression and realized it was all very real.

"Ronny, you'll have to tell Jose what we're doing when you bring back the tapes; otherwise, what the heck is he going to think if he sees the footage when he is copying it? He might freak out and think we are making porn or something weird," Chad declared with an urgency in his voice as the they drank their coffee.

"I will talk to him." Ronny realized Chad was right. He had met Jose only a few times, and his boyfriend was a big model agent. He felt he could trust him, but there was a chance he would talk to someone about what Ronny had done. It would be a disaster to not control who knew about or saw the tape. The morning slowly dragged on until finally it was an hour from the time of Chad's appointment at Santo's house. Ronny took a deep breath, considering one last time what he stood to lose. He stood up, and as he went to push in the dining chair to the small table, he noticed Nick's boxing gloves hanging on the back of the chair..

Chad sat on his bed as Ronny rang the agency.

"Ciao. It's Ronny. Could I have Paul, please? Grazie." Ronny waited patiently.

"Ciao?" Paul replied. He sounded busy.

"Hi Paul. I rang to let you know that Chad has just come down with food poisoning and he has been throwing up in the bathroom."

"Is he okay?"

"He said he will be fine; he just needs to rest. I know he had that appointment in an hour with Santo Diaz."

"I can just reschedule it for him."

"Well, I was wondering if you could ask Santo if I would be able to come in Chad's place to personally thank him for the photo shoot we did in Rio and show him my new portfolio. I'd really appreciate it, Paul, if you could do me a favor and get me in for a meeting with him. I could be there at the same time Chad was supposed to be."

"I'll check and call you back if that works for him." Paul hung up. Ronny sat in silence with Chad waiting for Paul to call back. After five minutes Ronny stood up.

"Guess it's not happening." His heart sank as walked to the kitchen. Suddenly the phone rang.

"He can see you," Paul said.

"Great. I'll get the address from Chad."

"I don't have to tell you how important this is. Don't let me down."

"I really appreciate this. Thank you," Ronny said as Paul hung up the phone. "He will see me," he said as he turned to Chad, who stood speechless. Ronny felt a little sick in his stomach now that this was becoming real. He took a deep breath trying to calm his nerves and focus. He got changed into a fitted black tank top and jeans and collected his portfolio and put it in the backpack.

"I made the backpack hole a little larger so there's no issue with sound," said Ronny as he fussed with the backpack.

"It's all good. You want me to go with you to his house?"

"I'm okay." Ronny embraced Chad.

"You crazy motherfucker. You got this, you know that! I'll be here by the phone if you need anything. Just let me know." Chad patted Ronny on the back as he left the room.

As Ronny walked toward the subway, his hands were sweating. His head was filled with a mix of emotions, including anxiety and fear that he may be caught and kicked out of Milan and have to go back to Brazil. As he rode the subway, he felt alone. He remembered feeling like this after he'd been kicked out of his parents' house. He looked up to see an old Italian man sitting opposite and staring at him; the old man nodded and smiled, his smile creating even more wrinkles on his face. He wished he had his camera with him so he could have captured the man's face. Ronny smiled back at the man and was reminded why he came to Milan—for his passion for photography and his need to capture images just like this one. Today he could lose that chance.

He took a mental photograph of the man's face as the train finally reached the subway stop in the wealthy Sempione district where Santo Diaz's house was located. He walked out of the subway and immediately noticed how green and manicured the neighborhood was and how beautiful the homes were. He checked the address on the paper he got from Chad and started walking down the block. He could feel his heart beating in his chest as he eventually arrived at the impressive stone villa with a large white wall in front with a security gate and cameras. He stood for a moment in front of the gate, wiped his sweaty palms on his pants, and then rang the buzzer. A few seconds later the gate lock clicked open and he entered the compound. As he walked up the grand steps toward the ornate entry, a handsome man in his late twenties with dark hair and blue eyes opened the door to greet him wearing a pair of white shorts and a white tank top.

"You must be Ronny. Ciao. I'm Paolo, Santo's personal assistant, please come in."

"Nice to meet you." Ronny smiled politely and walked inside, glancing up at the chandelier above the marble foyer.

"Here, let me take your bag."

"I'll hold onto my backpack. Thanks." He pulled back sharply from Paulo's hand as he reached for his backpack before laughing nervously, trying to seem like everything was fine. *Fuck!*

Paolo stood there with a blank expression before responding. "Santo is out at the pool. Please follow me." Paolo led Ronny through the grand foyer, around a marble statue of a male nude in the center of the room, and down the hallway. The villa was perfectly styled with vintage Moroccan rugs covering the floor, a large white leather sofa, and round glass coffee table with vases overflowing with flowers. Large paintings of landscapes and portraits hung on the walls in ornate gilded frames mixed with framed photographs shot by Diaz. Ronny was momentarily distracted by a Basquiat painting he had seen in a magazine. *Fuck, that's an original!* Ronny thought to himself as he walked through the opulent living area. In the distance he could hear people cheering, water splashing, and dogs barking. He took a deep breath and followed Paolo out through a large sliding door.

The pool area was lush and private with sun loungers positioned around a chic modern pool in the center. Three well-built naked young guys were swimming and playing with four well-groomed white standard poodles who were barking and jumping in and out of the pool. Santo was lounging on the other side of the pool in a Mancini robe with a cocktail in one hand and camera in the other. The sight of Santo waving refocused Ronny back to why he was there.

"Hey, Ronny!" called out one of the naked guys in the pool with the poodles.

"Josh? Oh, hey." Ronny was surprised to see Josh here, especially after his last experience with Santo when he was taken advantage of in the shower. Santo must have dangled a big carrot for a new campaign or magazine shoot to get him back. His mind raced as he surveyed the scene. *What about the plan? What does this change?* Santo got up from his chaise, put his camera down, and sauntered around the pool to greet Ronny. He smiled widely as he approached Ronny with an overly confident demeanor.

"Well, hello...what a surprise. So nice of you to come by," Santo said in his thick Latin accent as he slowly kissed Ronny on both cheeks. "I was wondering when I would see you again." Santo looked like the cat that got the cream. His skin was overly tanned and oiled, and his body lean. He ran his hand over his slicked back hair before removing his large purple sunglasses.

"Thanks for seeing me. I wanted to come and personally apologize for leaving your party so quickly in Rio and hope you will forgive me." He was hoping Santo had been too high at their last meeting to remember that he had almost pushed him through a bathroom wall after he groped his crotch. He tried to remain calm and deliver an apology that sounded genuine.

"I'm glad you came by. I loved shooting you in Brazil and would obviously love to work with you again." His voice was smooth and charming; his dark brown eyes traveled down from Ronny's eyeline to his body. His face became warm, and his heart felt like it was going to beat out of his chest. *Just breathe.*

"Coco! Lucy!" Santo called out to the two poodles fighting beside the pool. He rolled his eyes and smiled back at Ronny and took a slow deep sniff through his nose. Paolo appeared from inside the house carrying a tray filled with two cocktails, a bowl of olives, and a plate with a few lines of cocaine and a joint on it.

"Santo, there is a call for you. It's Marina from *French STYLE* magazine," said Paolo as he arrived with the tray.

"Excuse me for a moment. Help yourself, and I'll be right back." Santo felt Ronny's arm before walking inside. Ronny let out a deep sigh, realizing he had been holding his breath. He walked toward Josh and crouched down next to the pool.

"Hey, man. How you feeling?"

Josh swam over to the side of the pool where he was. "I'm great, man. I got a new tooth, and Santo is putting me up for the Mancini campaign."

"I thought you hated him? That story you told me about how he treated you in the shower?"

Josh reached for one of the cocktails Paolo had on his tray. "Hey, man, work is work. It's an amazing opportunity, and hell, maybe Annika is right. If I focused more on my career instead of pussy and partying things might be different."

He could tell by the way Josh was clenching his jaw and talking that he had been doing cocaine. He had been sucked back into Diaz's world and now he would do whatever it took to get another job and a paycheck. Ronny was reminded how much he was risking. *Maybe this isn't the right time. Fuck!*

"You should do a line. The coke is amazing," Josh said and then turned back to the other two guys in the pool. "Ronny, this is Donal and Brian." The guys waved as Brian positioned himself naked on an inflatable flamingo.

"Hey, you coming in?" Donal called out. Ronny smiled and gave an uncomfortable laugh. The whole scenario was starting to freak him out as questions raced through his mind. *What if Santo wants me to get in the pool naked with these guys and the poodles? Do I still turn on the camera?* Santo walked back out from the house.

"Sorry, a small drama with the *French STYLE* editor. She hates the hair on the latest cover I just shot and she wants to see more options. Fuck!"

"You have a beautiful home here," Ronny said.

"It's small, but I love the pool and so do the children." Santo looked toward the poodles as they continued swimming around. "Where's my manners? Did you get a drink?"

"I'll just have a water, thank you," Ronny replied.

"Paolo, can Ronny pleeease have a water."

"Still or sparkling?" asked Paolo as he appeared from nowhere.

"Huh? Oh, still. Thank you." *Maybe I should have a drink to help me relax,* Ronny thought to himself but decided to keep his head straight.

Santo turned to Josh, Brian, and Donal. "Why don't you boys dry off. I have an appointment with Ronny, and I need to do some work. We can continue the shoot with the children next week." The guys got out of the pool in all their naked glory and started drying themselves off.

"Paolo, can you dry the children please. The blow dryer is behind the bar. Grazie." Paolo appeared with a fresh basket of white towels and the blow dryer ready to dry off the poodles.

"Ronny, why don't you come inside where we can be comfortable," suggested Santo as he put his hand on Ronny's lower back. It took all his focus to not flinch and move away from his touch. Santo's hand lingered as Ronny turned back to the guys next to the pool. He waved goodbye to Josh as he walked back inside the house. He took a deep breath, trying to refocus himself. Paolo handed him a glass of water as he walked through the doors.

Can I do this? Can I really do this?

## CHAPTER 33

"Down here in my studio. It's quieter there," said Santo as Ronny followed him down the hall to a large modern white room with lots of natural light pouring in through huge black framed windows and a skylight. The floors and walls were all white, and in the center was a large leather couch, a glass coffee table covered in photography books, and against the wall next to a long desk were some studio lights, some photo equipment, and a few empty clothes racks next to several full-length mirrors. It was hard not to be impressed by the slick setup.

"Come sit down and show me your portfolio to refresh my memory," said Santo as he moved toward the couch and sat down, still with a drink in his hand. Ronny followed his lead and joined him on the couch. He put the backpack down in front of him and opened it to retrieve his portfolio that was sitting next to the video camcorder. He swallowed another huge lump in his throat. After he had passed Santo his portfolio, he noticed a generous mound of cocaine on the table on a gold tray with a small gold spoon on the side.

"Help yourself," said Santo after he noticed Ronny looking at the table. He just smiled politely. "Do you miss Brazil?" Santo continued; his expression became more serious as he opened Ronny's portfolio, sniffed loudly, and started looking at the photos.

"I miss my friends." Ronny paused briefly. "My family." He saw his mother's face; he felt his face getting warmer and tried to think of something else.

"I love Brazil and I loved these pictures we shot in Rio—so sexy. Paul talks highly of you, Ronny, and so does Lorenzo Mancini." Santo took a sip of his drink, put it down on the table next to him, and crossed his legs. The robe rode higher on his leg, and Ronny realized he wasn't wearing anything underneath it; his hands started sweating. Santo continued to peruse the portfolio and paused on one of the shots that he had taken of him on the beach.

"I love this photo, your expression, the light, your body. It's stunning. I know that Lorenzo booked you for the show because of these photographs, and then he talked to me about considering you for the Mancini campaign. What do you think about that?" Santo sniffed loudly.

"That would be incredible." He had mixed emotions as he sat there, trying to remain calm and focus on his plan. It was hard not to be distracted by Santo as he discussed the prospect of being shot for the Mancini campaign that would see his face and body featured all around the world. This would launch him in a major way as a model and give him a huge paycheck. Ronny found himself considering Santo's proposition. Then he considered this was probably the same pitch that he had given to Josh, Nick and who knows how many other young hopeful models.

"Lorenzo loves the idea of launching a new face and he feels that your face and body fits perfectly with his brand and represent where this industry is going. I must admit I was never a fan of grunge. Skinny, dirty models aren't really my idea of sexy. I'm sure you're familiar with my work?" asked Santo as he motioned to the coffee table in front that had several of his photography books on display.

"You have captured some incredible photographs. Especially with Lucia for *Italian STYLE* magazine." Ronny was a genuine fan of Santo's until he saw what went on behind the scenes of his beautiful photographs.

"Ah yes, Lucia. I have definitely created some amazing work for her." He noticed the way he responded when he heard her name and could sense there was tension there. Santo paused and looked up. "So, you know I am the one who shoots the Mancini campaign, and it's important that I'm confident that who I am shooting can give me what the campaign needs, especially this campaign as it's all about sensuality and the celebration of male sexuality. Mancini is launching the first male supermodel and whoever that is will be recognized all around the world." Santo looked back through the portfolio again and left it open on the coffee table on a shirtless photograph of Ronny. Santo pointed to the open portfolio.

"This is the kind of guy that we are looking for. This is the guy we need for the campaign." Santo sat back on the couch and finished off the rest of his cocktail before standing up. "I'd like to take some test photographs of you. Why don't you go and stand over there against the wall near the window." Santo walked to his desk to get his camera.

"Sure, can I just use the bathroom quickly?"

"In the corner over there," replied Santo as he pointed to the corner of the room. Ronny stood up, grabbed the backpack, and headed to the bathroom. He entered the large marble bathroom, turned around and locked the door. For a moment he stood with his back toward the door and took a deep breath, reminding himself this would all be over soon. He walked to the sink and turned on the cold water and splashed his face a few times. He wiped up the water and dried his face with the linen hand towel that was on the sink. He took a final look in the mirror to reassure himself.

He lifted the backpack up onto the counter and opened the zip and reached inside to make sure the camera was okay and in the right position; then he lifted up the flap on the side of the backpack and secured it with tape so the camera would have a clear shot. Ronny stood back from the backpack to look to see if he could notice the camera inside the opening and he felt a sense of relief that he couldn't. He opened the backpack one more time to push record on the camcorder, zipped the bag back up, and flushed the toilet before walking back into the studio carefully carrying the backpack.

Santo was back at the coffee table finishing off a large spoonful of cocaine with a strong sniff. Ronny quickly went over near the wall where Santo had asked him to stand and placed his backpack next to the window with the camera facing where he thought he would be standing so it wasn't too far away. He knew what was about to happen and the anticipation was causing him to feel cold and start to shiver. At least the camera was now in place. He stood against the wall as Santo collected his camera and turned up the music that had been playing softly in the background. *Shit. What if the music is too loud and his voice can't be heard on the tape?* Ronny could feel his hands starting to sweat again as Santo moved toward him.

"Okay, let's take off the top," said Santo as he stood watching Ronny remove it. "Ah, I remember that body. Let me see you lean against the wall and relax," purred Santo.

Relaxing was the last thing on Ronny's mind. He was tense and regretted not having a cocktail. His body continued shivering uncontrollably as he took a deep breath.

"I need you to relax. I want you to imagine we are shooting the Mancini campaign. I need sexy. I need you to give that to me through the lens. Let me feel it." Santo snapped off a few photographs then moved in closer. "That's better. Look towards the window, now bring your eyes back to me."

Ronny began to get into the zone giving Santo some of the looks he had been asking for. He had more modeling and photography experience since they shot together in Brazil, and he managed to give a series of poses that Santo liked. Ronny knew if things didn't go well, this would probably be the last time he would shoot with a big photographer in a studio like this.

"Better," Santo responded. "Now run your fingers through your hair, that's it, chin down and bring your eyes back to me, yes, yes. Bellissimo."

Suddenly there was a knock at the door. Ronny's heart stopped for a moment. *What now?*

"I'm busy, Paolo," Santo yelled in a stern voice.

Paolo opened the door slightly and spoke loudly to be heard over the loud music. "Santo, sorry to disturb you but Marina is on the phone again and she says its urgent."

"Fuck! Tell her I will call her back in an hour. I'm sure it can wait." Three of the poodles burst through the slightly opened door and into the studio. "Paolo! You need to keep the children outside. Now come in quickly and get them out." The poodles ran around the studio, play fighting with each other. Paolo came into the studio and tried to control them, but it wasn't easy. They ran over near where Ronny was standing and started wrestling near the window. Ronny watched as they rolled around on each other and managed to knock over the backpack and roll on top of it. *No!* He wondered if the camera had been damaged or turned off and if the flap was still not covering the lens.

"Paolo! The children!" screamed Santo as Paolo finally managed to catch the dogs and leave the studio. Santo followed Paolo and locked the door behind him after he left the room. Ronny seized that opportunity to quickly go over to the window and reposition the backpack and check that the flap was up, hoping the camera was still okay.

"I apologize for the interruption. Now where were we? Why don't you lose the jeans and I'll get a light ready." While Ronny took off his pants, Santo pulled out one of the lights on a stand, put it right in front of Ronny, and turned it on. The light was bright; Ronny momentarily closed his eyes. Santo went to the wall to push a control button; the window blinds dropped, and the skylight closed so the only light in the room came from the light Santo had just turned on.

"Santo, could we please turn down the music? My hearing isn't great, and I don't want to miss any direction," Ronny asked as Santo rolled his eyes and went to turn down the music.

"I believe you have the potential to go all the way and I can help you. I know you want to do well in this business," Santo said in his charming voice as he came in closer to him. Ronny couldn't see his face; he was silhouetted against the bright light. "All these campaigns I shoot, all these magazine editorials and all these clients. Their work is nothing without me. I have the final say on who is cast, who becomes a star. That could be you."

## CHAPTER 34

He could feel Santo was standing really close to him now.

"I need you to take a deep breath in, close your eyes, and relax for me." Santo directed. Ronny did as he asked and breathed in deeply. "Open your eyes." Santo reached out and touched him between the eyebrows. "I need you to relax this." He moved his hand down and placed it on his stomach. "And I want you to tense this."

Ronny tensed his abdominal muscles as Santo brought his gaze back up from Ronny's stomach to his face. He repeated the same direction a few times, and each time his hand got slightly lower on his stomach. A cold shiver went through his body and his teeth started rattling. He clamped his jaw down biting into the inside of his cheeks to distract his body from shivering.

"Let's take off the underwear," Santo said quietly as Ronny slowly blinked. *Was that what you asked Nick to do?* Ronny felt the anger inside him rise as he seriously wondered if he would be able to go through with this and not lash out at Santo and ruin everything.

"Why do I need to do this naked?" asked Ronny, hoping the level of his voice could be heard by the camcorder.

"Because I need to know you trust me." Santo took a few steps back so he could watch as Ronny slowly removed his briefs and let his hands come together to cover himself.

"I'm feeling a bit uncomfortable," Ronny added, knowing he was being recorded.

Santo came back in close again and repeated, "I need you to relax this and tense this. Relax this and tense this. Breathe, just breathe." He again touched him between his eyebrows and when it came time to touch his abdominal area for the final time, his hand brushed down touching his penis. Ronny froze as Santo moved back again and started to take some more photographs of him standing naked in front of him. Ronny tried as best he could to cover himself with his leg or his hand. After a few more shots Santo moved back in closer to him again.

"Your power is in your energy, and I need you to connect to where that energy is in your body. Put your hand where you feel the energy. Close your eyes and show me where you feel it."

He closed his eyes and lifted one hand up away from his crotch and placed it on his chest. He remembered what Josh had told them and knew where this was going.

"Now move your hand to where you feel the energy now. I want you to feel it."

Ronny moved his hand from one side of his chest to the other. Santo took his own hand and placed it on Ronny's. Ronny opened his eyes.

"I want you to feel where it's flowing. Find your power." Santo moved Ronny's hand down from his chest to his abdominal area. "Feel the energy, breathe into the energy." Slowly he guided his hand across his torso to the other side of his stomach and then very slowly down to touch his pubic hair. "Feel it." Santo guided Ronny's hand down farther onto his penis.

Ronny felt a deep knot in his stomach. He felt pain as he bit harder into his cheek and closed his eyes. Santo started to apply pressure to Ronny's hand, massaging his penis, encouraging it to get hard. The feeling of being violated was all consuming, he wanted to break down and scream.

"Stay there. Feel it," directed Santo as he moved back and proceeded to take some more photos. "Now open your mouth for me. Wider." Ronny swallowed the blood that was in his mouth from biting his cheek and opened his mouth as Santo moved in closer again and brought his hand up to touch Ronny's face. "Wider."

Ronny obliged as Santo slowly inserted two fingers into his mouth. Ronny closed his eyes, tasting cigarettes and cologne on his fingers mixed with the lingering taste of his own blood. *How much more of this can I stand?* He wanted to gag or clamp down and bite off Santo's fingers. The anger and humiliation he felt were boiling up to breaking point.

"The world is waiting for you, Ronny, and I'm going to bring you to them." Santo let his fingers stroke the top of Ronny's tongue as he slowly removed them now that they were moist. He brushed them over Ronny's lips to moisten them, and slowly he pulled back and let his hand travel down over Ronny's chest, massaging his firm pectoral muscle before letting his hand travel lower onto Ronny's dick.

Ronny felt sick. The tears he had been fighting welled up in his eyes and he was about to lose it. He bit down hard on his cheek again and sliced it open. He welcomed the pain that distracted him away from the torture he was subjecting himself to. The blood flowed freely inside his mouth as he swallowed. *How much more of this do I need on video? How much more can I stand?*

"I want you to touch yourself like this. Show me," Santo said as he massaged Ronny's penis in his hand, trying to arouse him, then proceeded to move back away from Ronny who could barely see Santo in the bright light. "Keep going, Ronny. Use your other hand to move up behind your neck and take your head back. Yes, that's it, that's it. Open your mouth. Again. Wider."

The camera kept clicking, but Ronny sensed that Santo was masturbating while he watched Ronny touching himself. Santo went silent. Ronny stood there powerless, unable to move, unable to scream. Unable to fight.

"Bellissimo," Santo said as he closed his robe and walked away toward his desk to put down his camera.

Suddenly the blinds came back up, filling the room with light. It was like waking up abruptly out of a nightmare that was over as soon as it had begun. Ronny stopped touching himself and felt physically numb and humiliated...broken. He quickly got dressed, wanting to get out of there as fast as he could. He swallowed the blood pooling up in his mouth and walked over to get his backpack, noticing that Santo was back at his desk wiping his hands on a towel. *Creep!* He felt violated, lost, and alone. He wiped the tears from his eyes and started walking to the door in a daze, in shock.

Santo turned around as he was leaving. "I will be seeing you again soon, I'm sure."

Ronny didn't respond, sensing that this was probably the end of his time in Milan. *I'm done. On so many levels.*

## CHAPTER 35

As Ronny walked across the foyer, he was stopped in his tracks when he heard Paolo's voice. "There's a hole in your backpack."

Ronny's heart stopped. "Huh?"

"Your wallet is on the floor; it must have fallen out." Paolo added.

"Oh yeah, thanks." Ronny breathed a sigh of relief. *Now let me get the fuck out of here.*

Ronny retrieved his wallet and turned to walk quickly out the front door and headed down the street in a daze, sweating, relieved that it was over. He spat out a mouthful of saliva and blood. The sounds around him were muffled, almost like he was in a dream. *What just happened?* He shook his head. He stopped in his tracks, bent over with his hands on his knees, and spat again. The taste of Santo's fingers and the blood lingered. For a moment he felt he might actually throw up. He sat down on a step and began to sob uncontrollably. The heat he felt in his head was intense, and he wanted to scream out the feeling of being violated. *Never again. It's over.*

Eventually the tears subsided as he slowly raised his head. In the distance he could see Chad walking toward him. He wiped his face a few times on his shirt.

"Hey, man, are you okay?" Chad asked in a concerned tone. He crouched down next to Ronny and put his arm around his shoulder; he made a muffled noise as if he were holding back tears in the face of what Ronny had endured in his place.

"I need a shower," Ronny eventually replied. It took his remaining strength to sound like he was doing okay and make light of the situation. "I'm surprised to see you here. I thought you had food poisoning?"

"Yeah, I feel a lot better." Chad wiped his eyes and smiled. "So, did you manage to get anything?"

"Fuck, the camera!" Ronny took off the backpack and unzipped it. He checked the camcorder inside, and it was still recording; he had forgotten to turn it off. He pushed the stop button on the camcorder and looked up at Chad.

"I think it worked, but I'm not sure. His poodles ran into the studio and knocked over the backpack. I tried to fix it but I don't know if the camera was okay." Chad embraced Ronny and slapped him on the back.

"You're a crazy Brazilian motherfucker," said Chad as they started walking back toward the metro. On the way back Ronny told Chad the story of what happened with Santo. Chad was silent for some time, letting the story sink in. Ronny could tell he was visibly shaken and probably relieved.

"I don't know how you did it, man. I don't know if I could have handled that, not for any campaign. Makes me sick trying to imagine going through that. I'm sorry." Chad added.

Ronny knew it would take time for him to really get over the ordeal. Chad put his arm around Ronny's shoulder; he didn't need to say anything. If he managed to capture the footage and he was able to use it to blackmail Santo, things may change; if not he would need to leave Milan. This had finally broken him, and he had had enough.

"If we hurry we can still make the lab before it closes. I need to see if I have something," Ronny said with urgency as they changed trains. Soon they arrived at Foto Aldo to meet Jose.

"Ciao, boys," called out Jose who had just finished up with a customer when he saw them enter. "How amazing is that camera!"

"Hey, man." Ronny sounded worried. "Yeah, it's great. I hope we managed to get some good footage." *Any footage.* Jose signaled to the guys to come in back with the camcorder. As the guys got settled around the monitor, Jose retrieved the tape, and inserted it into the player and rewound it. As it was rewinding Ronny put his hand on Jose's shoulder and spoke in Portuguese.

"Jose, I need to be honest with you. As you know Chad and I are here modeling, and powerful people are taking advantage of young models like us every day. Chad and I have been taken advantage of already, and we came up with a plan to film the people who were doing this to us and use it to blackmail them and try to stop this from happening."

Jose listened carefully with a serious expression on his face, nodding occasionally.

"The tapes show a very powerful photographer abusing me. I wanted to tell you about this because we need your help. We need to make sure the tapes are good quality and then have them copied without anybody knowing what we are doing. You can never tell anyone that you were in some way a part of this." Ronny left his hand on Jose's shoulder. Jose put his hand on Ronny's hand and squeezed it.

"Ronny, I think you're so brave. I know this goes on in the business for both girls and guys, and I am here to do whatever I can to help you. You have my word. Let me get you get set up here, teach you how the player works, and I will leave you to it. I can do as many copies of the tape as you need. I'll just be out front if you need me."

Ronny sensed that Jose would understand his circumstance. He knew he could be trusted. Jose left the room.

"Are you cool with me being here to watch the tape? I understand if you want to watch it by yourself," said Chad. Ronny realized what he might see and took a deep breath.

"We are in this together," he replied as he pushed play. Suddenly a shaky image appeared, then stabilized. He felt a wave of relief start to wash over him, but he couldn't relax until he saw the footage after the dogs came in. "This is where I carried the backpack from the bathroom." Eventually the camera stabilized. Ronny could be seen walking away from the camera and leaning against the wall. The framing was right, and the picture was clear. *Looks good,* Ronny thought. Then the music volume went up and Ronny was seen removing his shirt. Santo's voice couldn't be heard. *I knew that music was too loud.* Santo appeared on the edge of screen, appearing to take some photographs of Ronny. This continued for a moment until Santo could be heard yelling at Paolo and then the poodles appeared running on the far side of the set and moved close to the camera until finally rolling into the backpack and knocking it over.

He held his breath and Chad was silent. A few moments later the camera image moved again as Ronny tried to quickly reposition the backpack. Ronny watched in disbelief as he saw himself move back from the camera and out of frame to the left soon followed by Santo. The camera continued to record, but the new framing just missed where Ronny stood with Santo and filmed in the direction of the equipment area where nothing could be seen.

"No!" Ronny gasped. He sat down in the chair that was in front of Jose's desk and slumped over the desk. Eventually he lifted his head and smashed his fist down on his leg. He was crushed. Chad put his hand on his shoulder. The only saving grace was that the music was turned down and you could hear Santo speaking to Ronny, but without the visual it wasn't that damning. Ronny and Chad watched in silence as the tape played on. The studio went dark when the blinds were lowered, and only the dialogue between Santo and Ronny could be heard—an eerie reminder of what he had endured. After what felt like an eternity, the blinds went up and the backpack was lifting up, taken outside, and eventually the recording was turned off.

"You okay, man?" Chad asked in a soft tone.

"I can't believe it. I had it, and those fucking poodles knocked it over." Ronny rubbed his face with his hands. "What a waste." He felt despondent, angry, and violated. *All for nothing. Fuck!*

"Sorry, Ronny," said Chad quietly.

Ronny sat up, took a deep breath, and removed the tape from the player and cleared his throat; the disappointment he felt over the tape was consuming him. He didn't think he could feel any lower. Jose knocked softly on the door.

"How did the tape look? Did you get everything you needed?" he asked.

"Well, the camera angle was bumped and wasn't able to film what I needed."

"What about the audio? Does that help?" asked Jose.

"I don't know. I honestly don't know."

"Let me see if I can make the audio clearer so at least you have that. I'm really sorry you didn't get everything you need."

"Obrigado, meu irmão," Ronny replied as Jose moved forward and embraced him. He felt like an old friend.

"What did you say to him?" asked Chad as they left and walked back out onto the street.

"Thank you, my brother."

Back in their room Ronny had a long shower and decided to head to bed early.

"Do you want any food?" Chad asked.

"Thanks, but I'm pretty exhausted. I need to close my eyes on this day." Ronny lay on the bed, took a final look up at his photographs on the wall, and closed his eyes. He thought about a plan B, but without the visuals the evidence was nowhere near as strong and could be debunked by Santo. If he never mentioned the tape, then nobody would know he had tried to record it and he could continue to model and try and work. As he thought about work, though, he felt hopeless; he knew he could never put himself through what happened with Santo again.

He tried to distract himself remembering that Ella arrived back from her trip tomorrow. *How much should I tell her?* He realized that he had in fact missed her and looked forward to seeing her again. So much of his life felt uncertain that it felt reassuring to know he had real feelings for her.

# CHAPTER 36

The following morning the phone rang. It was Paul.

"Hi, Paul," Ronny said.

"Okay, you have a bunch of new go-see appointments this week, and of course you both have the Mancini show later today and the party afterwards. Santo Diaz has put you on hold for the Mancini campaign. He says he was really pleased with the test you did for him, I'm glad it went well. He said he may need to see you one more time before he makes a final recommendation to the designer."

Just hearing the sound of Santo's name was enough to turn his stomach and bring on a new wave of anxiety. "Am I the only person on hold for Mancini from the agency?" Ronny asked. Paul paused before continuing.

"There's a few guys he's interested in, but he said you're a favorite."

He knew that Santo would be using the Mancini campaign as a bargaining tool in order for him to take advantage of many other male models who were keen to get his favour.

"I almost forgot to mention that Chad showed me the contact sheet of the photos you did for him and they're really great. I knew you took photos for a hobby, but these are really strong; you definitely have the eye for it. I'd like to show the other bookers and talk to you about testing some of our other guys if you're interested."

"Sure. Thanks," Ronny replied. He wasn't as excited as he would have been if the Santo incident hadn't happened. He wondered if he had in fact released the tape of Santo what would happen to these sorts of opportunities. Would he be kicked out of the agency? Maybe kicked out of town? He thought back to Ella's story and how she was blacklisted. *Was it worth risking everything? Maybe there was a reason the video went awry?*

After Ronny got off the phone, Chad handed him a coffee. "How are you doing?" he asked.

"I thought I would be able to expose him. Change something." Ronny sounded helpless.

"I'm sorry, man. I wouldn't wish that experience with him on anyone."

Once they were dressed they walked out through the foyer of the Pola. Mama Pola looked up from her desk. "Ronny, there is a message for you from Jose at Foto Aldo. He rang while you were on the phone and asked if you could come by. He said it was really important."

"Probably something to do with the prints that Camille and Ella's agent are ordering. I wanted to order some more prints, too, so I can pass by there this morning," said Ronny to Chad. When he arrived at Foto Aldo, Francesco—the photographer that had tested him when he first came to Milan—was walking out the door.

"Oh hey, Francesco, good to see you."

"Ciao, Ronny. Nice to see you. Glad you're using Foto Aldo; they're really great."

"Yeah, I gathered you used these guys." For a moment he wondered if Jose knew that he knew Francesco and if he had told him anything.

"This is the only place I've actually ever used." Francesco smiled as he looked back toward the doorway. "Hey, how's your photography going?"

"Good! I've been testing and I'm just about to order some prints."

"Good for you, Ronny. Photograph what you love and keep shooting. See you soon. Ciao, Ronny." Francesco patted Ronny on the shoulder and headed off toward his parked vespa. *Nice guy,* thought Ronny as he walked into Foto Aldo and approached the counter where Jose stood.

"Bom dia, Jose," said Ronny.

"Ronny!" Jose didn't offer his usual smile; instead he motioned with his head for Ronny to follow him to the entrance of the back office. He started to feel nervous. *Did he speak to Francesco? Maybe he told his boyfriend about Santo. What's wrong?*

"You okay?" Ronny asked as he followed Jose.

"I have something I need to show you," Jose declared as he led him quickly toward the back office. "Close the door behind you and sit down." Jose sat down quickly in one of the two chairs in front of the screen on his desk. Ronny closed the door and sat next to him. "This equipment allows me to copy and edit video." Ronny watched as Jose injected a video tape and turned to face Ronny. "I was working on the audio of the video you shot. I started to play the tape, and I noticed something I think you'll find interesting." Jose pushed play on the machine and continued almost like he was commentating, "Here's the part where the backpack gets knocked over and you try and set it again but your angle was off and you missed recording him abusing you." Ronny wasn't enjoying reliving the experience and disappointment of not capturing the footage.

Jose continued. "Here's where the blinds go down, the room goes dark, and the studio light is turned on." Ronny watched as Jose stopped the tape and pushed a few buttons that started to zoom in on the image on the screen. "This is about the time when he started to molest you." Jose paused and continued to zoom in on the dark image. Ronny watched as the enlarged image came into focus and he could see the vague outline of the dressing mirrors that were along the side wall of Santo's studio. "Keep watching the mirror."

Ronny sat silent as he watched the footage reflected in the mirror come into focus and show Santo molesting him, in plain sight. He watched as Santo moved closer and put his fingers in Ronny's mouth. Jose zoomed in to show the disdainful expression on his face relaying the emotion he felt as the scene unfolded. Ronny swallowed hard remembering the taste of Santo's fingers. It was hard to watch.

"I worked on the audio, too," Jose said softly. Everything that Santo said was clear, and the shocking images were almost too hard for Ronny to watch as he relived the traumatic experience. Jose pulled the framing back slightly so Ronny could see Santo standing in front of him and watch as the action slowly reached the point where Santo retreated behind the studio light and started masturbating while he watched Ronny touching himself. It was humiliating to watch this with Jose. Ronny slowly shook his head, disgusted by the ordeal. Then it was over. As hard as it was to watch the tape with Jose, he felt a surreal wave of relief that it hadn't all been for nothing. Jose stopped the tape and turned to face Ronny who stood up and embraced him.

"Obrigado," he said softly. He was overwhelmed with emotion. Jose had given him back the chance to potentially change the game, to take back his power and see how far he could use this to stop the abuse. Ronny's felt his nerves and anxiety grow as he considered his next steps.

"I made you three copies. I can keep the original here for safe keeping. I also have some screen shots for you that I made into prints," Jose added as he handed him an envelope.

His mind raced as he reconnected with his original plan. *Shit!* The thought of it gave him an instant knot in his stomach, and immediately the doubt started rushing in.

"What if nobody cares and Santo turns the story around and makes it out like I was propositioning and blackmailing him to get work?" Ronny said as his fear of the powerful industry leaders crept in.

"You need to be strong. You need to stand up for what's right. I'm gay, but I'm not a creep like this guy and the people that enable him. It gives gay people a bad name when I see guys like this use their power to take advantage of people and play out their fantasies. Don't be afraid." Ronny knew Jose was right. His tone and passion reminded him of Milo. "I'm here to help you any way I can."

Ronny left and headed back to the Pola. The Mancini show was later that day, so he needed to get ready. As he walked he imagined the scenarios playing out in his head. It was so tough to know what the right answer was. One thing was certain—he knew this whole experience would influence his photography moving forward and how he treated people on set, especially women. If his ordeal with Santo Diaz had taught him anything, it was to know the kind of photographer he definitely didn't want to be.

# CHAPTER 37

When he entered his room, the phone was ringing.

"Hey, stranger." The sound of Ella's voice was a welcome distraction.

"I missed you," Ronny heard himself saying.

"I missed you, too. I was sorry to hear about your friend Nick. That's so shocking."

"He was such a great guy. I can't stop thinking about his family." Ronny glanced over to Nick's boxing gloves that hung on the back of the dining chair.

"Are you okay?" She asked. He felt that she could sense something was going on. He was holding it together but wanted so badly to let her know what had happened with Santo, but knew for the moment it was better to not mention anything.

"I'm doing fine," Ronny replied after a brief pause. "How was your trip?"

"The shoot went really well. I think they have a lot of work coming up, so hopefully they become a regular client."

"Can I see you tonight? Let's grab some dinner after I do the show?"

"I'd like that," Ella replied as Chad walked into the room as he hung up.

"You okay, man?" Chad asked as Ronny handed him the photographs Jose had printed from the video footage. It was embarrassing to share images like that of himself, but he trusted Chad, and he was so glad he finally had evidence that the molestation actually happened. It wasn't just his word against Santo's anymore. Chad took a moment, sat at the small table, and wiped his face. After looking at the first photograph in silence, he shuffled uncomfortably before handing it back to Ronny, apparently unable to continue looking at what would have been his fate if Ronny hadn't taken his place.

"Jose was able to enlarge the video image and found that all the footage I needed was recorded in the reflection of the mirror in the corner of the room."

"Now you have what you need," Chad replied softly.

"I hope Brett was right about Lucia and her feelings about Santo. I know Brett's a gossip and maybe he exaggerated what had gone on between them or got it wrong completely." Lucia would definitely be at the fashion show, and it would be the ideal place to at least start a conversation and gauge if I can trust her.

"Ronny, don't start second-guessing yourself. You have managed to get the evidence you needed. You've already done something nobody else has been able to do."

"But what if nobody cares?"

"I think they will." Chad reassured him. Eventually it was time to head to the venue for the show. Ronny was nervous about meeting Lucia.

"Stick to your plan. It's worked well so far, hasn't it?" Chad said.

"Yeah, I guess you're right. I'm starting to get sweaty. Thanks for reminding me."

"Just breathe, man. Breathe and focus!" Chad patted Ronny on the shoulder in encouragement.

"Now you sound like a coach."

"Let's get going or we'll be late."

They arrived at the backstage entrance to the Mancini show, which was being held at an abandoned building in downtown Milan. They checked in with the two security guards wearing black suits and earpieces and walked through the large industrial doors into the backstage area, which was surrounded by twelve-foot-high black curtains that had been erected to hide all the rough interior walls. A woman with a wireless headset and clipboard greeted them and took their names as they walked in.

"Ciao. Come this way." She quickly ushered them past a few large empty backstage metal boxes, scaffolding, and lighting stands. In the distance they could hear loud music playing and someone yelling. The woman turned back briefly. "They're doing a sound check right now. You will be needed for a rehearsal walk-through in an hour, so let's get you into hair and makeup."

They followed her down the corridor as the room opened to a larger area lined with more black curtains and high ceilings that had been spray-painted black. In the center of the room were rows of about twenty lit mirrored hair and makeup tables manned by hair and makeup artists, and to the side were racks of clothing. There was an electric energy in the room and about thirty shirtless male models already there, some standing talking and some getting their makeup and hair done as music played in the background. It was hard not to be impressed by the size of the production. Ronny felt a nervous excitement knowing this was his first show and the reason why he was brought to Milan by Mancini.

"Ronny, your rack is over here and, Chad, yours is right next to his. Ronny and Chad are here," she called out to Flavio who was running around getting the racks organized.

It felt surreal seeing Flavio again. He was part of that elite club that Ronny wanted to bring down, and his time was running out. Ronny was in no mood today to deal with being felt up, so for Flavio's sake he had better not test Ronny's patience.

Flavio waved them over. He wore his trademark kimono, this time in dark green, and his hair in his signature ponytail. "Bianca, my assistant, will be dressing you guys. I am dealing with Tiana Taylor. It seems she can't find her fucking shoes."

"Hi, guys. Nice to meet you," said Bianca, a short young blonde girl dressed in a black T-shirt and jeans. "Sorry it's a little hectic. Tiana, Liliana, and Caitriona are in town to attend the show and they are on the other side of the room having their hair and makeup done and final fittings for the red carpet."

At least with all the drama going on, Flavio won't have any time to be hands-on with us.

"Flavio? Flavio? I need you over here," Tiana yelled across the room.

"Darling, can I get you another pair of shoes?" asked Carlotta, who was running across the room with a dress in her hand.

"I want the gold ones for the red carpet, and I can't wear these to the after-party. How can I dance—my feet are already killing me!" demanded Tiana as Flavio started to visibly sweat.

"Of course the pair of shoes that goes missing is hers," Chad said.

"Leave your bags here under you rack, take off your shirt, and let's get you in hair and makeup," said Bianca as she led them to the hair and makeup table. "Serge, this is Chad and Ronny. Serge will be looking after your hair. Once you're done with hair and makeup, just make your way back over to your rack and we will call you for rehearsals."

"Thanks, Bianca. Ronny, I remember you from the shoot in Rio with Santo," Serge said in his French accent.

"Nice to see you again, Serge." Ronny remembered he was one of the friendlier people on the set that day. Ronny's mind raced as he took a moment to take a deep breath. He had a lot on his mind besides the fact that he about to be walking in his first fashion show in front of the whole industry.

"Chad, darling!" They turned to see Carlotta moving towards them wearing a body-hugging yellow dress, high gold heels, and a large gold bracelet. Her hair was perfectly styled and she looked stunning. "Ciao, Ronaldo." Carlotta kissed both guys on the cheek. "I see you have met Serge, the genius. Make sure you take care of these two. I know you are going to be fabulous. Chad, I spoke to Lorenzo, and you will be opening the show. I will see you afterwards to celebrate. Enjoy the show."

"Thanks, Carlotta. We are so excited to be here," replied Chad as she blew air kisses and rushed away in the direction of Tiana. Carlotta's news seemed to catch Chad off guard.

"How amazing, you're opening the show!" said Ronny as he slapped his back. He could tell Chad was nervous.

Serge smiled. "Carlotta is a bit stressed dealing with Tiana at the moment. Even at the men's show, she seems to need all the attention. Okay, guys, grab a seat. I will be doing your hair, and the fabulous Dotti will be doing your makeup." Serge nodded toward an edgy blonde-haired girl standing at the next table wearing glasses, a black tank top, and skinny black jeans. "Dotti, this is Ronny and Chad."

"Hello, lovers. I'm almost finished here, Serge," Dotti said in an Australian accent.

The guys sat down facing the mirror as Serge and his assistant set about giving them a trim and then blow drying out their hair and styling it.

"We want big hair and big energy today, boys," Serge said.

As unassuming as he was, Serge was the top hair stylist in the world and did all the biggest fashion shows and campaigns. Ronny had seen his name appear in many of the credits on the editorial photo shoots in *Italian STYLE* magazine. Soon he and Giuseppe, his assistant, had finished the guys' hair, and they were sent over to Dotti to do their makeup with clips in their hair to hold the style and shape.

"Sit down, boys. Let Dotti do her magic." Like Serge, Dotti was a leader in her field. Mancini only worked with the best in the business. Dotti and her assistant began with a face massage using oils.

"Wow, that feels incredible," said Ronny.

"You boys don't need much help; you already look delicious, so it's going to be light and luminous."

Dotti proceeded to cover up a few small spots and add a layer of translucent foundation and then bronzing powder to finish off the makeup.

"When you're dressed, I will finish you off with some light oil. Lick you later, darlings," said Dotti with a wink and a cheeky grin.

"Okay, time for the rehearsal," called out Bianca. "Let's go, boys." Chad and Ronny walked toward the back of the curtain that opened out onto the runway. Ronny made sure to take in all the details of the styling, hair, and makeup. The whole backstage experience was an exciting one, and the fact that this could be his last modeling job if things didn't work out with Lucia was a reality that weighed heavily on his mind.

"Hey, Josh!" said Chad when he saw him walking toward them.

"Hi, guys," replied Josh. He seemed a bit flat and not his usual positive loud self.

"You okay, buddy?" asked Ronny, who could sense something was wrong.

"I feel bad that Nick's not with us."

"Sorry, man," said Ronny. "It's shocking. He was such a cool guy."

"Let's have some attention here, please," called out Orlando the main producer for the show. Everyone stood together listening for instructions. Lorenzo Mancini appeared from behind the curtain, followed by two assistants.

"Ciao, ciao. Nice to see you all here. Thank you so much for being a part of this show. The Mancini man is confident, sexy, and he enjoys the finer things in life. He knows what he wants. We are launching a new man this season: the Mancini man. Walk with purpose and enjoy this moment." Lorenzo added as everyone applauded.

Orlando stepped forward. "Okay, guys, you will line up in the order that we give you, then you will come out and walk down the righthand side of the runway, pause at the end for photographs, and then turn and walk back on the right side of the runway passing the next model on your left side. You each have three outfits, so the changes need to be fast. Let's stay focused. Okay, let's go. Chad, you're up first. Then we have Peter, Gustavo, Ronny, Norberto, Pierre, Marcus, Brian, Donal." He continued to read through the list of names, and everyone got in line. Ronny patted Chad on the shoulder as he moved to the front of the line. Ronny could see many of the other models were staring at Chad, wondering who this unknown model was and how he landed the main spot.

*Maybe they will think he was the one Santo Diaz wanted for the show. Maybe I'm being paranoid.* Ronny felt the excitement build as he heard the music pumping, and then he watched Chad disappear behind the curtain and onto the runway. Soon it was Ronny's turn. The producer tapped him on the shoulder. "Go, Ronny."

Ronny walked out past the curtain onto the stage and was awestruck by the size of the room and the number of seats that lined the runway. The blue tinted spotlight coming from the end of the runway was bright and caught him off guard. He hesitated and squinted as he adjusted his eyes and continued down the runway, which seemed to go forever. The rows of empty seats would be filled with people in less than an hour, and he knew he wasn't supposed to acknowledge anyone. After passing several of the models, he got to the end of the runway and stood for a moment before turning and walking back past the other guys that were now walking out. He knew his mother would have loved to have seen this although it was so different walking on a stage compared to the hallway he had practiced in with Brett at the agency. Ronny was relieved that was just a rehearsal. Backstage he saw Chad was looking anxious.

"I can't believe I tripped when I first went out there. I wasn't ready for the lights," Chad said, sounding slightly panicked.

"Chad, darling." They turned to see Carlotta coming up to him, smiling. "I know this is your first time doing this and it's a bit nerve racking, but I believe in you, and I need you to relax and be confident."

"I appreciate that, Carlotta. Honestly, if you want to swap me out with any of the other models for the first spot, I'm cool."

"Chad, look at me." Carlotta replied as Chad raised his eyes to meet hers. "I know a star when I see one. I need you to focus. I need you to own this moment and I need you to trust me. You got this!" Carlotta gave Chad a hug and kiss on the cheek, smiled at Ronny, and walked away.

*Tough love.* Ronny was excited for Chad; this was a huge break for him to open the show, and with Carlotta's support who knows where that might lead.

"Grazie," Chad responded. He looked at the ground, took a deep breath, and blew out the air quickly, almost like he was psyching himself up for a wrestling match.

"Okay, let's get dressed and do final hair and makeup checks. The show starts in thirty-five minutes," the producer called out again after the last model came back from the runway. They made their way back to their rack.

Ronny reached into his backpack to retrieve an apple and saw the yellow envelope that contained the photographs and tape of Santo Diaz. He had no idea how Lucia would react, and in many ways he was glad he would be trying to approach her after the show and not before. He was nervous but knew there was no turning back. Not now.

## CHAPTER 38

Well, I'm glad we had a run-through," said Ronny, wanting to help ease Chad's nerves.

"First outfits, please," Bianca said as she appeared from behind the rack. Ronny got dressed into a suit, black tank top, a shoulder bag, and sandals. Serge waved to get their attention.

"Let me take out your hair clips and finish off your hair," Serge said in an urgent tone. Ronny looked in the mirror and saw his hair quaffed up into an almost Elvis like shape.

"Looks cool. Thanks, Serge," said Ronny, who had only worn his hair one way his whole life. A few flashbulbs went off as backstage photographers moved around the room capturing the hair and makeup direction for the show.

"Over here, darlings!" called out Dotti, who was ready to finish off the guys' makeup. "Well, don't you look fabulous," she said as she added some more bronzing dust to their faces. "Let's give that body a bit of love, too." Dotti proceeded to put a small amount of oil on her hands. "Do you mind if I apply this to your chest and stomach?"

"That's fine. Thanks for asking," Ronny replied. Dotti looked up over the top of her glasses with a cheeky smile. Ronny looked in the mirror and admired the image of himself looking like a stylish Mancini man.

"Final checks, everyone!" called out Orlando as outfits, hair, and makeup were checked by the dressers and teams of hair and makeup artists. The room was abuzz with chatter and the occasional production person yelling out something urgent. The producer stood next to the entry to the runway. "Chad, let's have you up here and ready, please. Models, let's get lined up in order."

Ronny nodded at Chad. "You got this, Iowa."

Chad moved forward, and Ronny could see that Lorenzo was standing next to Orlando just behind the curtain looking at the monitor displaying the live feed from a camera positioned at the end of the runway so the producer knew when to send out the next model so they were evenly spaced. Orlando spoke into his headset. "Okay, everyone is seated in the front row. Let's have house lights down."

Ronny watched as Chad briefly closed his eyes then opened them, focused and ready. Ronny imagined this is what he would have done before a wrestling match.

"Let's start the music. Lights up and go, Chad." Orlando tapped Chad on the shoulder. A remix of Grace Jones' "Love Is the Drug" filled the space as Chad walked out onto the runway. Soon it was Ronny's turn. "Go, Ronny!" Orlando touched Ronny's shoulder, and he walked past the curtain and onto the runway. His adrenalin was pumping as he walked with purpose, striding forward down the center of the runway, letting the music be his focus. His body felt strong as he got to the end of the runway, slowed down, and struck a pose, standing in the blue spotlight. He slowly brought his eyeline up to the flashing cameras, keeping a wrinkle on his brow. As he turned and walked back up the right side of the catwalk, the next model passed him. Back off the stage he finally took a deep breath; he couldn't remember breathing during his walk. *What a rush.*

"Bravo, Ronny." Ronny heard Lorenzo as he walked backstage. This is what success in this business felt like, and it was hard not to want more of it. When he got back to his clothes rack, Chad was already changed into his swimsuit and sandals; he was all bronzed up and looked amazing. Ronny got changed quickly into his swimwear and was back striding down the runway as he looked around with his eyeline above the seated crowd. He owned this moment. *Bittersweet,* he thought to himself as he stood at the end of the runway and the photographers flashbulbs went off. As he walked back to the start of the runway and back through the curtain opening, Lorenzo stopped him.

"I knew when I saw you in that magazine spread with Tiana that you were right for this show. Thank you for being here."

"Grazie." Ronny smiled at Lorenzo as he continued back to his rack.

Chad and Ronny walked one more time in their final outfit, and as they walked back from the runway finale following Lorenzo Mancini, they were on an incredible high. Chad gave Ronny a high five as the celebration going on backstage was already underway. The applause and cheers rose when Lorenzo walked back behind the curtain. Lorenzo started thanking the models and his team as the VIP front row audience started to make their way backstage to congratulate him.

Grace Jones was towering above the crowd as she entered the room and waved at Lorenzo, making her way through the crowd to kiss him. Supermodels, celebrities, the world's top fashion elite were all there to celebrate Lorenzo and the beginning of men's fashion week. Ronny got changed quickly and grabbed his backpack. He scanned the room looking at the entering crowd to see if he could find Lucia. Many of the people that came backstage were looking at Chad, and a few came up to him to introduce themselves.

"Chad, I'm Silvio, the editor of *British Man* magazine."

"Nice to meet you, Silvio," Chad responded as he gave a quick sideways glance to Ronny with raised eyebrows.

"I will be in touch with your agent to discuss a cover story." Silvio pulled out a pen and paper to write on and scribbled some notes. "Carlotta has said that you are the image of the Mancini man, representing a new wave of male models to launch a new image for men, one that is athletic, sensual, and masculine. What do you say to that?"

"I'm so thankful to Carlotta for believing in me and giving me a chance to walk in their show. It's been incredible."

Ronny was happy for Chad's success and knew if Carlotta had anything to do with it, he stood a good chance of getting cast for the Mancini campaign. Chad elbowed Ronny to indicate that Lucia was in the corner. She was wearing a chic black dress, her blonde hair held back in a ponytail. She smiled at people as she walked up to greet and congratulate Lorenzo and then posed with him for a few photographs before getting into a conversation with Carlotta.

"Nice to meet you, Silvio. Please excuse us." Ronny nodded politely as they made their way through the crowd. He asked Chad to distract Carlotta to give him a chance to speak to Lucia. He took a deep breath to calm himself.

"Have you met the fabulous editor of *Italian STYLE*, Lucia?" Carlotta said as they approached.

"Carlotta, congratulations on the show!" replied Ronny. "Nice to see you again, Lucia. We met at the Mancini party when we were with Paul." As Carlotta moved forward to kiss Chad, Ronny positioned himself closer to Lucia so he could speak to her discreetly. He knew didn't have a lot of time before someone else came to speak to her.

"Yes, I remember," Lucia answered.

"I have something I'd like to share with you that I think you will find very interesting."

"Why do you think I would find it interesting?" she quickly replied, giving him a curious expression. He locked eyes with her, trying to read her expression. His nerves almost overcame him. *Just tell her. Now.* Ronny whispered in her ear, "Because I have evidence that could destroy Santo Diaz's career, and I wanted to get your advice on what you think I should do with it." Ronny moved back so he could see Lucia's face and gauge her reaction. Lucia turned toward Carlotta and touched her on the shoulder.

"Congratulations again on the show. Bellissima!" Lucia said as she gave Carlotta a kiss on each cheek. *Fuck!* Ronny thought. Maybe he had overstepped the mark and offended her. Lucia came back in close to Ronny. He held up the envelope with the photos and tape, and she put out her hand to stop him from giving her the package.

"Meet me at the Savini Café at nine tomorrow morning," she whispered to him before turning and walking away, almost as if she didn't want anyone to see them together. Ronny stood shell-shocked. He wasn't sure exactly what that meant.

"I knew you would be amazing, Chad," Carlotta gushed. "Everyone is asking who you are. This is only the beginning for you."

"Carlotta, can we get a photo of you and Chad, please?" A photographer interrupted their conversation, and Chad stood posing next to Carlotta as the camera flashes went off.

"Have you met Ronny? He took the most amazing photographs of me," Chad said as he pulled Ronny in to join him and Carlotta in the photograph.

"A man of many talents," Carlotta said as she smiled at Ronny. "Ciao, ciao for now." She walked into the crowd to continue greeting the other guests.

"I'm meeting Lucia tomorrow morning at nine," Ronny quietly told Chad.

"No turning back now, bud."

*Let's hope what Brett said was true.*

## CHAPTER 39

Ronny knew that Santo would be at the Mancini party that evening, so he decided not to attend and go and catch up with Ella instead. When he got back to his room at the Pola, he was on a high, still buzzing from the experience of walking in a fashion show. He took a moment to call Milo to let him know that he had gone through with the plan to film Santo.

"Are you okay?" Milo asked without a hint of judgment. "I know that must have been a lot for you to deal with."

"I'm pretty shaken but I needed to take a stand."

"You've got the evidence. Nobody can deny that."

He was right. Ronny noticed that Milo sounded tired and not his usual motivated self. Losing Nick and knowing how soulless working at the club must be for him he decided to try and help in any way he could. "How are you doing? You sound a bit tired. Everything alright at the club?" asked Ronny.

"I know I can't keep working there. It's just not sustainable. I've been doing drugs just to get me through the night."

"If you're open to it, Luiz has a lot of good contacts for work, and I think he could really help you get something organized.

"I need to do something different. It would be cool to see your brother. I haven't seen him for ages."

Ronny gave him Luiz's number to call, hopefully his brother would know someone who could give him a job. After the call he called Ella and went to meet her in front of the Pola. When he walked out on the street, Ella was already there leaning on the wall. Her smile lit up his heart, and when she embraced him, she squeezed him tight then pulled back briefly to give him a kiss. It felt so natural to be with her, especially after the last few days.

"So rumor has it that you missed me," Ella said.

"Is that what you heard?" Ronny replied as they started walking down the street from the Pola to the pizza joint close by.

"I'll tell you what I heard. That my agency loved the photographs you took and they want to meet with you to discuss testing other girls."

"They really liked them?" Ronny said as he stopped and turned to face Ella and squeezed her hand. This was a big deal. If they let him shoot upcoming models, it would be amazing for his portfolio, and he could make some money doing it.

"I'm happy for you, Ronny. Your work deserves to be seen."

"So, what are your plans for the rest of the year?"

"I am supposed to be back home in Australia in the fall to go back to school, and honestly, I don't want to go."

Ronny thought about her leaving and didn't want her to go either. If Nick's suicide had taught him anything, it was to value what he had while he had it. He fantasized that they could spend time traveling together. "What are you studying?" he asked.

"Arts and humanities."

"You must be loving being here surrounded by art and all the history. Do you have a favorite Italian artist or piece of art in Italy?"

"Probably Michelangelo's statue of David," Ella said as she burst out laughing and Ronny rolled his eyes and laughed.

Obviously she had heard the stories about Carlotta calling Chad the statue of David.

"I think Chad's head's almost as big as David's. Have you ever seen David?"

"Yeah, my roommate is sleeping with him."

"Come on!" Ronny laughed. Once the two were seated at the table they ordered two beers. "What was it like growing up in Australia?" Ronny asked as Ella picked up a bread roll that was on the table, pulled off a small piece, and took a bite.

"Well, I spent most of my childhood on the beach; we lived in a treehouse."

"A real treehouse?"

"Well, it looked like a treehouse. My dad's a builder so he built it around these huge fig trees, and when you're in the house you feel like you're actually living in a treehouse. It's pretty cool. I have a little brother, Scott, and he always loves to collect spiders and bugs; it drives my mum crazy."

He was enjoying getting to know Ella. In the past he had never taken the time to do so—never allowed himself to get this close. After dinner they headed back to the Pola and went back to Ella's room. They sat on the bed, and Ella leaned over and opened the drawer in the side table. The same draw where she kept her condoms.

"Do you want to see my brag book?" asked Ella as they sat back on her bed together.

"I'll just say yes; I'm not sure what a brag book is, though." Ronny was relieved that she hadn't pulled out a condom, he was enjoying their conversation.

"My mum put it together for me when I first left Australia. It's a little family photo album and I've always kept it." Ella showed Ronny the small album which featured photos of her family, her dog, and pictures of her with her surfboard on the beach.

"Wow, that beach is beautiful. Your family looks really cool, too." Ronny remembered when he was younger and his family was together enjoying holidays. He felt so close to Ella in that moment. "I remember each year we would all pile into my dad's car and drive up the coast to Bahia, a beautiful surf town. My brother and I would play beach volleyball with my dad and uncle." Ronny took a moment then refocused his eyes on Ella. "Seeing the photos of your family made me remember when my family was together and happy. My dad was my hero, and he adored my mother. I miss those times."

Ella moved in closer and softly kissed him then lay back on her bed with him. She ran her fingers through his thick dark curls and rested her head on his chest.

Ronny lay silent as he considered what their future might hold. Was a relationship even worth exploring knowing she would be leaving to go back to Australia to school, and who knows what was to come of his plan with Santo. What was his future now in Milan? Was it all worth it? As much as he tried to block out his appointment with Santo, he wasn't sure he could continue modeling. Without it, however, did he have what it took to survive here and get established as a photographer, and how long would that take? *How could I support myself and pay back my brother?* So many thoughts and questions filled his head.

"How's the photography going?" Ella asked.

"I'm not sure," Ronny answered. "I need to tell you something." He needed to trust her; he needed to let her in.

Slowly Ronny told her about the appointment with Santo and what his intentions now were. He talked about his mother, Milo, and his father. It wasn't easy to open up, but he felt Ella was someone who would understand, especially after she shared her own story. Occasionally he paused as Ella listened, touching his chest.

"I'm sorry. I know it's not easy to talk about, but what you are doing takes courage," Ella said as he turned toward her.

"Brave or stupid. I may be throwing away what I came here for to try and make a difference that might backfire. I really don't know what's going to happen."

"Sometimes doing the right thing is scary. At least you have evidence. What were your plans after the season?" asked Ella.

"Honestly, I'm not sure. It depends if I get kicked out of Milan or not."

"You came here to follow your dream, Ronny. Don't give that up."

He knew she was right. Only time would tell if that was possible or not. It had been an intense few days, and as they lay silently on Ella's bed he softly stroked her head and they drifted off to sleep. Eventually Camille knocked softly on the door and woke them up. Ronny kissed Ella and quietly headed back downstairs to his room.

The next morning Chad made coffee as Ronny got ready to head off for his meeting with Lucia.

"How was the party?" Ronny asked.

"As you would expect, it was pretty over the top. I had a great time until Santo came up to me towards the end of the night. He was pretty messed up and was feeling me up telling me that I was the favorite for the Mancini campaign but I had to test with him first." Chad looked shaken. "I managed to get out of there. I know I couldn't test with him after knowing what you went through."

"Hopefully you won't have to." Ronny added.

# CHAPTER 40

He arrived early at Savini Café to get a discreet seat in the back. It was an old café filled with mostly old men and women who wouldn't know or care who Lucia was. The smell of warm pastries and hot coffee filled the air as Ronny made his way to the back of the café where he sat in an old burgundy leather banquet. He sat down feeling nervous and anxious, wondering what her reaction would be and if she would even show up. On the way to the meeting, he had second thoughts about going through with the plan. His hands were unconsciously opening and closing the flap on the envelope that he put on the table. At 9:03 a.m. Lucia walked into the café looking stylish with large sunglasses on and her blonde hair tied back in a loose bun; she had an effortless chic style about her.

"So here we are," Lucia said as she sat down and ordered an espresso and a water from the waiter who appeared at the table. She was polite enough, but Ronny sensed she was being cautious.

"Thank you for coming, Lucia," replied Ronny as he took a deep breath to calm his nerves. "I wanted you to see these. I'm hoping you may be able to help me." Ronny pushed the envelope on the table toward Lucia who was looking at him with a blank expression.

"I'm intrigued to find out how you think I can help you." Lucia kept her eyes fixed on Ronny. *Maybe I miscalculated.* Ronny's hands started sweating.

"In this envelope are still photographs taken of video footage I have recorded of Santo Diaz doing what he has been doing for years—taking advantage of young male models." It felt strange to say this out loud to someone he didn't know, almost like he was getting a dirty secret off his chest. Lucia took the envelope and looked back at Ronny as he continued speaking nervously. He was still unsure whose side she was really on, but it was a risk he was willing to take. "I had an appointment with Santo last week knowing what would happen by what other models have told me. I planned to record him so I could use the evidence to hold him accountable and stop him from abusing anyone else."

Lucia's espresso arrived. The waiter put down her coffee and left; she took a sip and opened the envelope and pulled out the photographs. Ronny watched her closely, observing her reaction. Slowly she looked at each photograph of Santo with his hands touching Ronny's crotch, another one with his fingers in Ronny's mouth, and then finally Santo masturbating as he took photographs of Ronny standing against the wall. Lucia was quiet and stone-faced as she looked over the photographs again. It was hard to gauge her reaction. Ronny took a sip of the water that sat on the table.

"You took quite a risk doing this. Santo is a very powerful man. I had heard rumors of his behavior, but seeing this evidence is a different story." Lucia's expression softened; she looked visibly taken aback by the photographs. Ronny could tell by her expression that she knew the weight of this scandal and how it would impact Santo's career and his work with A-list celebrities and advertising clients. It would be devastating for him. Lucia looked back up at

Ronny and took a slow deep breath. "So why would you come to me with this?"

"Because so many people are aware of what happens in this business but are too afraid to try and change it. I see you taking risks with the editorial shoots you do for Italian STYLE so I thought you might be able to help me."

"What about your agent?"

"Paul is well aware of what Santo is doing and has no problem sending him new young models in the hope that one will score the next big campaign and the agency will get their commission. He's a part of the problem," Ronny replied. *Maybe she doesn't want to get involved. Maybe Brett got it wrong.* "I need someone in the business that isn't afraid of Santo and who won't stand for this. Someone who can give me advice and help me get it into the right hands. Someone I can trust," Ronny added.

Finally, Lucia spoke. "You're a brave young man, but I'm sorry, I can't help you. I do have my issues with Santo, and as much as I would like to see him go down for this, my hands are tied. If it was found out that I was responsible for helping you get this out, I'm not sure what the ramifications would be for me."

Ronny was crushed. He felt the disappointing weight of the situation and put his hand up to rub his forehead.

"All I can tell you is that a year ago, a few male models came forward with accusations of abuse against Santo, and because they had no evidence their charges were dropped. I'm sure if they had what you have, things would have been different. I heard that a news article exposing the abuse was going to run in the *London Daily Mail* with respected fashion journalist Trent Fraser. The story was killed by a powerful fashion editor in New York. Nobody found out about the abuse. I didn't tell you this." Lucia touched Ronny on the arm. It was obvious she was talking about Liz Kirby, the

American editor for *STYLE* magazine. "I'm sorry I can't be more helpful. I'm truly sorry."

Ronny felt his face getting warm. He felt small again. He played his hand and fell short. Who knows who Lucia might speak to about this. Lucia quickly gathered her things and put her sunglasses back on before standing up. Ronny stood up next to her as she hugged him. He sat back down as she walked out of the café to her awaiting car. As powerful as Lucia was, she was still trapped by the industry that paid her bills and made her famous. Ronny collected his things and walked out of the café. He continued to walk for several blocks letting the walk signals guide his direction. He was in a daze, needing some time to get his thoughts together. As he approached the Pola, he saw Chad sitting outside against the building.

"How did you go with Lucia?" Chad asked as he quickly got up to greet him.

"It didn't go anywhere. She was concerned about how it might affect her career if it was found out that she helped me." Saying it out loud made the situation seem even more hopeless.

"That really sucks. I just spoke to Paul and I have to meet with Santo this weekend." Chad shook his head. "You and I are both on hold for the Mancini campaign and they will be making decisions soon. I don't know what to do."

"You don't need to go, Chad, if you don't want to. Remember you're not guaranteed the job. Look what happened to Nick." Ronny added. Chad shuffled on his feet and started rubbing his head. "I'm sure Carlotta has a lot of say as well. She wouldn't have put you first in the lineup at the fashion show if she didn't think you were right for their brand," Ronny hoped that would calm Chad's nerves.

"I guess so. I just don't know how many other guys are on hold and who Santo has been promising the campaign to. It's such a huge opportunity. I'm sure a lot of guys would do anything to book it. What are you going to do now that Lucia won't help you?" Chad asked.

"Honestly, I don't think I can stay here modeling, sell my soul, and continue to pretend all this isn't happening behind the scenes. There's obviously nothing I can do to change it and I'm done with the hustle. I'm done being a victim. Photography was why I took a chance to come here, and what I've realized is that I can do that anywhere."

"What about Ella?" Chad asked.

"I know. That's a tough one. Besides you she really is the best part of my time here." He knew he wanted to continue seeing Ella, but maybe Milan wasn't the right place for that.

"I'm sorry things didn't work out," Chad said.

"Maybe they did," Ronny said as Chad looked at him with a curious expression as he continued. "Before I came here I was judging my mother for staying with my father in an abusive relationship and judged my best friend Milo for being a sex worker to support his family. I realized they needed my support, not my judgment. Seeing how this business works has been an eye-opening reality check, and in trying to change it I lost a part of myself in the process." Chad touched Ronny on the shoulder. "I'm going to swing by Foto Aldo to pick up the prints from our photography test. I need a distraction."

When Ronny walked into Foto Aldo later that day to collect the prints, Jose greeted him with a smile.

"How's it all been going?" Jose asked as Ronny indicated to move to the side of the counter so their conversation wasn't overheard by anyone. He told him what happened with Lucia and what she had said. Jose could sense his disappointment. "I'm sorry. I know you hoped to get more support from her, but this business is a tough one, and not a lot of people have the courage to rock the boat or try and change things. I have your prints. They're beautiful." Jose retrieved a box of prints for Ronny of the images he had selected from the test. He opened the box and handed Ronny the twelve prints to look at. Ronny felt a wave of excitement as he started to study the prints.

"How would you like to have your photographs exhibited on the walls right here at Foto Aldo?" Jose added.

"What do you mean?" he replied.

"I just had a meeting with the management here, and we were discussing the plan for the upcoming exhibitions, and I showed him your prints and talked about the other photographs you took in Brazil, and he was really interested. Every year we select a few young upcoming photographers that we think have a lot of potential and showcase their strongest work. The images are also published in a respected photography magazine that sponsors the event with a profile of each photographer. He agreed to have you be part of the exhibition and include six of your photographs. So what do you think?" Jose said as Ronny was left momentarily speechless.

"Are you serious?" He waited for Jose to say something, but he just smiled. "I think that sounds incredible."

"We will do the printing for you, and we have frames we use, so it won't cost you anything. You can invite whoever you like to the first night when we have some drinks and food provided by the photography magazine who sponsors the event. A lot of people from the industry come to the opening so it's great exposure."

"Obrigado. This means more than you know." Ronny paused as Jose listened. "I had virtually given up on staying here. I just couldn't deal with modeling anymore, and I wasn't sure what to do next with my photography. This is amazing news."

"Honestly, if you are over modeling, your photography is strong enough to make money from paid tests and to start assisting an established photographer. You should be proud of yourself." Jose patted him on the shoulder.

As Ronny left to walk back to the Pola, he fist-pumped the air. "Yes!" he called out. Finally—a chance to have his work seen by a larger audience. He couldn't wait to tell Ella. On his way back to the Pola, he walked past an old lady selling flowers in front of the subway station. She had long grey hair and light blue eyes. Ronny stopped to ask if he could take her portrait. He retrieved the camera that Francesco had given him and snapped a few frames before thanking her. The moment felt free; it reminded him of why he loved photography. When he walked into his room, he stood in front of the photographs on the wall, considering which photographs were his strongest. The phone rang. When he picked it up, he heard Luiz's voice.

"Is everything okay?" Ronny asked.

"It's Mom," Luiz finally replied.

"What happened?" His heart sunk. *What now?* "Is she okay?" Ronny sat down on the bed and put his head in his hands.

"She's here," Luiz replied.

He sensed he was holding something back. "What happened?"

"Mom finally told Diego she was leaving him, and he hit her. She called the police, and he's been arrested."

"He hit her?" Ronny's heart raced. He had been worried this would eventually happen.

"She's fine, just shaken," Luiz assured him. There was a slight pause.

"Ronny?" His mother could be heard speaking on the phone. She sounded like she had been crying.

"Mama. Are you okay?" His voice broke as he felt relief that she was okay and that she had finally left. The anger and hatred toward his father rose.

"I'm okay now. I finally told him I was leaving. I have been so scared of what might happen if I left. Worried about what I would lose. I kept thinking about you being so courageous to follow your dreams and I felt it was time I found my strength. You gave me the courage I never knew I had."

Despite having been hit by Diego, she sounded like she had finally got her power back.

"I'm so sorry I left you. I just couldn't stay there." Ronny started to cry. "I'm so glad you're there with Luiz," he added and wished he was there with her.

"Don't cry, sweetheart. You couldn't have stayed. It wasn't safe. I'm sorry I stayed here as long as I did. I was just so scared to be on my own, and I thought that maybe your father would change. I couldn't sit back and be a victim anymore. I realized life is too short to be treated like that." He hadn't heard his mother talk like that for a long time. She had finally found her voice again. "How are you doing? Is everything okay?" she asked.

"I'm fine. I'm fine. I'm just glad you're okay. I love you." He rubbed his face and felt a wave of relief that she was finally free. He missed his family.

When Luiz got back on the phone, he reassured Ronny that she was doing fine and she was staying with them. They were together again as a family.

"We all miss you here, Ronny," Luiz added.

Ronny didn't think he had any tears left. He wiped his face as he hung up the phone relieved that his mother was no longer a victim and neither was he. *Courage.*

He knew what he had to do.

## CHAPTER 41

He went up to Ella's room and knocked on the door. She answered wearing a T-shirt and denim shorts.

"Oi, linda," Ronny said with a smile.

Ella gave Ronny a kiss. "Who's Linda?" she asked with an amused expression.

"Oi linda is 'hi beautiful' in Portuguese," he answered as she laughed. Ronny embraced her and held her.

"Is everything okay?" she asked.

"It is now. Can we talk?" He moved to sit with her at the small dining table. Ella's expression became serious as she sat down and pushed her hair back behind her ears.

"I've decided not to pursue modeling and to focus on my photography. I just got asked to exhibit some of my photographs at Foto Aldo and I'm going to start doing paid tests and try and get an assisting job."

"Good for you. You deserve it," Ella said. Ronny knew she was genuinely happy for him.

"I wanted to tell you that I've never met anyone like you, and you have honestly been the best thing to happen to me," Ronny said as Ella reached out and touched his arm. "For years I watched my parents' relationship deteriorate. A home filled with love and laughter turned into a prison, especially for my mother. I lost faith in love. My mother finally got the courage to leave my father and the abuse she was being subject to." Ella's unconditional support for him through this crazy time had shown him that she truly saw and understood who he was, her vulnerability was something he had never witnessed before. "I really want to see where this goes with you if you are open to it. I know I'm just starting with the career and completely understand if this is all just too complicated," he said as Ella squeezed his arm.

"I'm so grateful that you trusted me enough to open up and let me in. I feel the same way." Ella paused and smiled softly at Ronny. "I know photography will work out for you. It's your passion. The good news is that you can do it anywhere...Milan, Brazil, New York, even Australia," Ella added with a smile as Ronny leaned in and started kissing her. Ronny pulled back slowly to look at her eyes and softly caress her face. He knew he'd made the right decision.

"Hey, by the way, what happened with Lucia?" Ella eventually asked.

"Unfortunately, she wasn't able to help. But she did give me the name of a journalist with the *London Daily Mail* that might be able to help me. I'm going to find his number and leave a message for him. Can I call you later?" He stood up and embraced Ella. They held each other as he savored the feeling of her in his arms. It felt like the start of a new chapter for him, one he didn't need to experience alone.

It was easy to get the contact information for Trent Fraser from the copy of the *London Daily Mail* at the international newsstand at the end of the block. Ronny called and left a message on his answering machine saying that he had recorded evidence of Santo Diaz abusing a male model.

Trent called him back within two hours. He sounded like a trustworthy person on the phone, he told Ronny about the previous story that had been killed and the other male models who had come forward. Ronny took his time to tell Trent what had happened to him, to Nick, Josh, and the other models he knew about. As uncomfortable and humiliating as it was to share the story again with someone he had never met, he knew why he was doing it. He told him about the people around Santo that directly enable him, like Paul, and mentioned other people in the industry who were also abusing models, like Flavio the stylist. They talked for about an hour, and when he talked about the tape and photographs, Trent confirmed that someone from the paper would come by to collect everything within the next few hours.

"Do you want to press charges or seek compensation?" asked Trent. "I know a good lawyer."

Ronny hadn't really thought about any legal action. He just wanted the abuse to stop. "I just want to do the right thing and not have anyone else have to deal with what I went through," he replied.

"You are a brave young man. Thank you for doing this. With your evidence I can now run the story that was killed. You have no idea how many people you are helping," Trent said as he hung up the phone.

Chad walked into the room as the call with Trent was ending. "That sounded pretty serious," Chad said.

"That was a journalist from the *London Daily Mail*. Lucia had told me he was doing a story on a bunch of male models that were being abused by Santo, but the story was killed because of lack of evidence, and Liz Kirby—the editor of *American STYLE* magazine—was protecting him."

"Are you worried about what Paul will say about everything knowing how close he is to Santo?" Chad asked. Ronny took a moment. He knew Paul would be implicated in the story, too.

"I've decided I'm going to leave the agency and focus on my photography. I know it's going to be tough to start, but I need to try." Despite feeling a sense of relief knowing he wouldn't have to deal with the abuse anymore, he knew he would miss his daily routine with Chad.

"That's huge, man." Chad paused, taking in what Ronny was saying. "Does that mean I'm losing my roommate?"

"After you shoot the Mancini campaign, I'm sure you won't be sharing a room anymore," Ronny replied in jest, but he honestly hoped Chad was the one that got the campaign.

"Your lips to God's ears, as my mom says."

"Hey, I almost forgot I have some prints from our shoot." Ronny passed Chad the box of prints he had collected from Jose.

"I love these," Chad commented as he started looking through the prints. "Ella looks incredible. Have you told her what's happening?"

"I saw her earlier. She knows everything, and we have started officially dating."

"Good for you. She is an amazing girl."

"I finally got out of my own way, I don't want to lose her."

Eventually Chad stood up and went to the kitchen, the phone rang. It was Mama Pola letting Ronny know there was someone downstairs to collect an envelope for Trent Fraser. As Ronny handed the envelope over, he felt nervous even though he knew it was the right thing to do. He headed back upstairs and pulled out all of his prints and negatives and put them on his bed and the floor in an attempt to distract himself and edit down his work. He continued to work on creating a portfolio to show agents so he could be considered for paid tests and at the same time consider the images he would exhibit at Foto Aldo.

The following day Ronny went to meet up with Jose at the lab to help him decide which photographs he was going to exhibit. He felt pressure knowing that they would be the first impression on a larger audience, and he wanted to choose them carefully. Thankfully, Jose had a great eye and was able to help him choose the strongest images for the exhibition and put together a portfolio of his work.

Early the following morning there was a knock at the door.

"You need to turn on the news," Ella said as she quickly entered his room and went to turn on the small television in the corner. She sounded anxious, which made Ronny nervous. Even though the news was broadcast in Italian, Ronny could clearly see the news reporter speaking at his desk with an image of Santo Diaz in the corner of the screen. The photographs taken from the video of the test with Ronny appeared where Santo could be seen touching him. Ronny's face has been masked out, but he recognized the images. Ronny sat down on a chair, realizing all this was happening in real time. Everyone stood in silence watching the television. Several reporters were shown gathered outside Santo's house, waiting for a comment. Ronny felt nervous as he recognized the building.

"Apparently it's all over the press," Ella said.

"He can't hide anymore," said Ronny. "None of them can." He felt a weight had been lifted off his shoulders, despite not knowing what the fallout from all of this would be. "I'm a little freaked out, I have to say." His mind raced as he continued to watch the news. The phone rang. Ronny knew it was for him; he picked up the receiver and heard Jose's voice.

"Ronny, I gather you've seen the news. Are you okay?" Jose asked.

"To be honest, it's a bit scary," Ronny replied.

"Just know you did the right thing," Jose tried to reassure him.

"Thanks, I appreciate that, man. What have you heard?" Ronny asked.

"The news of the scandal has sent shock waves through the industry. Santo released a statement denying any wrongdoing and claims that he was set up. Paul from BAM Models is denying any wrongdoing as well and has resigned."

"What?" Ronny replied. He felt anxious as the weight of the situation closed in on him. He was unable to control how it played out. Ella touched his shoulder.

"Apparently, the other models that had come forward in the past that were in the unpublished story were all represented by BAM Models at the start of their careers, and they all said that Paul knew about the abuse and had ignored their concerns," Jose said. Ronny felt bad for Paul, but knew that he had enabled Santo for many years and now his time was up.

"Is Foto Aldo still okay to have me exhibit my photographs?" Ronny asked.

"Of course! What you have done took courage. You have no idea how many people this will help. I'll make sure your photograph is the one used on the invitation for the opening," Jose replied. Ronny felt a huge relief knowing his dream of having his work seen by a larger audience was still happening. He took the risk to make a stand for all the people in his life that had been abused: his mother, Milo, Nick, Ella. He looked forward to having all this behind him. When he hung up the call with Jose, Chad walked out of the kitchen and handed him a coffee.

"This will definitely shake things up," commented Ella.

"Damn right," said Chad.

Ronny looked up to see Santo Diaz on the television making his way past reporters, escorted by police and getting into a car without making a comment. A chill ran up his spine seeing Santo's face.

"He's probably trying to leave the country," Chad said.

"He can't run away from this," Ronny replied.

The phone rang again, and Ronny picked up the receiver. It was Lucia.

"I wasn't expecting to hear from you," Ronny said.

"I wanted to call you and apologize for not helping you. Santo is a powerful man, and I'm sorry I couldn't find the courage to support you. Are you okay?" Lucia replied.

Ronny was surprised by her call and change in tone. "It's a bit overwhelming, but I know it was the right thing to do. What do you think will happen to Santo?"

"The story came out in the *London Daily Mail*, and parts of the video have been released. The abuse you suffered matched the abuse that all the other models described. Santo just got arrested and will be charged. He has been dropped by all the major publications and clients he was working for. Paul and Flavio were also named in the article, and both will deal with consequences. I believe Paul has already resigned and Flavio has been blacklisted." Ronny imagined the sleazy smile being wiped off Santo's face as he realized his whole world had come crashing down. "Again, I'm sorry I couldn't help you. If there's anything I can do for you in the future, please let me know," Lucia added as Ronny quickly considered her offer and decided to take a chance and make a request.

"I appreciate that, Lucia. Actually, there is something. I never told you that my real passion is photography, and next Thursday I have a few of my photographs being showcased at Foto Aldo in a group exhibition. If you have time to come by, I would love to hear what you think of my work." Ronny was nervous even asking but felt like at this stage he had nothing to lose.

"I will try my best to come by. Thank you," Lucia replied.

Ronny hung up the phone. "That was Lucia. She apologized for not helping me and told me that Santo has been arrested and will be charged. He has been dropped by all publications and his clients," he said to Chad and Ella.

"You did it, man. You really did it." Chad hit him on his back.

"I don't know what to say. It feels like a weird dream." He feared that one of them would somehow seek revenge on him for what he had exposed.

"You hungry?" asked Ella.

"I'm okay. Sorry, there's a lot going on." Ronny touched her hand.

"I've got to run to an appointment, I'll be back as soon as I can." Ella kissed Ronny then stood up.

"If you can get a copy of the *London Daily Mail* article that would be great. Thanks." Ronny looked back to the television to see Santo's face appear again. The news station was running the footage of him being arrested on repeat. His expression was one of disbelief and shock. He no longer looked like the confident tanned photographer who lived a lavish international lifestyle surrounded by the world's rich and famous. Finally, justice for all the times he took advantage of so many young men just trying to catch a break and get ahead. As Ronny sat down on the chair with Nick's gloves hanging on the back, he thought about how much had changed since he left Brazil. He took a chance to do what was right, and only time would tell if it completely paid off and didn't affect him and his efforts to get ahead as a photographer in a negative way.

When Ella brought back the *London Daily Mail*, he opened it to the page with the headline, "FASHION WORLD SEXUAL ABUSE SCANDAL EXPOSED." Ronny slowly read the article, which featured several photographs of him being molested by Santo Diaz. Fortunately, his face and private parts had been covered up. The article named Santo, Flavio, and Paul.

After the support he had received from Milo, he wanted to update him and called to tell him what happened and that he was okay.

"It's happening. The tape and photographs I managed to record as evidence allowed a bunch of models, who had a case against Santo, to be able to prosecute him. He has been arrested," Ronny said to Milo.

"I knew you could do it. That's incredible news. You must be relieved it's over," Milo replied. It was so good to hear his voice.

"The whole thing is surreal. I'll be honest, it's freaked me out. I keep thinking someone is going to take revenge on me in some way."

"You did the right thing. Don't forget that."

"Thanks, man. On a side note I'm feeling better now that my mom finally left my dad and is now with Luiz."

"I spoke to your brother, and he told me. I'm so happy for you. I know that was really tough on you to see her dealing with Diego. By the way, Luiz also helped me find a job, so I don't need to work at the club. Ana misses the extra cash, but I couldn't do it anymore."

"That's such good news. Good for you."

"Are you coming back soon?" Milo asked.

"You know, I have been thinking about it and I've really been missing home," Ronny replied. As much as he had wanted to escape his life in Rio for such a long time, he now realized how many things he had taken for granted. "I have a bunch of things I want to get set up with my photography, but I think I'll come back for Christmas. Turns out Rio's not such a bad place to be after all."

# CHAPTER 42

After Ronny left BAM Models, Mama Pola managed to get him a studio room at Residence Pola so he was able to stay close to Chad and Ella and pay the same amount of rent. And Ella could spend the night with him without disturbing Chad. Keeping busy was also a perfect distraction from the whole situation with Santo Diaz. It was amazing how many more people in the industry were inspired by Ronny to come forward and tell their own story of abuse. So many people were grateful for what he had done.

When Ronny walked into Foto Aldo with Ella for the exhibition launch, he felt nervous wondering if anyone would come and what they would think of his work. Looking at the other photographers' work on the walls was a little intimidating. He had never seen his images printed in a large format and framed professionally on the wall. When he hung them earlier that day with Jose, he stood back and studied each one, the portrait of his mother captured her eyes that tried to mask her sadness. The portrait of Ella dancing was a perfect moment that showed her vulnerable expression and incredible body shape.

"Your prints look beautiful" Ella said as she looked up at his work and squeezed his arm. "You know you really made a difference with what you did," Ella said as she ran her fingers through his hair. They had spent several evenings together since the article came out.

"It's been a bit surreal, I have to admit. I think the whole situation with Santo being charged woke up a lot of people. The other models that brought charges against him are now starting a website to support models dealing with abuse with advice and legal help. I'm just glad I didn't get kicked out of Milan," Ronny replied as he took Ella's hand.

"I'm glad you didn't get kicked out either." Ella kissed him as Jose came up to greet Ronny.

"Congratulations! How amazing do they look? Such powerful portraits," Jose said as he offered them two glasses of champagne.

"Thanks, Jose. Honestly, you've been so amazing. I'm so excited to be a part of this." Ronny added. Jose had helped him crop and reprint a few of his photographs to add to a portfolio of his work to show agents.

"It's only the beginning for you, Ronny. Enjoy the night." Jose moved to offer drinks to the other guests.

"So which one is your favorite?" Ella asked as she nodded toward Ronny's photographs.

"Now that's tough. I love them all, but the one that makes me smile is the one of you. That was the first time I really saw you." Ronny kissed her and turned to see if there were more people coming into the room.

"Congratulations, Ronny," Lucia said as she approached them.

"Lucia. Thanks for coming. This is my girlfriend, Ella," Ronny said. It felt natural to call her his girlfriend. Ella squeezed his hand.

"Nice to see you. I came early because I have a dinner. I really like your photographs, you have a good eye. I would love to see more of your work," Lucia commented.

"That would be amazing. Your magazine has been such an inspiration for me."

"Give me a call this week," she said as she handed him her business card and kissed him on both cheeks and left.

"Wasn't that Lucia, the fashion editor?" asked Chad as he walked up to Ronny with Camille.

"It was. I had invited her, and I can't believe she came."

"She knows you're a photographer now," Ella said. Ronny smiled at her. She was right; he was a photographer and this evening was a taste of what it would be like to have his work seen. A warm sense of pride came over him as the room filled with people.

"Congratulations on your photographs," Camille said as she kissed Ronny and Ella. "By the way, somebody's got some big news."

"Did you get confirmed for the Mancini campaign?" Ronny asked Chad with excitement.

"Yes, it's official. I'm going to be a supermodel," Chad replied in his best Superman voice then laughed. Ronny and Ella cheered and hugged Chad.

"Now just don't let your head get any bigger or we won't be able to get you out of this room," Camille added.

"That's a huge deal, man," Ronny said. "Congrats!" Chad really deserved the campaign and Ronny couldn't be happier for him.

"Thanks, man. I can't thank you enough for what you did," Chad said to Ronny with his hand on his shoulder. Chad never had to do a naked shoot with Santo Diaz, a bullet he dodged thanks to Ronny's evidence.

Ronny turned to see Francesco standing against the wall and approached him.

"Thanks for coming. I was hoping you got the invitation," he said and shook his hand.

"Congratulations on your photographs. Really great work, and what a turn out," Francesco said. "Seeing your work exhibited on a wall never gets old."

"Thanks, that means a lot coming from you," Ronny replied with relief that he liked his work and excitement that he had turned up. They spoke briefly about what happened with Santo. Even though he didn't disclose any details of what had happened to him, Ronny could sense that something had in fact happened to Francesco, and in his own way he had tried to warn him.

"I wanted to thank you," said Francesco.

"For what?"

"I'm shooting the Mancini campaign. It's my first really big break, and I got it after Santo was canceled."

"Good for you, man. You'll be shooting my friend Chad. He is amazing. Hey, if you need an assistant, please keep me in mind," Ronny mentioned again. Getting to assist someone like Francesco would be a huge opportunity for him.

"My second assistant is leaving in a month, so why don't we meet for a coffee after the weekend," Francesco replied as he patted Ronny on the shoulder.

"That would be incredible. I will give you a call to organize it." Ronny replied and moved back to where Ella was standing.

"I'm so proud of you. Remember this moment," Ella said softly.

"I came to Milan thinking I knew what I wanted." Ronny looked around the room acknowledging his work on display. "But I got so much more than I dreamt of," he said as he took Ella's hand.

Later that evening back in his room, Ronny took a moment and dialed Luiz's number to check in on his mother. She sounded lighter and more optimistic than she had in a long time. It was good to know she had Luiz and Maria to look after her. It felt like old times as he heard her laughing about Luiz's cooking. He wished he was there with his family.

"We are moving into a bigger place," Luiz said as he was passed the phone. "We need a room for the baby."

"What? Really? That's amazing news!"

"Yes. We just found out. Mom will live with us to help with the baby."

"There will be room here for you too, Ronny," his mother added as she took the phone back from Luiz. "So when are you coming home?" she asked. Hearing her sound like her old self brought tears to his eyes. His heart was full as he felt his smile grow and his face getting warmer.

"I'll be home for the holidays. I need to be with my family. I guess I needed to get away to realize how lucky I was."

"I'm so glad to hear that," Adriana said. Her voice softened. "I can't lose you again." He could hear her voice starting to break as she handed the phone to Luiz.

"We love you, Ronny," Luiz said before he hung up.

Ronny lay back on his bed and closed his eyes feeling relief that his mother was finally safe with Luiz. He savored the moment as his tongue ran across the scar on the inside of his cheek. A reminder of what he had been through and what he sacrificed to get here. He slowly opened his eyes and looked up at his prints on the wall above the bed. A smile appeared on his face.

Now he wasn't the only one that would get to enjoy them.

# FIN

# BOOK CLUB CONVERSATION

### CHARACTER DEVELOPMENT:
How did Ronny's character evolve throughout the story, especially considering his challenging background and experiences within the fashion industry? Were there specific moments or relationships that significantly influenced his growth?

### INDUSTRY CRITIQUE:
The novel sheds light on the darker aspects of the fashion industry, including abuse, drug use, and the pressures faced by models. How did the author portray these elements, and what impact did they have on your perception of the industry? Were there moments that surprised you or challenged your preconceptions?

### FRIENDSHIPS AND RELATIONSHIPS:
Explore the dynamics of Ronny's friendships, particularly with Ella and Nick. How did these relationships contribute to Ronny's journey, and in what ways did they help or hinder his pursuit of his dreams? Did you find the portrayal of friendships and relationships realistic?

## THEMES OF RESILIENCE AND PURSUING DREAMS:

Ronny faces numerous challenges in pursuing his dream of becoming a fashion photographer. Discuss the theme of resilience in the story and how Ronny overcomes obstacles. How does the character of Ella play a role in supporting Ronny's determination to follow his dreams despite the hardships?

## MORAL DILEMMAS AND INDUSTRY SECRETS:

The plot takes a turn when Ronny decides to uncover the truth behind Nick's death and expose the industry's secrets. Discuss the moral dilemmas Ronny faces in this quest for justice. Do you think his actions were justified, and how did they impact your perception of the characters and the fashion industry as a whole?

# ACKNOWLEDGMENTS

I want to personally thank my friends and family who have always been there to support and inspire me as I continue my journey as an artist.

Special thanks to my dear friend Rich LeMay who I told this story idea to years ago and who has always been there to inspire me to write it and keep going. I would also like to thank Tiffany Yates Martin (Fox Print Editorial) for editing this manuscript and really pushing me to grow as a writer. Your feedback and insights were invaluable.

Finally, I would like to thank my amazing husband Brian McGrory who I am lucky enough to share this incredible journey with. You and our beautiful daughter Dylan have been the greatest gift.

.

# ABOUT THE AUTHOR

**FOLLOW JAMES:**

www.houstonphoto.com

Instagram: @jameshoustonphoto

Australian born James Houston is a first-time novelist, award winning film maker and has enjoyed a global career as one of the world's leading beauty and body photographers based out of New York.

James originally started taking photographs while modelling in Japan in 1982. As a successful model for seven years James was featured in over 100 commercials and travelled the world modelling and taking photographs as a hobby. Besides Tokyo James modelled in Europe, South Africa and Australia.

After his last contract in Japan James returned to Australia to focus solely on his photography career and launch his first published photography book RAW at an exhibition in Sydney. He focused on the Australian market and after several years he was shooting covers for Australian Vogue and major advertising campaigns.

In 1999 James moved to New York City to further his photography career. His tenacity and determination eventually paid off and he began working regularly on international fashion and beauty campaigns for clients such as L'Oreal Paris, GAP, Donna Karan, Hugo Boss. His eye for beauty also made him popular with celebrities such as Jennifer Lopez, Blake Lively, Jessica Alba, Emma Watson and Hugh Jackman. Editorially James has worked for American Vogue, UK Glamor, Interview Magazine and Harpers Bazaar.

Five Award Winning international books have been published on his work, including *MOVE* (PowerHouse Books), which was created to benefit various HIV/AIDS charities and raised close to US$500,000. The book project, titled *MOVE FOR AIDS* was launched in 2006 with the support of Elton John, Hugh Jackman and Baz Luhrmann.

While working on *MOVE FOR AIDS*, Houston was shocked to learn about American attitudes towards adolescent sexuality and the impact it has on U.S. teens. This discovery inspired Houston to raise over 1 million dollars to fund his first feature documentary film titled, *LET'S TALK ABOUT SEX* which was aired on TLC in 2011. The Award-winning film takes a revealing look at how American attitudes towards adolescent sexual health affect today's teenagers.

James's last published book project titled *Natural Beauty* raised funds and awareness for the environment and benefitted The Global Green Foundation. For the project James photographed the world's top models including Karlie Kloss, Arizona Muse, Irina Shayk and Christy Turlington and celebrities Emma Watson, Caitriona Balfe and Adrian Grenier. The project was launched in New York at MILK Galleries in 2013 with a high profiled event sponsored by W magazine and Dom Perignon. James also directed a web series on the making of Natural Beauty which was released on YouTube to support the launch.

As a passionate activist James has used his talents and network to bring awareness and raise millions of dollars for various causes through his books, exhibitions and launch events. James now lives with his husband and daughter in Los Angeles. Scouted is his first written book.

*1st edition.*
*This book was first printed in March 2024.*

Printed in Great Britain
by Amazon